SOULSTONE

Katie Salidas

IMMORTALIS SERIES: BOOK 4

Soulstone
SECOND EDITION
Copyright © 2010 by Katie Salidas
Second Edition © 2015 Katie Salidas

Editing by Sharazade
Cover Art by DJ Rogers
Interior Design by Katie Salidas

Published by Rising Sign Books, LLC.
http://www.RisingSignBooks.net
ISBN: 978-0-9851277-5-6

For my son, Hunter.
Let your imagination soar and wonderful things will happen.

THE IMMORTALIS SERIES:
All 6 Books Are Available Now

Becoming a vampire is easy. Living with the condition... that's the hard part. Join Alyssa as she stumbles through the world of the "Unnatural."

BOOK 1: IMMORTALIS CARPE NOCTEM - Newbie vampire Alyssa never asked for this life, but now it's all she has. Rescued from death by Lysander, the aloof and sexy leader of the Peregrinus vampire clan, she's barely cut her teeth before she becomes a target. Kallisto, an ancient and vindictive vampire queen – and Lysander's old mate - wants nothing less than final death for her former lover and his new toy. She's not above letting the Acta Sanctorum, and its greatest vampire hunter, Santino, know exactly where the clan can be found. With no time to mourn her old life, Alyssa's survival depends on her new family. She will have to stand alongside Lysander and fight against two enemies who will stop at nothing to destroy them.

YOU ARE READING **BOOK 2: HUNTERS & PREY** - Rule number one: humans and vampires don't co-exist. One is the hunter and one is the prey. Simple, right? Not for newly-turned vampire Alyssa. A surprise confrontation with Santino Vitale, the Acta Sanctorum's most fearsome hunter, sends her fleeing back to the world she once knew, and Fallon, the human friend she's missed more than anything. Now she has some explaining to do. However, that will have to wait. With the Acta Sanctorum hot on their heels, staying alive is more important than educating a human on the finer points of bloodlust.

BOOK 3: PANDORA'S BOX - After a few months as a vampire, Alyssa thought she'd learned all she needed to know about the supernatural world. But her confidence is shattered by the delivery of a mysterious package - a Pandora's Box. Seemingly innocuous, the box is in reality an ancient prison, generated by a magic more powerful than anyone in her clan has ever known. But what manner of evil could need such force to contain it? When the box is opened, the sinister creature within is released, and only supernatural blood will satiate its thirst. The clan soon learns how it feels when the hunter becomes the hunted.

BOOK 4: SOULSTONE - It's a desperate time for rookie vampire Alyssa, and her sanity is hanging by a slender thread. Her clan is still reeling from the monumental battle with Aniketos; a battle that claimed the body of Lysander, her sire and lover, and trapped his spirit in a mysterious crystal. A Soulstone. Unfortunately, no amount of magic has been able to release Lysander's spirit, and the stone is starting to fade. Weeks of effort have proved futile. Her clan, the Peregrinus, have all but given up hope. Only Alyssa still believes her lover can be released. In despair, Alyssa begs the help of the local witch coven, and unwittingly exposes the supernaturals of Boston to unwanted attention from the Acta Sanctorum. The Saints converge on the city and begin their cleansing crusade to rid the world of all things "Unnatural." In the middle of an all-out war, but no closer to a solution to the dying stone, Alyssa is left with an unenviable choice: save her mate, or save her clan.

BOOK 5: MOONLIGHT - Good girls don't wear fur, or fight over men, and they certainly don't run around naked, howling at the moon. But then, no-one ever called Fallon a good girl. As a human unofficially mated to an Alpha werewolf, Fallon is being pressured to "become"...or be gone. Her mate Aiden, the interim leader of the Olde Town Pack, is in a position that demands he either choose a wolf mate...or leave the pack forever. No matter how hot the sex with Fallon is, he can't ignore centuries of tradition. Become a wolf or not. If only the choice were that simple. Fallon's options are further clouded by the overt presence of other females desperate to be the Alpha's mate. And when these bitches get serious, it's not just claws that come out. If Fallon wants to keep her man and take the title she'll have to exert a little dominance of her own.

BOOK 6: DARK SALVATION - A gathering storm of violence is on the horizon. Whispered threats of the Acta Sanctorum's return have the supernatural world abuzz. Only recently aware of the other world hidden behind our own, Kitara Vanders has barely scratched the surface of what being supernatural truly means. A special woman in her own right, she possesses unique telepathic abilities, gifts that have recently come under the scrutiny of the Acta Sanctorum, a fanatical organization whose mission is to cleanse the world of anything supernatural. Targeted, and marked for death, Kitara's only hope lies with the lethally seductive yet emotionally scarred warrior, Nicholas.

Knowing full well the atrocities the Acta Sanctorum is capable of, Nicholas is all too eager for the battle to begin. Fueled by pain and rage from the loss of his mate, he's itching for a fight, but one thing stands in his way, Kitara: a beautiful dark-haired woman with unique psychic abilities and an unusual link to the Saints. Despite his resolve to remain focused on his mission, a purely physical relationship binds them together in a way neither of them expected. And when her life hangs in the balance, Nicholas finds his own is teetering on the edge too.

ACKNOWLEDGMENTS

I'd like to thank three very special people for helping me see this book to completion.

Dana. Your enthusiasm for this series has kept my spirits up. Thank you for being a wonderful critiquing partner. During the many times I wanted to throw in the towel you were there practically begging me to get to the next chapter and the one after that. I don't know that I would have completed this book without you.

Willsin Rowe. Not only are you my favorite cover artist, but you're also one of the best beta readers I know. Even down to the last few minutes prior to publication, you were there finding my mistakes and helping me correct them. You've definitely got a keen eye!

Sharazade. Feel free to beat me up anytime for my coma usage. You're an awesome editor and friend. Thanks for always being there to answer my emails and dumb grammatical questions.

1

Down the creaky steps I walked, alone, heading for the basement.

Visiting Lysander had become my nightly ritual. I'd wake up in my bed, reach out to the empty sheets, and feel nothing but crushing emptiness. It's hard to believe that the absence of someone can bear such a heavy weight on one's soul, but it does. That's when realization would hit me, and I'd relive that terrible memory of seeing Lysander, my love, my mate, dive into the flames. Only after coming downstairs to the dark, dungeon-like basement, would I feel better.

I took a deep breath and stepped down onto the cold concrete floor. To my already tepid skin, the ground felt icy. Winter's chill had frozen everything, and the basement was no real shelter from the cold. I probably should have worn something more than socks, but in my desperation to see him, I'd ignored basic necessities. I shook off the chill working its way up my spine and continued on.

"Good evening sweetie." I said it as if he could hear me.

His spirit could, I guess, but Lysander had no voice with which to respond. Still, it made me feel better to talk to him as if he were alive and in front of me.

"It's snowing outside. Boston is a winter wonderland. Zuri took us shopping for coats and boots." Lysander had lived the last fifty years in Las Vegas. I had grown up there, before becoming a vampire. So for desert rats such as us, snow was as infrequent as rain, which made them special. Now that we were on the east coast, both were very common but neither had lost their beauty, at least to me they hadn't. "I wish you could see it, honey. It's just gorgeous out there. Everything's covered in white."

No response, as always. Not that I had really expected one. Hoped for, yes. But, at this rate, my hope was beginning to wear thin.

Too much time had passed since he'd been trapped inside the crystal that now served as his prison. The fragile hope I held of saving him was almost gone. I grew restless for a resolution. His spirit felt weaker. The warmth of his presence was almost … transparent.

Ariana, our resident witch, had not yet come up with a solution. She'd managed an impressive feat, trapping Aniketos back into the Pandora's Box. But because she'd used her own spells instead of the original ones from the old scrolls, Lysander had been trapped too. His spirit now resided in a large blood-red crystal.

She'd said her coven might be able to help; however, weeks later, we still had no resolution. Others in the house had already given up. I could feel it in the way they avoided any talk of Lysander or the crystal. They'd always find a way to change the subject. A few times, I had the sneaking suspicion that they were purposefully avoiding me so as not to have to talk about it.

I reached up and pulled the chain, flicking on the over-head light. The basement was small and bare. Brownstones in the Back Bay area of Boston were built tall, not wide, so the basement didn't take up much square footage. Lysander's coffin sat in the middle. Just a plain pine box that reminded me of ones from the old westerns I'd watched as a kid. It had been quickly constructed, and wasn't a show-piece; just a simple, almost flimsy box, only meant to hold Lysander until we could find some way to release his spirit.

Seeing it there, sitting all alone in the cold dark room, caused my heart to seize. Each time I set eyes on the coffin, for a brief moment, my world crumbled into dust—like everything important had been destroyed, except the reminder of the act that put him in this coffin.

For as long as he'd been lying there, I hoped he was comfortable. Part of me felt guilty, like the others and I should have gotten him something a little nicer to sleep in. That thought too made the permanence of death seem more real. A tear welled up in my eye, and I wiped it away.

The pine box is fine. He won't be in it much longer.

I pushed aside the lid and leaned it against the side of the box. Inside, Lysander lay, looking as if he were sleeping off his terrible injuries.

Where his body wasn't scabbed or bruised, the skin ap-peared ashen in color and almost plastic-looking, as if not really skin at all, but a sort of waxy coating. I shivered at the gruesome sight. He'd been so beautiful before the fire charred him. His once-gorgeous chocolate-colored hair had been singed away in the blaze, leaving only a few patches here and there to remind me of its original color. The tips of his fangs poked down from behind dry, parched lips. I'd tried to give him blood, hoping it might restore him, but it hadn't had any effect. His body was frozen in the moment his spirit had left it.

The fire had almost destroyed him before his spirit had been caught. Ariana had suggested to me that Lysander had already died and his spirit was moving on when she trapped him. She told me that if we freed it from the crystal, he might not return to his body.

I wasn't ready to accept that. I could still feel his presence, though weak, emanating from the large soda bottle-sized crystal. Whether in his body or not, his spirit was still with us. That had to count for something. He was still here with us and alive, for all intents and purposes. And until we knew otherwise, I did not want to hear talk of him "moving on."

I hoped and prayed to every deity out there that when Ariana did find the answer, Lysander could be returned to his body. Even if he remained charred and burned, I'd still love him. I didn't want to face eternity without him.

I'd placed the crystal on his chest and folded his arms across it. There it had rested for the last two weeks while I tried to find answers. I hoped keeping the two together like this would help in some small way.

"Alyssa the widow is back to mourn again," said an overly chipper voice from the top of the stairs. "Shouldn't you be wearing black?"

I craned my head to look up and found Ian standing at the top of the stairs. As usual he was dressed for a night out: raven-black hair slicked back with just a few strands framing his face, skin-tight t-shirt and tight-legged jeans to ensure nothing was left to the imagination, and topped off with a leather coat. I often wondered if he had been a greaser before being turned. He certainly looked the part.

"Widow implies death, Ian," I said with as much snark as I could put into my mournful voice.

"Widow also implies… available." Ian beamed down with his thousand-watt smile. "I've had enough of this moping. You're coming out with me tonight." He took the stairs at a trot.

"No, thanks. I don't need to hunt tonight." I looked down at Lysander again. "You have to come back, honey. Look what you're leaving me with."

"I'm not taking no for an answer." Ian's breath blew across my ear. I felt the closeness of his body almost pressing against my back. "And I prefer to be the one on the hunt."

I jumped in response, and my head collided with his. "Ugh. Ian! Stop it. I'm not one of your waitresses or barmaids. Leave me alone." A spike of pain radiated through my skull. I could only hope I'd done more damage to Ian. The nerve of him, hitting on me in front of Lysander.

"No, you're not. Which makes the hunt all that much more fun for me. Tricky little prey, aren't you, Alyssa?" If I had injured him, he didn't show it. In fact, whatever pain I'd caused him, he might have even liked.

I groaned in frustration and rubbed the sore spot on the back of my head.

"Oh, c'mon. Try me. You just might like it." He winked.

I couldn't help but roll my eyes. "I don't want to try anyone, especially not a sleazy vampire that'll sleep with anything that breathes."

"Not fair. I didn't sleep with your human friend, Fallon."

"That's 'cause she's with Aiden."

Ian grimaced for a brief second before his smile returned. "She's off limits."

"And so am I."

"Just come out and have fun."

"Fun for you is getting in the sack."

"Look, you might see me as sleazy. I prefer the term 'promiscuous'; it has a nicer ring to it. But the bottom line is, at least I'm out there living life, not moping around in some dingy cellar, waiting for a man who'll never return." His typically cheerful tone had all but vanished. "I'm trying to help you."

It was the first time I had ever seen Ian serious. Beyond that, he almost looked angry. His blue-gray eyes narrowed on me and his lip curled ever so slightly. "You have to know when to give up." He inclined his head toward the coffin. "Let a lost cause go."

I stared at him while anger and grief fought each other to be the dominant emotion inside me. My jaw quivered. I mashed my teeth together so it wouldn't show.

"Lost cause? Lysander's not a lost cause." My eyes watered. I blinked and turned away. I didn't want to melt down again. I didn't want anyone seeing me like this.

"Look, I'm sorry I hurt your feelings," Ian said, softening his tone. He smiled at me, but it didn't have its usual brilliance.

"You don't know what this feels like. To know that your mate is here, lying as if dead. But I feel him. I know he hasn't gone yet. Yes, Ian. I can feel his spirit. Right here."

I picked the crystal up, off Lysander's chest, and held it for Ian to see. "He's not dead and gone. I know you can't feel it, but I can. That's what makes this so difficult."

"I get it. You've been so maudlin lately. I'm just trying to lighten things up. Put a smile on that pouty face."

I huffed. There was no getting through to that man. How could I expect him to understand the loss of a mate? He was the pathological playboy of the immortal world. Sex was his answer for all life's problems.

"I'm sorry. Let's try this again." Ian's wide eyes suddenly narrowed on the crystal. "Hey, didn't that used to be all red?"

"What?" I pulled it closer to inspect. When Lysander had been trapped, the crystal had gone from completely transparent to a deep red color, as if it were made from blood itself. To my surprise now, the tip had turned clear.

"What does this mean?" I mumbled more to myself than to Ian.

"Good news, probably. Maybe the longer you keep that thing on Lysander's chest, the more his spirit can seep back into his body."

Oh, how I wished he were right! Ever the optimist, Ian had given me a little more hope. Maybe the spell would reverse itself after a short while, and Lysander would heal and return to us.

"Ariana is coming by later. You can show her then."

I gave Ian a genuine smile.

"There it is. That's what I've been looking for. You look so pretty when you're not moping. Now, let's go out and celebrate this good news."

Part of me wanted to. I'd been cooped up for the last two weeks, researching and staying by Lysander's side. It would be nice to get out and enjoy the city.

Ian took a step, closing the gap between us. He was a tall man, six foot or better. He pulled me into a hug and cradled my head to his chest. "It's not a crime to go out and have fun. You have to live too. Otherwise, what's immortality good for?"

I pulled back and looked down at the crystal in my hands. It seemed to pulse, as if Lysander were trying to tell me something. The warm, tingling sensation of his presence briefly flashed through me. Maybe he was saying the same thing: *You shouldn't forget to live.*

I held it up and gently kissed the smooth sides. "I'll be back soon," I said, and then placed it against his chest.

"Atta girl." Ian's full blinding smile returned. "Let's turn that frown upside down, permanently. We're gonna hit the town and have a little fun."

"I'll go out with you tonight, on two conditions," I said as I closed the lid to the coffin.

"Name them."

"Quit with the cheesy lines. You need some new material."

"Ouch. I think I might be insulted," Ian quipped.

I shook my head. "Oh, poor baby. It couldn't hurt that bad. I doubt anything in the world could damage that ego."

"You're so feisty and full of anger. I know a way to relieve some of that tension." He waggled his eyebrows.

I gave him my best I-don't-think-so look and drummed my fingers on the top of the coffin.

"Can't blame a guy for trying. Either way, you're still smiling." He smirked. "What's the other condition?"

"That you talk Zuri into coming with us."

"Spoil sport." Ian shot up the stairs, leaving me alone with Lysander's body.

I had to laugh. Ian just didn't give up. That, in its own funny way, gave me more hope. Maybe he was right and Lysander might actually make a comeback. That was a reason to celebrate, even if it was with Ian. I took one last look at the coffin. "Are you sure I should go out with him?" I mumbled to the box. As expected, there was no response, but I still felt Lysander's spirit.

I wished, just once, that he would answer. With a sigh, I headed to the stairs, pulling the chain for the light as I walked by. "I'll see you later honey. Don't you go waking up without me, okay?"

2

As I went upstairs to get ready for my night with Ian, I stumbled upon my clan members seated around a large cherrywood table in the formal dining room. I stepped inside to see if any of them wanted to join me for a night out on the town. I opened my mouth to speak and caught the awkward glances that Nicholas, Crystal, and Drew were giving me. Silence enveloped the room, as if my presence were unwanted.

"Did I miss dinner?" I asked, hoping to break the awkwardness of the moment with a little humor, but none of them laughed at my bad joke.

Nicholas folded his hands in front of him on the table. He shook his head and clenched his jaw as if he wanted to say something but was holding back. Drew looked down at the dining table, pretending to be intensely studying the grain of the wood, while Crystal sat back in her chair, picking at her long, manicured fingernails. If I wasn't mistaken, they seemed to be avoiding eye contact with me. This was one of those many times I wished I were an older vampire and had developed the ability to read thoughts. Being a newbie, as I was, I had almost none of the nifty abilities that the more experienced vampires had. I could sense emotions, but that wouldn't do me much good here. I did, however, have the sneaking suspicion they'd all been talking about me.

"Okay then," I said to break the silence. "Lysander's crystal is in the coffin if anyone is looking for it. I noticed something different about it today. Possibly a good thing. Fingers crossed. When Ariana gets here we need to have her take a look at it. Maybe the spell is reversing itself. Wouldn't that be great?"

Crystal glanced up for a brief second and smiled awkwardly at me.

Drew cleared his throat and it sounded like he said, "Okay," but didn't bother to turn and look in my direction.

I found it odd that none of them bothered to comment on what I had said about Lysander or the crystal. Come to think of it, they'd been acting funny for the last few evenings; avoiding me, ignoring me, and spending a lot of time in their own little group. Did they know something I didn't? And if they did, why weren't they telling me? I wanted to blurt these questions out but knew better. If they were trying to hide something from me, the direct approach wasn't going to get me any answers. I'd have to keep a close watch on them to find out myself.

"Anyway... Ian is dragging me out of the house. We're going to hit the bar. If anyone else wants to join us, I'd love to have you. Please come."

Crystal shook her head and folded her arms across the table, but maintained her silence.

"Drew, Nicholas, either of you guys want to tag along? Don't make me go out with Ian all by myself." I figured that would at least get a rise out of one of them. They'd been like overprotective brothers, and Ian was just the kind of guy that brothers kept away from their little sisters.

"Actually, that might be best." Drew said in his usually chipper tone. "You get along well with the Boston crowd. I feel you should go out with them more often. It would do you good."

"I'm sorry… what?" To say I was startled would be an understatement. "Remember we're talking about Ian here. Mr. Wannabe Casanova. You want me to go out with him tonight?"

"You can handle him," Drew responded.

"What I think Drew is trying to say," Crystal said softly, "is that we want to see you going out and having fun. We're worried for you. The Boston crowd is younger, and you can relate to them better. Maybe that's what you need to move on."

"Move on!" I said a bit louder than I wanted to. "Nicholas, back me up here. Have you moved on from Rozaline?"

I realized about two seconds too late that I probably shouldn't have reopened *that* wound. And I was right. Nicholas's face tensed. His jaw clenched. His eyes zeroed in on mine, and without needing to hear the sound I knew he was still screaming in pain on the inside.

Rozaline, Nicholas's mate, had died days before Lysander had been charred and trapped in the crystal. We'd all watched her decapitated and drained at the ghostly hands of Aniketos. Her death had been gruesome and very final, and

I doubt even the coldest heart out there could have gotten over that pain so quickly.

"Sorry, that was wrong of me. I didn't mean it to come out like that. All I'm trying to say is, she died and he is allowed to mourn. Lysander isn't dead, and you all seem to want to act like he is. There is nothing for me to move on from."

Crystal stood and walked purposefully toward me. "We just feel like you might be holding false hope. We don't want you to hurt more if things don't work out."

"At least I have hope." I couldn't hold back the raw emotion in my voice. "At least I want things to be better. What are you all doing? Have you lost your humanity completely? This is no different than if he were in a coma in a hospital. If we were human, I'd be by his side every day, because I love him. That's what you do when you love someone."

She put her arm around me. "You're not wrong to care. And we do want things to be better. Even if that means letting go."

I jerked away from her.

"Not of your hope," she added. "Let go of some of the pain. Don't forget you have to live too. Transfer that energy into something productive, so you're not constantly dwelling on the uncertainty of his situation."

"And what if I'm not ready to let go of the pain? What if all I have is my pain?"

"You know that's a lie." She pulled me back into her arms. "You have us. We care… in our own way."

Drew stood and joined us. His massive height dwarfed both Crystal and me. "So go out tonight. Have fun with Ian and Zuri and anyone else you can drag along with you. Get out of this house. That's all we want."

"Then I want you all to come too." If I was to be forced into going out and having fun, they should have to go too. It was only fair.

"We've already hunted," Drew said with an obviously fake smile. "And I don't really care much for the dance clubs here."

"There is nothing you can say that will get me to go to another bar," Nicholas said with a note of finality.

I knew better than to push him. We shared a common pain, though not exactly the same, and I wouldn't blame him at all for locking himself away to mourn. Losing a mate with whom you have shared eternity is not something you can just walk away from. He'd been ready to join her, offering himself as a sacrifice, but that too had been stolen from him when Lysander took his place.

"Well, I know Crystal will go with me." I gave her my best you're-not-getting-out-of-this look. Crystal liked to go to parties and clubs. She'd been the first to take me out dancing after I'd been turned. "No excuses. If you don't go, I don't go."

She sighed and for a brief moment, I almost believed she was angry at me for giving her an ultimatum; but then a smile blossomed from her tight lips. "Oh, all right. I'll go out tonight."

Drew cleared his throat. "I thought we had our own plans for tonight." He put his arm around his mate. "Remember, just the two of us?"

She stammered for a moment and looked up at her mate with confusion in her eyes. "Oh… yes… I completely forgot. Alyssa, let's have a girls' night some other time."

I couldn't put my finger on it, but they were all acting very suspicious. I sighed in disappointment. "Fine. I'll see you all later. Will someone call me if Ariana gets here before I return?"

"If we're home." Drew said with a cocky tone that didn't suit him.

Something was definitely up.

"Yeah, okay. If you're around, give me a call," I said, and then turned and headed toward my room to get ready.

3

Maybe everyone was right. I should enjoy a night out on the town. And, deep down I wanted to, but things just felt out of whack, and it had nothing to do with the fact that Ian was the one to get me out of the house. It was as if the feeling part of me had been left with Lysander while my body traveled to the bar. The smells and sounds of surrounding humans didn't even entice my hunger, though I hadn't hunted in a while. Even sitting in my new favorite bar with Fallon, my closest friend, I felt strangely disconnected.

My thoughts floated from the bizarre way my clan members had acted to the fading crystal housing Lysander's spirit. *Could that really be a good sign? What will happen when—or if—the crystal completely fades?*

"See, this is one of those times where being a vampire must suck," Fallon said as she took a swig of her beer. "Alyssa, you look like you could use a good stiff drink."

Ian's eyebrow arched and a crooked grin spread from one side of his lips to the other. "I've got something stiff…"

"Finish that sentence and you'll meet the business end of a wooden stake," Fallon snarled.

"Well, well, well. Look who became an Amazon woman once she started dating a wolf," Ian retorted.

I couldn't hold back the laugh that bubbled up from my chest.

"I'll take that as a compliment," Fallon said with a smile and turned to me. "Glad to see you laughing again. It's been a while."

"Sorry, guys. I know I've been a downer lately. I've just got so much on my mind."

Fallon reached out and placed her hand on mine. "I know, and I feel bad I haven't been around much for you, and I'm sorry."

I lifted my head and met Fallon's deep brown eyes. She hadn't been around *at all*, and part of me hated her for it. She'd begun seriously dating Aiden, one of the Olde Town wolf pack members and practically fallen off the face of the earth. The other part of me, however, understood the pull of a new relationship.

"Yeah, and the one night you're here, I'm not." I sighed, slouched into my seat, and started picking at the label on Fallon's empty beer bottle.

"Really, I hadn't noticed. So, what's on your mind tonight?" she asked in her most sympathetic voice.

"Have you talked to Crystal or Drew lately? They were acting really strange at the house."

She shook her head.

Ian shrugged. "They're no stranger than they've been since they got here. No offense, but your whole group are a melancholy bunch."

"Ignore him," Fallon said. "The whole clan has been through a lot, and it's not like we're all home and living the comfortable life back in Vegas…"

The waitress, a fair-skinned, freckle-faced redhead sauntered up to our table. "Need another round, or are you all set?"

"We're good, thanks," Fallon said with a hint of annoyance, and held up the bottle she was still nursing.

Ian flashed her a devilish smile and ran his hand through his slick back hair. "I'm all set, but if you need anything, don't be afraid to ask."

The waitress turned on her heel, mumbled something that sounded like "Jerk," and sauntered off.

"Ian, go flirt at the bar or something," Fallon said, and then turned toward me. "We've all been through a lot in the last few weeks. There's bound to be some weirdness."

"I get that, but they're acting weird toward *me*. Like they're hiding something."

Fallon took another swig from her beer. "What makes you say that?"

"When I went up to ask them if they were going to come out with us, they got all quiet. It was like they were having some secret meeting and didn't want to include me."

Ian leaned back into his chair. "Did you ask them what they were talking about?"

"Well, no." I scrunched up my face in confusion. "I assumed if it was clan business they would tell me."

"That's your first mistake. Don't blame them for not telling you something if you didn't ask."

I didn't appreciate Ian's mocking tone. "That's not the point. It doesn't matter what they were discussing. It's how they were acting about it that bothers me."

"Well, you've been very moody lately." Fallon cringed as if she were expecting a backlash. "Maybe they were just trying to act cautious around you."

"Moody… and how would *you* know?" I realized a second too late that I was yelling. A sudden silence filled the air, and I sensed the eyes of the humans around us zeroing in on me. I shrugged sheepishly. "Sorry, but you haven't been around much to see me being moody."

"See, this is exactly what I mean. Look at how you're snapping at me, just because I pointed out something you didn't want to hear."

Embarrassment sent heat creeping up to my cheeks. She was right; even if she hadn't been friend enough to be around for my mood swings, I'd been on edge since the incident with the box. "Okay. I see your point there. It still seems odd, though. And they didn't even flinch when I mentioned the crystal was fading."

Fallon's eyes widened and she choked on her beer. "What? The crystal is fading? What does that mean?"

"See. That's the reaction I expected to see when I mentioned it to them. Instead, they just smiled and nodded as if I'd said the sun had come up this morning."

"Yeah, that *is* a bit weird."

Ian sighed loudly. "Well, if you ask me… Not that anyone has, thank you… I think it's a good thing, and you ladies need to just relax. The whole point of this evening was to paint the town red, not blue. Remind me never to take you two out again."

My temper momentarily got the better of me. "You know, Ian, if you're not having a good time, you can leave."

"I'll do one better." He winked over Fallon's shoulder at a tall blonde girl wearing a miniskirt and knee-high boots.

"Tell Chlamydia I said hi," Fallon said with a smirk.

For the second time tonight, I couldn't help but burst out laughing. Ian, seemingly unaffected by our mockery, stood up and headed toward the bar—and his next conquest.

"That's what I wanted to see. Smiling and laughing." Fallon tapped me on the shoulder. "I knew my old friend Alyssa was in there somewhere."

"Thanks. I needed that. And you got Ian off our backs too. Good job."

"He's right, though. We aren't having much of a night on the town."

"I want to be happy and have fun, but I'm worried about Lysander, and I just can't shake the feeling that there's something going on. And for whatever reason, I'm being kept out of the loop."

"Should we just go back to the house then? Call it an early night and maybe veg out in front of the TV."

"Ariana was supposed to come by tonight."

"So that's it. You want to get home early so you don't miss her."

"Do you hate me?" I asked sheepishly.

"Nah. I get it. Lysander is your man. I'd be the same way if something happened to Aiden."

"How's that going?"

"He asked me to the next full moon revelry. He wants to formally introduce me to the pack as his girlfriend."

"Oooh, sounds serious."

"For them, it is. You know these wolves… everything is a ceremony."

"See, you should have become a vamp. We're very low-key."

She narrowed her brown eyes at me. "I'm not becoming anything, thank you."

"Oh, so you're not thinking of signing up to be Mrs. Werewolf?" I said playfully.

"Lyssa, we've only been dating a few weeks."

I gave her a knowing look, and then stood and turned toward the door. "Back to the house then?" "Yes, and hopefully Ariana can put all your fears to rest." Fallon took a final swig of beer and walked with me to the door.

4

"We're back," I called as I walked through the front door of Zuri's house.

But no one answered.

In a house filled with supernatural creatures, it was common courtesy to announce yourself. This avoided any problems that could arise with surprise guests. Vampires and were-wolves have excellent hearing, and even if someone were on an upper floor of the old brick row house, they should have heard me call, and responded.

"Hello," I shouted louder. "Anyone home? Nicholas, you here?"

Fallon walked to the stairs and turned her head skyward. "Aiden... honey, are you home?"

Still no response.

Fallon followed me into the foyer, through the main floor parlor and dining room. It seemed like the place was empty; yet all the lights had been left on, and a fire was still burning in the fireplace.

"Strange. Why is no one answering?" I mumbled. "Something's not right."

Fallon removed her coat and tossed it over the back of a large L-shaped sectional sofa in the parlor. "Don't be so worried. Maybe they stepped out for a minute." She flopped down onto the couch, kicked up her feet on the oversized ottoman, and started fishing in the cushions for the remote.

Crystal and Drew had mentioned plans, so I assumed they would be gone. I knew Zuri was on duty, watching the tourist spots for rogue vampire activity, so I hadn't expected to see her. But Nicholas should have been home; he'd been in a state of mourning since Rozaline's death, and hardly left the house.

"I guess you could be right, but where would they *step out* to? It's not like anyone is going to run down to the corner market for some bread."

Fallon cleared her throat. "Excuse me…Not all the people in this house are dead, you know. Some of us do eat real food."

"I'm not dead; my heart still beats. How many times do I have to remind you of that?" I didn't bother to hide the aggravation in my voice. "And I seriously doubt Aiden stepped out for a loaf of bread, okay?"

"You're right." She stuck her tongue at me. "He'd probably grab a burger… or ten. My point is, I'm sure whoever left the fire going didn't plan to burn the house down. They'll be back soon. He and Brady are probably outside smoking a cigarette."

"Nasty habit." I joined her on the couch.

"Don't start with me," Fallon warned.

I'd been trying to get her to quit for years, but it wasn't working.

A loud crash rumbled through the house. It shook the floor below our feet.

"What the hell?" I yelled and jumped to my feet. "That doesn't sound like someone stepping out for a smoke."

Fallon and I exchanged worried looks.

The door to the basement burst open and Nicholas came rushing out, coughing. A trail of smoke followed in his wake.

"What the hell happened? What the hell are you doing down there, and why the hell are you smoking?" I asked.

"I don't smoke," Nicholas snapped at me.

"I mean, you're on fire. Turn around and let me see."

Nicholas grumbled something under his breath as he turned his back toward me. There were no flames, and the smoke had dissipated, but his shirt had a large scorched area in the middle. Thankfully, his skin looked undamaged.

"You're fine, but that shirt isn't. Is everything okay? What was going on down there? Is Lysander—"

"Take a breath," he said dismissively. "Everything is okay. What are you doing home anyway? Aren't you supposed to be out?"

"I didn't really feel much like painting the town red. What were you doing down there?" I started heading toward the basement door, but quick as a blur he stepped in front of it, blocking my path.

"What the hell, Nicholas?" I was really beginning to get sick of the strange way the members of my clan were acting. They were definitely excluding me from something, but what? "Let me down there."

"You're not going into the basement right now." His words came out stern but the concerned expression on his face told me he was more worried about what I might find than just imposing his will.

Fallon was at my side in a moment. "Why can't she go down there? What have you done?"

"*I* have done nothing, little human. Stay out of this." His concerned expression turned into sneer.

"It's okay, let them come." Ariana's voice floated up from the basement.

"When did she get here?" I pushed past Nicholas and barreled down the creaky steps.

In the basement, Crystal and Drew were busy lifting Lysander's coffin back onto its stand. Smoke cleared out of the room through two small windows near the ceiling. Broken glass lay on the floor next to a greenish colored substance. Below Lysander's coffin lay a charred body.

I rushed to the coffin. "Oh my God!"

"No, it's all right," Crystal said soothingly. "We were just trying something. We thought we could free Lysander, but it didn't work."

"What about the smoke and why is the body? That's not…"

Her eyes followed the same path mine had taken and focused on the charred body lying at our feet. "On, no! That's not Lysander. Everything's okay. That was a human we used for blood."

My hands shook on the lid of the coffin. Part of me needed to open it to confirm her words, while the other part of me was too scared to look.

"That was my doing." Ariana lowered her head as if ashamed and wiped her hands on her jeans. "My potion backfired and sort of exploded."

"Why didn't anyone tell me what was going on?" I shot angry glances around the room. "You all had this planned and didn't include me. Why?"

The room fell silent. Crystal bit her lip and looked away from me, toward the open window. Drew and Nicholas exchanged serious glances. But none of them appeared to be willing to speak. Even Fallon, who had followed me down the stairs, remained silent where she stood.

I turned to Ariana. "You I could understand keeping secrets, but not the rest of you. And yes, I'm including you too, Fallon." I pointed a finger at her. "You've been too busy to hang out for the last couple of weeks and then suddenly tonight of all nights, you're able to go out." I flung my hands up in exasperation. "I can't believe you would all do this to me. He's my mate, and you were all keeping secrets from me."

Drew opened his mouth as if he wanted to say something, but Crystal cut him off. "We didn't know if what we were doing would work."

"That doesn't matter," I yelled. "You still should have told me."

Crystal reached out to me. "We wanted to spare you the pain—"

"Well, you fucked up there, didn't you? You just caused me more pain. How can I ever trust you?"

I finally mustered the confidence and opened the lid, expecting the worst. Thankfully, to my great surprise, I found Lysander still intact, and if possible, looking better than he had earlier in the evening. The crystal too, residing on his chest, looked as if it had been rejuvenated. It had returned to a deep crimson again, as if it had never begun to fade. I reached out, hesitating as I touched it, and quieted my mind to sense Lysander's presence. Like a beacon, it was there, stronger than before.

"What did you do?" I whispered. Whatever it was, it had strengthened him, and for that small part I was thankful.

Ariana was the one to speak this time. "We thought that maybe he needed to be stronger to break free from the crystal's hold. We tried experimenting with blood and a summoning spell, but something went wrong and my potion backfired. I'm not sure what happened."

Those words angered me even more. "Then why are you messing with magic you don't know? You could have killed him!"

"And that's precisely why we all thought it was best you weren't around for this." Drew's voice boomed through the room. "You want him back, right? Well, you have to take some risks. Untested magic put him into that crystal, and it's likely that untested magic will get him out."

The anger in his voice shook me to the core. I'd never in all my time heard Drew yell. It was generally Nicholas who threw his authority around, and many times Lysander, but never Drew. I gulped back the angry retort I would have said. No matter how mad I was at them, they were trying to help.

"Now, if you'll quit throwing a temper tantrum and help us clean up this mess, we can sort out what happened." Drew sounded a little calmer now, but the authority was still there in his voice.

"Fine. I'll grab a broom for the glass," I said.

Ariana's phone rang, playing *Black Magic Woman* as her ring tone. *Fitting*, I thought as I started heading up the stairs to the kitchen.

When I came back down, broom in hand, she looked very excited.

"I'll tell them right now. Full moon is only a few days away… That's why they call you the High Priestess." She snapped the phone shut and that moment, all eyes were on her. "That was Mysti, high priestess of our coven. She's been through all of our magical library and thinks she has located a spell that should free Lysander from the crystal and return him to his body."

"Wonderful news!" Crystal turned to me. Her face clearly said "See, I told you we'd do it!"

"Do you really think it will work?" I asked, my voice wavering with cautious happiness.

"She said it will take a majority of the coven, lots of magic. And it will have to be done under the full moon since that was when he was originally trapped, but it's the best chance we have. Trust me, she knows her stuff. If she thinks this will work, it will."

"That's good enough for me. What do we need to do to prepare?" Drew asked.

"Nothing yet. She's going to gather the necessary items and find the location to perform the ceremony. Once she has that, then she'll tell us and all we have to do is bring the body and the crystal. You should have your leader back by the end of the week!" Ariana turned to me and smiled. "And your boyfriend too."

Do I dare hope that this will work? My whole body shook with excitement. I dropped the broom to the ground. *My Lysander. I'll finally get him back!*

"You okay, Lyssa?" Fallon asked me.

"Yeah… yeah… fine. Just a little jittery. Excitement."

"I understand." She hugged me tight. "If this works, everything will be good again. Well, almost everything." She turned toward Nicholas and gave him a silent nod.

"Yes, it would be good to have my brother back," Nicholas said but his voice didn't carry the same level of excitement.

I knew why. We might be able to save Lysander, but Rozaline could never return to him. No one has power over death.

The overall mood of the room became awkward, and Ariana must have sensed it. "Okay, well, lots to get ready for. I'll call you guys when Mysti gives me the location," Ariana rushed up the stairs. "Be ready. Full moon is in a few days."

5

Three days later, Fallon dropped the bomb on me, saying she wouldn't be with us for the full moon.

"What do you mean you won't be there?" I shot Fallon an angry glare, but I was more hurt than anything else.

She stood in the parlor, arms crossed, looking as if she wanted to cry. "I would go under any other circumstance. Believe me, I want to go, but I'd already promised Aiden I'd be there for this full moon."

I let out a growl. "Aiden, Aiden, Aiden. That's all I ever hear these days. I'm getting really fucking sick of him."

"Hey. I didn't give you this kind of crap when you ran off with Lysander," she shot back at me.

"That was different. I was supposed to be dead to the world. I couldn't come back and just hang out. And if you don't remember, I risked everything to get you back as my friend."

"And I am not discrediting that. I just made a promise, and I have to be there for Aiden and the pack." Fallon snatched her thick coat off of the back of the couch and tossed it on. She pulled the faux-fur-lined hood up over her head covering her short blond hair.

I turned away. "Fine. Just go."

"Lyssa, don't be like that," she pleaded.

"You have your thing, and I have mine. Just go."

"Everything will be fine, you'll see. And I promise I'll make it up to you later."

The front door opened, sending in a frigid rush of air. Then, just as quickly, it closed. Fallon was off with her werewolf boyfriend to celebrate the full moon and be introduced as his mate for all intents and purposes. Meanwhile, it was time for the rest of my clan to head out with Lysander's body and the crystal to the witches' circle. I wanted so much to believe things were going to work out. I wanted to hold Lysander in my arms again, but deep in the pit of my stomach, I felt uneasy. Perhaps it was just my nerves getting the better of me. Not having Fallon there with me really hurt. I had a feeling that things were not going to be as easy as Ariana had said. And if they went wrong, Lysander could be lost forever. I wasn't ready to face that possibility alone.

"Open up," Nicholas's voice boomed from behind the basement door.

I rushed over and pulled it open just in time for Nicholas and Drew to walk up the final steps with the large coffin in their arms.

"Thanks," Drew said as he passed me by. "Grab something to toss over the box and then get the front door, too."

I did as he said, pulling a large blanket out of a chest next to the fireplace in the parlor. I hoped Zuri had been able to grab a parking spot in front of the house. It would look pretty odd to have two men carrying a coffin, covered or not, out of the house and down the street.

As I opened the front door, the cold air rushed in along with flakes of snow. It wasn't a heavy fall, but there was enough coming down to make driving an adventure.

Zuri had a large van she borrowed from the wolf pack. It was parked just a few car lengths away from the house.

"Careful on those steps, they look icy," I cautioned the men as they carefully walked the coffin down the few steps to the sidewalk.

"Hope the full moon makes an appearance soon," Zuri said as she walked up to the front door. "I think that's part of the ritual."

"Great, something else that could go wrong. Weather related screw-ups!" I groaned.

"We'll be fine, girl. Seriously, you need to chill." She turned and walked inside.

I shivered; the icy wind was starting to chill me to the bone. My poor circulation, a curse of being a vampire, made winter extremely annoying. It felt as if my blood would freeze under my skin. I turned and called after Zuri, as I followed her inside. "What else do we need before we load up?"

"That's it. Ian and the rest of the boys are in the car. Just grab a coat, get Fallon and Crystal, and get in the van."

"Fallon isn't coming." I didn't bother hiding my aggravation.

She stopped in her tracks. "What? Why?"

"She has to go with Aiden."

"That's right." She nodded and took another step toward the coat closet. "I completely forgot the monthly revelry. Big night for her."

I huffed. "She's just being paraded around the pack. She could do that any other full moon. Tonight is important. Lysander's life could be at stake here."

"Wolf politics are different than most. They're a different animal, literally. This isn't just her meeting the family. Aiden is second in the pack. He's the one to take over if something were to happen to Connor. His choice in mate is important. By introducing Fallon tonight, he's making a formal commitment to her and solidifying her place in the pack."

After hearing that, I felt bad. Sure I wanted her to be with me for moral support, but it hadn't even crossed my mind that she might have needed me to be there for her.

"I probably shouldn't have given her crap then," I mumbled.

"Girl, you shouldn't be doing a lot of things lately. I'm not trying to be a bitch, but you've had a serious attitude problem. I know you lost handsome and all, but you have to snap out of this crybaby bullshit. There are other people here besides you."

Zuri was right; they all were. I'd been moody and selfish lately, and everyone around me had suffered for it. "Sorry."

"Don't say sorry to me. Just quit with the pity party, everyone-is-against-me attitude, okay?" She opened the closet by the front door and pulled out a heavy navy blue winter coat.

I nodded, not really having anything else to add.

Zuri tossed me the coat.

Crystal came up from the basement, carrying Lysander's crystal in her hands. "I'm ready when you are."

"Boys are in the car. They're just waiting on us," Zuri said. "Let's get moving."

***

With the snow and heavy traffic, our trip took longer than we had planned. The witches had picked an area close to the wildlife preserve the wolves used. I recognized the long stretch of road that seemed to go nowhere. However, just before we would have turned to enter the wolves' sanctuary, we made a sharp left and took a small dirt path deeper into the forest.

"Is it safe to be so close to the pack during their full moon revelry?" I asked.

"Don't see why not," Zuri answered. "We'll be just out-side of their borders. They're pretty good about keeping the party in their safety zone. Connor runs a tight pack."

"Yeah, you don't break Connor's rules," Ian chuckled. "He'll break your face."

"Sounds like someone has personal experience," I said.

"Me? Never." Ian shrugged and flashed me his best in-nocent smile.

"We're here," Zuri said as she turned the van and drove it into a small clearing. Other vehicles had been parked in no particular order; however, we only saw two people huddled around a small fire.

One by one, we hopped out of the van.

Nicholas took the lead and headed straight for the two people who were warming their hands by the small blaze. "Where is the rest of the coven?"

A man looked up and pushed back his hood. He met Nicholas's eyes with no apprehension, which surprised me. The witches knew about vampires, and almost every human we'd met had some level of healthy fear upon learning what we were, even if they knew we posed them no threat. There was no hint of anxiety in the air at all. He was either brave or stupid, or maybe both.

"We were wondering when you'd show," the man said gruffly. "They're all assembled in the circle. Follow us." He stood, and so did the woman beside him.

Not waiting to see if we would follow, they hurried into the tree line. Ian and Drew unloaded Lysander's coffin and carried it carefully into the forest behind Nicholas. I walked behind the men with Crystal and Zuri.

In the distance, I heard chanting and smelled the burning of wood and spices. My stomach felt queasy, but it wasn't the pungent aroma turning it. I couldn't quite put my finger on it, but things just felt... off.

I looked above at the patches of sky that could be seen through the skeletons of snow-covered tree branches. The snow had stopped falling, and bits of sky were becoming visible through the hazy clouds. *At least now we might see moonlight.*

Our trek into the forest seemed to go on forever. And as we walked deeper into the darkest parts of the forest, I felt the eerie sensation of unseen eyes on me. Unlike the feeling that accompanied a strange vampire nearby, this felt more ominous and less supernatural. I took fleeting glances around but couldn't spot the person or persons who might be setting off my internal panic alarm. I did, however, see what I thought was blinking red light, though it was not coming from the direction we were heading. It was then that the scent of fresh blood hit me. Tangy and sweet, it called out to my more beastly senses. I hadn't hunted in a few days, and instinctively my mouth watered in anticipation. I had to push back the urges. We had more important purposes. If this worked out, Lysander and I could hunt together. That pleasant thought helped soothe the beast.

"It's going to be okay," Crystal said. "I know you are worried, but try to relax."

I wondered if she had read my thoughts or just knew instinctively how *on the edge* I felt. "Thank you." I wanted to let out all the worries I had been feeling, but I'd done plenty of that these last few weeks. They'd put up with enough of my whining and complaining and worrying.

Ahead, the glow of a large fire lit our path, and I let out a sigh of relief.

"Welcome," a female voice called to us. I spotted the blonde woman, wearing a floor-length white robe tied at the waist. She stood in the center of a large circle that had been marked on the ground. At four points, a different colored candle had been placed. In the center where she stood was a large table covered with dark fabric, candles, a knife, and a large bowl. To her left were two sawhorses, presumably to hold up Lysander's coffin.

Ariana walked to us with two men trailing behind her. "These guys will take the coffin. I will take the crystal. Unfortunately I can't let you into the circle. I hope you understand."

That sent my nerves on high alert. "Why not?"

"You are supernatural beings. Your presence inside the protected circle might cause problems with the spell."

I eyed her suspiciously, but before I could respond, Crystal nodded and handed the crystal to Ariana.

"Relax. They're on our side," Zuri whispered in my ear.

"I'm sorry, Alyssa." Ariana feigned a smile. "But this is how it must be. You'll see, things will work out."

I let out an exasperated sigh, reminded myself that I was supposed to stop being such a whiny baby, and returned her smile. "Go ahead. Do what you have to. I trust you."

"Thank you," Ariana said, and turned toward the altar.

The blonde woman flicked a lighter and began pacing the circle, stopping at each point to light the candle and mumble a few words. When she finished she looked to the assembled crowd. "The circle is cast, enter now with open minds and open hearts."

Upon hearing this, the gathered assembly began to enter one by one. As each passed the woman inside, she mumbled a few words and they responded with, "In the light and love of the goddess."

Once the crowd entered, the two men carried Lysander's coffin in and set it upon the sawhorses.

Ariana followed last, reverently holding the crystal containing Lysander's spirit. "High Priestess Mysti, I bring forth the cursed object for cleansing under the light of the full moon." She held up the crystal for all to see and then handed it to the blonde woman. She and the high priestess walked together to the altar, where Mysti placed the crystal in a large bowl.

Mysti turned one full rotation, recognizing all members of her assembled coven, and then held out her hands. "We gather tonight to rejoice by the light of the moon. We celebrate the season of darkness, knowing that the next turn of the wheel will bring light. We use this time of darkness for thought, introspection, and growth. As the moon above, so the earth below."

The assembled crowd responded, "Blessed be."

Behind me, there was a snap of branches and a metallic click. I turned, and bright white light flooded my eyes.

6

My eyes burned as if I had looked directly into sunlight, but no warmth hit my skin. In an instant, my vision failed. Everything became white, and for a brief moment there was complete and utter silence. Not even the chirp of a cricket could be heard. That moment was shattered by a loud explosion and the thunder of frantic footsteps heading my way.

"What the hell is going on?" Disoriented and blind, I stumbled around amid the sounds of screaming people and the discharge of weapons. Someone bumped into me and knocked me down.

Another loud blast went off as I hit the ground. The scent of blood permeated the air around me, rich, thick, and fresh. It was so close I could taste it, feel the spray of it on my skin.

I reached out, wondering if someone had fallen with me, when something hard and heavy crushed my left hand. It felt like the rigid bottom of a steel-toe boot. My eyes watered with pain. I bit back a cry, unaware if whoever stood on me was friend or foe, and waited until the pressure released to yank my hand free and roll away.

I waited a moment to see if I'd been spotted. No one, no sound indicated anyone knew I was there. More shots were fired nearby. Something behind me fell to the ground with a soft thud. Panic had me twitching in every direction, and being blind didn't help. I sat up, clutching my wounded and throbbing hand to my chest. I tried to blink away the haze in my vision, needing to see what was happening. Everything around me was unbearably bright; shapes and figures were all washed out as if just a smudge on a flat canvas.

It was no use. My eyes refused to focus through the white haze. I knew I couldn't sit still and be a target for whoever or whatever had attacked us, so I scooted backward, feeling the ground behind with my uninjured hand until I butted up against a large tree trunk. At least, I hoped it was a large tree. To my left felt like bushes or perhaps some low-lying branches. I ducked my head underneath, hoping the foliage and the darkness of the forest would keep me hidden until my vision returned.

Heavy footsteps approached from my right. I heard a male voice say, "Alpha team, to the north."

My heart raced with sudden panic. I couldn't run. I couldn't see. The only thing I could do was make myself as small as possible. I crouched into a ball, hoping to remain hidden.

The footsteps halted. They sounded close. Right in front of me.

I held my breath and covered my mouth with my hand, thankful that as a vampire, I really didn't need to breathe. My normally slow-beating heart thundered in my ears. I was surprised the man near me couldn't hear it.

"Block their escape and push them east. Leave no survivors," the man said.

A different, garbled, static-filled male voice replied, "Affirmative."

"I'm going after the cargo," the voice in front of me said, and then his footsteps began to retreat.

When I could no longer hear him, I let out a sigh. *Cargo? What cargo?* It took a moment to hit me. *Lysander. What if this had been planned? What if they, whoever they were, had been after Lysander?*

A woman screamed in the distance, "We made a deal." Her shrieks were followed by a quick burst of gunshots.

The male voice again called out, "Cargo secure. Holy Cross, cover me." His voice trailed away. Whatever he had come for, he got it. I doubted he could have carried Lysander's coffin by himself. *He must have been after something else. But what?*

Another pair of footsteps came up slowly behind me. As they grew louder, so did the frantic beating of my heart. I thought for sure I had been found this time and braced myself for whatever might come.

"Alyssa, Crystal, Zuri?" a familiar voice whispered.

I let out a loud sigh of relief. It was Drew and he had to be close; he sounded like he was right on top of me. I reached out and grasped hold of fabric and pulled. "I'm here," I whispered back.

"Are you okay?" he asked, and it sounded as if he'd crouched down to my level.

"The light… I've been blinded." I tried again to blink away the haze in my vision and could almost make out his blurry figure.

Another loud blast went off nearby. This time, I saw the flash. It had the same intensity as the one that had blinded me. My good hand flew over my eyes to shield them from the harsh light.

"They are using some kind of phosphorous weapons to disorient us," Drew said. "Whoever they are, they came prepared."

"Yeah, I'd say their plan is working. I can't see anything."

"Try not to look directly at anything. Relax your eyes. Your vision should return soon enough."

"Who did this? Was it the witches?"

"Witches use magic, not guns. No time to talk. We have to get out of here." He yanked me up by my arm and pushed me forward.

I stumbled a few steps and caught myself on a large tree. "No use," I groaned. "I can't see where I'm going."

"I'm not leaving you behind. Hold on to me and try to keep up."

I did as he said and grabbed hold of the thick, pillowy fabric of his winter coat. He moved forward, tugging me in his wake. Drew's pace was quick, and I stumbled over what felt like large tree roots or rocks, but as we moved I heard the sounds of the battle diminish.

"What about the others?" I asked.

"We scattered when the first blast went off. I can still sense Crystal and Nicholas. They can't be too far away."

Fast steps headed our way, crunching leaves and twigs behind us as they pounded the ground. "This way," Drew whispered. He yanked me left, and took off running again.

In the darkness of the forest, my vision started to return. I was soon able to make out the trees as we passed and the rocks before I tripped over them. It was then again that I had the sudden eerie feeling of being watched. The cold prickling sensation tickled the back of my neck and made my hair stand on end.

"Do you feel that?" I asked.

"Shhh." He halted, and together we ducked behind the trunk of a tree.

"I wouldn't take any more steps in this direction," a familiar gravely voice called out to us. "There are traps set up all over this forest."

I knew that voice. At one time it had struck fear into my heart. *Santino*. Until recently, he had been the Acta Sanctorum's best hunter. He had a reputation as the one man no supernatural creature could escape. But that was before he helped us fight his once and hopefully former masters.

"What the hell are you doing here?" I asked. "Join forces with your old religious buddies again?"

"You still haven't learned to shut that smart mouth of yours. My old buddies, as you call them, want you dead. Would I warn you of the trap if that was what I wanted?" he replied, and though I couldn't see it, I could hear the smirk in his voice. "I could kill you myself if that would make things easier."

"If you have no business with our enemies, then leave us alone, Santino. We have a truce, remember?" I said.

Drew took a few steps forward, still tugging me behind.

"If you choose to ignore my warning, so be it," Santino said coolly. "There's an anti-vampire claymore mine with a special RF sensor three steps ahead of you. Trip that sensor, and if the blast doesn't kill you, the silver-wire bolo rounds will certainly make you wish you had died."

"Why tell us this?" Drew asked with a snarl. He and I both backed up a few paces. "Think you'll earn more prestige by bringing us in alive?"

I squinted through the remaining haze in my vision and spotted a small red light not too far ahead of us. For whatever purpose, Santino had told us the truth.

Santino sighed. "We worked together to destroy the West Coast branch of the Acta Sanctorum, I save you from what might certainly be a bloody and painful death, and yet you still cannot trust me."

"You'll have to make up for more than five hundred years of slaughter before I will ever trust you, Saint," Drew replied.

"We can settle our differences later," I said with an exasperated sigh. "Santino, if you're here to help us, then do that. Drew, we need to find the others, get Lysander, and get to safety."

"Saint," he laughed at the word. "I haven't been called that in quite a while. It may have been my title once, but not anymore. I gave up that life when we destroyed Quentin. Now, unless you wish to be destroyed as well, back up three more feet, then turn and follow the sound of my voice."

Drew grumbled, but did exactly as Santino had instructed. We backed away and headed toward the direction of his voice. When we reached him, Santino pointed back in the direction we had just come from. "See the light?"

It was the same light I had spotted. I nodded, and Drew grunted in agreement.

"RF trip wire. Cross the beam, and it sets the mine off."

Nearby, I felt the sensation of another vampire heading our way. In the distance I heard gunshots and what sounded like a group of men running. I turned on my heel. My vision had cleared, and I was able to see the figure running with a healthy lead, and three men carrying rifles giving chase.

"That's Ian," Drew said with sudden alarm in his voice. "He's heading for the mine."

"We have to stop him," I said.

"Get the soldiers."

"No," I heard Santino shout behind me as I took off at top speed with Drew at my side toward the three soldiers.

Whether they saw our charge or not, I will never know, but suddenly, they halted and turned to run away. I caught up with the straggler on the end. He wore an all-black uniform of cargo pants, flak coat, and helmet with night vision goggles. I pounced, jumping onto his back, tackling him to the ground. The heel of the rifle in his hands came back and smacked me in the chin, snapping my jaw closed. My eyes watered with pain, but I held on tight to his back. He squirmed and tried to roll and knock me off, but I wasn't going anywhere. I clung to him tighter, like a rodeo cowboy riding his bucking bronco, while I looked for a good place to bite down.

I bent down, to the crook of his neck, finding my target. My teeth made contact, sinking like a knife through hot butter into the soft skin of the soldier's neck. His adrenaline-fueled blood gushed into my mouth. He moaned in pain but quickly went limp under me.

"Take cover!" Santino's voice boomed loudly.

I knew better than to ignore a warning like that, especially from him. Still latched on to the soldier's neck and clinging tightly to his back, I threw all of my body weight to the ground, and managed to get him to roll on top of me.

I heard the sound of an explosion and felt the break of wind, like a rushing wave across both my and the soldier's body. A moment later, Ian cried out in pain.

7

I left my unconscious victim on the ground and headed toward the moaning and writhing form of Ian.

The scent of his blood weighed thickly in the air. Splatters of it dotted the surrounding trees, glistening in the moonlight. With all the blood around, I was surprised that Ian was still conscious.

I reached him, and though my inner beast begged for a sample of the life-giving fluid, my stomach lurched at the carnage. Ian's left arm had been severed just above the elbow. It lay in pieces around him. So too was his right leg below the knee. The remainder of his body resembled something like Swiss cheese, it had so many holes. Blood oozed out on to the ground making it sticky and slippery.

"Oh God!" I fell to my knees beside Ian and pulled his head into my lap.

He wailed in pain as I moved him. Blood loss usually made a vampire fall into a comatose-like state. Something was different now. Ian was wide awake and though I had no connection to him, I could sense the terrible pain he was feeling, almost as if it were my own. He needed blood, quick. I bit into my wrist and held it firm to his mouth, stifling his cries of pain.

"Drink, Ian. It will be okay. Just drink." Though I spoke words of comfort, I didn't believe them. He'd been so badly hurt, and there were still so many unknown enemies around. We could be attacked at any moment, or worse, another one of those weapons could go off.

I felt the pull of his mouth on my wrist and let out a sigh. At least he still had the strength to drink. The pain I sensed from him lessened as he swallowed. Immortal blood was a powerful healing agent. I just hoped I could spare enough to help him before it took its toll on me.

Santino came up behind me. "He's a lost cause," he said coldly.

If I hadn't had Ian attached to my wrist I'd have punched him for that. Santino never seemed to care for anyone or anything. How could he be so heartless? "Ian's still alive, and he needs blood to heal."

Santino huffed. "You'd be kinder to put him out of his misery. Not all of those wounds will heal."

"Why is everyone so quick to give up?" I asked.

His words echoed the sentiments others had said about Lysander. Was I the only person willing to try to save someone?

"Do something helpful," I snapped at Santino. "Grab that soldier over there—"

Before I could finish the sentence, I heard Drew approaching. I turned to see that he had one of the three soldiers we'd chased draped over his shoulder. He dropped the unconscious man to the ground near me.

"Hope it helps," he said, but his voice suggested otherwise.

"He'll never walk again. You don't regenerate missing limbs. Do you think he will want to live eternity in a wheelchair?" Santino asked.

"That's for him to decide," I growled the words, both in anger and from the loss of blood making me cranky. I'd need more myself soon too, but Ian needed as much as he could get *now*.

I pulled my wrist away from Ian's mouth, and he cried out for more. The sensation of pain radiating off him overwhelmed me. As quickly as I could, I bit into the soldier's wrist and then pushed it to Ian's mouth.

Drew bent down to inspect Ian's body. He ripped open the shredded remains of Ian's coat and the layers of shirt underneath. Some of the wounds were closing. Bits of metal had slowly pushed their way to the surface. I watched as one seeped out of his still-bleeding wound.

"What the hell is that?" I asked.

Santino bent down to take a peek at the wounds. "I warned you they were special mines. Built to maim and kill unnatural creatures. That's probably just a bit of shrapnel. His body will try to expel it all as it heals. If he were a werewolf, he'd be dying right now."

Drew bit into his own wrist and allowed his blood to drizzle over Ian's chest. "We need to get him somewhere safe. He's going to take a while to heal and needs rest."

"But what about the others? And Lysander? His coffin may still be out there."

"You don't even know if they are still alive. I warned you, there were many traps like this in the forest. My guess

is those soldiers were trained to push you into them."
Santino said matter-of-factly.

I stared up at him coldly. "You know, for someone who
isn't supposed to be on their side, you know an awful lot
about their plans."

Santino matched my frigid disposition with his own
chilly, biting tone. "Which is why I was able to save you two
from this fate. You should be a little grateful. I could have
just as easily followed them instead. Then you all would be
lying in a puddle of your own blood."

Drew looked up toward the sky and closed his eyes. He
took a few slow deep breaths as if centering himself. "I still
sense Nicholas and Crystal. They are alive. I'm going to
assume Zuri is with them."

"Thank goodness for that." As a young vampire, and
especially one not bonded to any of the other elders via a
direct blood link, I wasn't able to feel their presence.
Lysander had been the only one I was directly linked to by
blood. He'd been both my maker and my lover, and that
made our connection doubly strong.

"Then we need to find them," I said and shot a stern
look at Santino, daring him to question me or say anything
to the contrary. "We don't leave our people behind to die."
At that moment, I was never so happy to have been ditched
by Fallon. She would have never survived. She was in the
safest place possible, surrounded by her werewolf friends.

The ghost of a smile crossed Santino's aged and scarred
face. "I may not agree, but I admire your loyalty."

Drew stood. "I'll collect the other soldier's body and
bring it here. Then I'll find the others. Feed Ian as much as
you can while I'm gone." He met Santino face to face.
"You, keep them both safe until I return."

"I did not come here to babysit," Santino grumbled.

"What *did* you come here for, then?" I asked.

Santino let out a defeated sigh. "To help Lysander."

"How did you know…"

"For your help back in Las Vegas, I felt I owed it to him to keep an eye out for your clan, at least for a little while. When I heard of your troubles with the Pandora's Box, I came as quickly as I could, but I was too late. I know what has happened to Lysander, and so does the Acta Sanctorum."

"Shouldn't they be happy? Lysander's gone." It hurt to say the word. Lysander wasn't gone, he was just indisposed. But I still missed him all the same.

"Yes, indeed, because you have created a powerful magical instrument. A crystal that can trap a vampire's spirit. Think of the application if the Acta Sanctorum could duplicate that kind of magic. It would make their job of ridding the world of unnatural elements much easier."

My eyes widened in shock. "Back there. In the forest. I heard someone say they had secured the cargo. They were after Lysander the whole time."

"Yes. And I had come here to help you, but again, I was too late."

"But why would the Acta Sanctorum willingly use magic? Wouldn't that make them just as *unnatural* as us?" I air quoted as I said the word.

Santino let out an almost boisterous laugh. "Child, are you that naive? The double standard has never applied to them. I'm proof of that. Quentin was proof of that. They do not care what they have to do to stop the unnatural, they just do it."

"Then… if they have the crystal … we're fucked!" I couldn't hold back the panic in my voice.

Drew looked to me. "We'll get it back." Then he turned to Santino. "And by 'we,' I mean our clan… all of them. Stay here and protect her and Ian while I find the rest of our group."

"I will babysit if I must," Santino growled. "But it would be best to move to a safer location. There could be more Saints lurking in these woods."

"The wolf reservation is not far from here." I offered, remembering Fallon again. She was in the safest place possible. And not too far away.

Santino winced at the mention of the wolves. "They would kill me on sight."

I let out a chuckle. "The brave Santino, afraid? When did this happen?"

"It is the full moon, and the entire pack is assembled. I haven't survived all of these years by being careless with my talents. I have strength, cunning, and speed on my side, but the sheer number of them would negate all of those benefits."

"Call it what you will; you're scared to go in there. The wolves are our friends and we are members of the pack too. Theirs is the safest place for us to go. I doubt the Acta Sanctorum would step foot there tonight, for exactly the reason you mentioned. The whole pack would massacre them."

"Good plan, Alyssa. Go as soon as you can. We will regroup there," Drew said, and took off running.

Santino grumbled his annoyance, but said nothing further.

Ian squirmed in my lap. The pain he radiated had lessened, but the human's blood was not working as well as mine had. He still needed more. I listened, but couldn't hear the heartbeat of the soldier Ian had been feeding on. It was time to switch to the other that Drew had brought over.

"Hang in there, Ian. We'll get you more blood and take you somewhere safe," I whispered and patted his head gently.

Santino paced behind me as I attempted to yank the unconscious soldier's arm closer. With Ian's head in my lap, it was no easy task.

"Little help here," I said, not bothering to hide my annoyance.

Without a word, Santino dug his foot under the soldier's body and flipped him up into the air. He landed with a thud and crunch beside me, dead.

"Thanks for nothing."

"We're wasting time. Let's just move him now before your enemies return."

"My enemies, huh?"

"We can argue semantics later." He bent down and scooped Ian into his arms. Ian cursed and hissed in pain, but Santino paid him no attention. "Which way to the wolves' den?"

"Don't you know?" I asked with as much snark as I could muster, and jumped to my feet, ready to run.

"Best to enter via the front door than to sneak in through the back, wouldn't you agree?" he replied with an equal measure of attitude.

I shrugged. There was no use arguing with him at the moment. Getting somewhere safe, and doing it quick, was all that mattered.

"Your guess is as good as mine. I'm lost. Lead the way."

Santino let out a frustrated groan. "Follow me then, and let's pray we do not stumble into a hunting party."

8

The moment we entered the wolves' territory, we were surrounded. No doubt the scent of Ian's blood had alerted them. Werewolves' noses, if possible, were better than that of any vampire, and on a hunting night, they'd be especially keen to the scent of blood.

At least ten gray and black wolves surrounded us, baring their teeth. I recognized them as werewolves by their size and the way they immediately organized a tight circle around us. None of them hid in the brush; they all walked uniformly toward us, forcing Santino and me to stand side by side.

"Be very still," I whispered to Santino. "Let them learn our scent."

Werewolves, though primarily human in thinking, tended to take on their more animalistic side when in wolf form.

It was best to approach them with extreme caution until they showed signs of recognizing who you were.

Thankfully, Santino listened. He stood still, holding Ian in his arms, and allowed the largest wolf to approach.

I recognized the thick, shaggy dark-gray fur and let out a small sigh of relief. Aiden.

When the wolf finished circling and sniffing Santino and Ian, he moved on to me. My inspection took no time at all, and when he finished, Aiden sat on his two hind legs and began to change.

The air around us took on almost an electric charge. As the fur fell from his body, the wolf began to twist and contort. Each movement was accompanied by a strange popping sound like the cracking of knuckles. His muzzle shortened, bones began moving and shifting underneath bare skin. It was hard to witness as it looked so painful, but Aiden did not cry out as he continued to shift.

When he finished, Aiden let out a small groan, stood up, and stretched his newly transformed body. He stood completely naked in front of us, not bothering to cover himself. He sneered at Santino. "You brought a Saint here, into our territory. Why?" An animalistic growl accompanied his words.

The surrounding wolves echoed Aiden's growls.

Worry shook me to the core. I was an honorary member of this pack and was still new to their laws, but I knew the consequences of breaking them were severe. What if coming here had been a bad idea?

"He's no longer a Saint," I said, my voice warbling with fear. "And… we are in desperate need of sanctuary."

Ian mumbled incoherently in Santino's arms. The scent of his blood began to turn sour, as if infection had set in, though I knew that was impossible; vampires are immune to human disease. There was no time to waste in getting him to safety and figuring out what was going on.

"Ian is hurt," I blurted out. "We were ambushed. There could be more still in the forest."

"And you risk bringing them straight to us? How stupid are you?" Aiden snapped at me with all the command and intensity of a drill sergeant.

He was right; if they had followed us, then we would have led them straight to the pack. That would reveal their location if the Acta Sanctorum hadn't already known it. Either way, it was the pack's duty to protect their members. That was one of the oaths we had all taken when being made honorary members. I held my head up and tried to banish the fear from my voice. Wolves respect you more when you're confident. "We had no choice. As a member of this pack, I ask for your protection."

Aiden, second to the Alpha, had the authority to grant us sanctuary. If he did, no other wolf would challenge it. He paced the space in front of us and stroked his smooth chin, while pondering what to do. All of the wolves surrounding us turned their eyes on Aiden, waiting on his order.

My heart pounded as I waited on his decision. Why wasn't he simply saying yes and letting us pass?

"C'mon, Aiden, it's me. Please, we need to get somewhere safe, and Ian needs help. He might be dying."

The circle of wolves growled, as if telling me to shut up and wait for their leader's decision.

"They do not want me here," Santino said matter-of-factly. "They think I am a spy."

"You are more than that, Saint," Aiden spat the word out. "You are a death-bringer to all. You may have fooled Alyssa, but you do not fool me. I know of Gareth's pack in

Colorado. None escaped that massacre. I should rip out your throat on principle alone."

"My past is well documented. I will not argue that," Santino said, with no hint of remorse.

If I wasn't mistaken, he sounded almost proud as he said those words. That would do nothing to help our cause.

"He has done many bad things, but if it weren't for him, we wouldn't have destroyed the Acta Sanctorum's operations on the West Coast." I hoped that bit of information would sway the vote.

Aiden turned to me and eyed me suspiciously. "You would vouch for this… Saint?"

I met his eyes in a defiant stare. "He's not a Saint anymore. You have my word."

The moment I said that, I felt a sinking weight in the pit of my stomach and had to turn away. Vouching for someone, in the wolf pack, meant putting your life on the line for them. Though I knew Santino had done good, and I hoped he was firmly on the side of good now, I still wasn't a hundred percent sure. If he screwed us over, I'd pay the price with my life.

"You give your word… knowing the consequences?" Aiden asked.

I gulped down the lump forming in my throat, and then turned to Santino and mouthed the words, "Don't fuck me over!"

Santino gave a nod.

"Yes," I said, meeting Aiden's eyes again. "I'll vouch for him."

"I hope you know what you're doing," Aiden said, and I detected worry in his voice. I could only imagine what he must be thinking. His girlfriend, or mate, or whatever wolves call their significant other, was my best friend,

Fallon. I didn't suppose it would go over well if he ever had to kill me.

"I hope so too," I whispered, hoping and praying that I had made the right choice.

"Then follow us." Aiden crouched down and began to transform back into his wolf form. Gray hair sprouted all over his body. His hands and feet shrank, accompanied by the sound of popping knuckles. The sound grated on my nerves like nails on a chalkboard, but Aiden showed no sign of discomfort as his body contorted and reshaped. In a matter of minutes, he had regained his animal form and took off running into the woods.

The circle of wolves broke and chased after their leader. Santino and I followed close behind.

Wolves are fast runners, but vampires are just as quick. We had no trouble keeping up with the pack as they zigzagged through the forest and bounded over large boulders.

For a moment, I let myself enjoy the feel of the crisp winter air against my face and the thick pungent aroma of the damp forest. There was a certain feeling of freedom in running with the wolves. I made a mental note to join in on their next full moon revelry. At the very least, I owed it to Fallon to be there for her.

In no time, the light from a bonfire told me we were nearing the main building of the Wildlife preserve. The wolves had been smart when they set up their territory, placing it within the boundaries of protected lands. This ensured that the pack was always able to have a safe and secluded place to come to.

The large rectangle building came into view as we approached, and I could see Fallon, bundled up in her large winter coat, warming her hands by the fire.

She turned as we broke free of the tree line and the look on her face went from excited to frightened in the space of a heartbeat. "What happened? Alyssa, Ian, what's going on? Why is Santino here?"

There was no time to sit and explain. "We need to get him inside, quick," I shouted, not stopping on my way to the main building.

The preserve didn't really have what most people would consider an infirmary, but it did carry a large supply of bandages and first aid equipment, and a lot of open space to lay someone out. Wolves were a somewhat aggressive breed of supernatural creature and fighting was a way of life for them, which meant lots of injuries to heal.

The building was empty. Most of the wolves were still out on the hunt, and I was glad for that. I didn't want to have to defend myself or Santino to any other people at that moment.

"Put him in here," Fallon said as she followed us inside and pointed toward an empty meeting room off of the main lobby. "I'll grab some bandages."

Santino set Ian on a large oak conference table.

If possible, Ian looked worse than before. His pale skin had become gray. His eyes seemed to have sunk into their sockets. The wounds dotting the exposed portions of his chest were still open and oozing blood.

Vampires heal quickly, or at least we usually do. Something was definitely wrong, and the smell emanating from his body was turning my stomach. It was a sharp, metallic scent that caught in the back of my throat. It reminded me of the dead cow's blood I had once attempted to drink to avoid killing and stave off hunger.

Dead blood was not a good thing to a vampire. Since we cannot make any of our own, we must consume it. Live blood was what kept our bodies functioning. If Ian smelled of and was oozing dead blood, then something was severely wrong with him.

"Why isn't he healing?" I couldn't hide the panic in my voice.

"This is most unusual." Santino's voice remained calm. "There must have been something else in that shrapnel besides silver."

"But what?"

"I don't know," Santino said in frustration. "The Acta Sanctorum is constantly looking for new ways to fight back. It could be anything, blood thinners, anti-coagulants, mercury…."

"You know everything else about what has happened tonight, except this."

"Lots of things affect blood. How am I supposed to know exactly what was used? It is not my weapon."

I threw my hands up in frustration. "Then what can we do?"

"I told you, it was best to put him out of his misery."

"That's not an option." I growled the words. I was sick to death of him wanting me to let Ian die. "Now, either tell me what we can use to try and save him, or I'll rescind my word to the pack and let them have their way with you. "

Santino's face blanked of all emotion. If I didn't know better, I'd say I shocked him with my threat, but he was not one to be bullied.

I put my hands on my hips and glared at him. "Well, what's it going to be? Because I am done playing around. We either save him, or I watch two people die tonight. Your choice."

Santino sighed. "We will need to remove as much of the shrapnel as possible. Check every inch of his body. Then, he will need blood, lots of blood. Even then, he may not completely heal."

"Well, at least that's a start."

Fallon returned moments later. "Aiden is informing Connor of what happened. I've brought a few bandages, but I really don't know anything about vampire first aid. What else do you need?"

"Something to dig out the bits of metal in the wounds," Santino replied. "And something to muffle the screams."

"What about pain relief?" she asked in shock. "Or antiseptic?"

"That doesn't work on our kind," he grunted, then bent down and ripped Ian's shirt in half. "We just have to stabilize the damage and see if his body will repair itself."

Ian moaned as his body was jostled left and right while Santino went to work stripping him naked.

The marks and holes were everywhere, many of them still bleeding.

"The bloody ones are where we need to concentrate." He bent to whisper in Ian's ear, but spoke loudly enough for even Fallon to hear, "This is going to hurt."

9

"He didn't deserve this!" I paced the lobby of the wildlife preserve, awaiting news and the arrival of the rest of my clan. Fallon kept in step with me as I attempted to wear a track into the slate floor.

Ian's agonizing screams, though muffled by walls, assaulted my ears. I wanted to be there, holding his hand, helping him through the pain, but I couldn't bear it. And for that, I felt terrible. At least he had Aiden by his side to keep watch while Santino worked to remove all of the poisonous pieces of shrapnel.

"I feel so terrible that I wasn't with you," Fallon said.

"No!" I turned on my heel and came face to face with her. Fallon's mournful, deep brown eyes told me exactly how sorry she was, but there was no need for apologies. "If you'd been there, you'd be dead. I'm so glad you weren't, and I feel ashamed for acting like a bitch to you earlier."

"Don't be so hard on yourself, Lyssa. I get it—you were trying to save your man. If not for the promise I had made to be here with Aiden, I'd have never left your side."

I pulled her into a tight hug. "You're a true friend."

She groaned. "And you're squeezing me to death."

"Sorry." I let go and stepped back.

Before either of us could say another word, the front glass doors flung open. Crystal limped in. Her thick winter coat was in tatters and her pants were shredded and bloody.

I rushed to Crystal's side to help her. "Are you okay?"

She nodded weakly. "The others are coming."

Zuri and Nicholas followed right behind her, carrying Lysander's coffin. They too looked battered and caked in dirt, but thankfully, not bloody. That was a huge relief.

Drew entered last, carrying an unconscious Ariana in his arms.

"Were there any other survivors?" I asked.

"None that we saw." Crystal's voice was strained. She was suffering but attempting to put on a brave face. I could see wounds like the ones Ian had suffered on her legs. Her jeans were completely shredded below the knee and fresh blood trickled down her leg, dripping on the stone floor below. Just as with Ian, the wounds were not healing as they should. That had me worried.

What kind of chemicals were the Acta Sanctorum using that could have this effect on my kind?

Another of Ian's ear-splitting screams rang through the lobby, reverberating off the walls.

"Is he any better?" Drew set Ariana down on a cushioned seat in the center of the room. The concern in his voice was palpable. No doubt he knew his mate shared the same type of wounds and would soon be making those sounds.

Not wanting to worry Crystal, I tried to sound as positive as I could. "Santino said these wounds will heal once the shrapnel has been removed, but his missing limbs will never regenerate."

Nicholas and Zuri set the coffin down on the ground.

"Just how bad were his injuries?" Zuri asked.

"He lost a leg and an arm," I answered.

"Oh hell, that's bad!" Zuri gasped and her hand shot up to cover her mouth.

"How is he?" I asked, inclining my head toward Lysander's coffin.

"No harm came to the box," Nicholas responded and patted the lid. "However, the crystal has gone missing."

"Not missing." I said angrily, remembering what I'd heard in the forest. "Stolen. That was what the Acta Sanctorum was after." I pointed a finger toward the sleeping form of Ariana. "Her coven made a deal with them."

Zuri quickly placed herself between me and Ariana, as if expecting a fight. "No! Ariana's cool. She'd never do something like that."

"Well, she and her witchy friends just did," I shot back at Zuri.

"Easy... easy. No need to jump to conclusions yet." Nicholas held up his hands in peace. "That's a serious accusation you're making, Alyssa. Not that I don't trust you, but how do you know this?"

It aggravated me that Nicholas thought to question me instead of taking me at my word. "When the first flash went off. I was blinded, but I managed to hide and heard one of them mention a deal."

"Who?" Nicholas's eyes widened.

"I don't know." I reached back into my memory to try and remember the name. "I think it was … Mysti. Yes, it had to be her. She was trying to stop a soldier from advancing on her. At least, that's what it sounded like. She said plainly, 'We made a deal.' That was right before he shot her."

Nicholas turned to Zuri. "It does sound like they double-crossed us."

"Not Ariana, no!" She turned and looked with horror on the unconscious witch. "I can't believe it. She'd never betray us. We've known her for years. She and her coven have always been there to help us out."

Drew spoke up before I had a chance. "Santino told us that the Acta Sanctorum knew about the crystal. That was the reason he'd come to help us. He knew they would be after it. It stands to reason that they might strike up a deal… offer the witches something of great value… whether they meant to hold true to their word or not. Perhaps they enticed the witches to get us to a vulnerable place. Just look at how well orchestrated that attack was. They had traps set up all over the forest."

"Would they really pretend to work with witches?" Nicholas asked. "Or could they have spied on the witches and learned where to attack?"

"Does the Acta Sanctorum really ever work with anyone?" I scoffed.

"You see?" Zuri jumped into the debate. "They weren't really working with anyone. The Acta Sanctorum must have followed the witches' movements. They learned of their circle and set the trap."

"I'm inclined to agree with Alyssa here," Nicholas said. "Think about it. They knew exactly when and where to attack. We were late arriving, and still the attack was carried out flawlessly. Not to mention, you said it yourself." He pointed directly at me. "One of them said, 'We made a deal.' 'Deal' implies prior knowledge. You can't deny that."

"No." Zuri huffed. "I just can't believe she would betray us. There has to be a better explanation."

"Maybe there was a reason for it," Crystal said. "I'll play Devil's advocate here for the sake of argument. Let's say they were afraid of the Acta Sanctorum. Maybe the Saints were coming after their coven, and that was the deal they made. Save their coven instead of our clan."

"Witches couldn't possibly fear the Acta Sanctorum in the same way that you do," Fallon said.

"Witches have plenty of reason to fear religious organizations. Need I remind you about the Salem witch trials? They weren't that long ago," Crystal said.

Confusion wrinkled Fallon's face. "But witches today are more accepted. They're out in the open now. Hell, they have their own religion—Wicca."

"True." Crystal nodded. "Practitioners are common. Real, powerful witches are not. Those like Ariana's coven would have reason to fear discovery."

"Then they're stupid to charge for their services," Fallon scoffed.

"And greedy," I added with a dirty look toward the unconscious Ariana.

"Not all are out for personal gain. And magic supplies cost money too, you know," Crystal said, and I could hear the pain in her voice. She was getting weaker. We needed to get that poison shrapnel out of her leg, fast.

"Good point," Drew said. "Everyone has their price, and protection of their coven might have been enough, at least in their eyes, to turn our clan in."

Nicholas nodded. "It would make sense."

"I just can't believe that anyone would be that stupid," I said. "Even the greatest treasure in the world is not worth trusting the Acta Sanctorum over. They destroy anything unnatural. And since witches are just as unnatural as we are, they had to expect that they'd be next on the hit list."

"The Acta Sanctorum works under the pretense of maintaining the greater good," Santino said, startling me as he entered the lobby. "Their methods may be called into question, but ultimately they work for the side of good, and that may sway the vote of trust their way."

"The road to hell is paved with good intentions," Crystal snarled at Santino. "Claiming to work for the greater good is not actually working toward it." She tried to stand and fell back onto her seat.

Drew was up in an instant and at her side. "Don't try to walk yet. We have to work on your leg."

Santino held up his hands in surrender. "I wanted to let you know Ian is resting now." He looked to Crystal. "I know you do not want me here. Please understand I'm here to help, but only if you accept it. If you all wish to proceed without me, I'll leave."

"See that you do," Crystal's voice was full of venom.

Santino nodded, turned, and walked back into the room with Ian.

"We might need his help," I said. "He knows the Acta Sanctorum better than anyone else."

"I don't trust him," Crystal spat the words. "I'll never trust him."

"We've worked with him before."

She sneered at me. "Yes, and I wasn't happy about it then either."

"Save the bickering for later," Nicholas said in his most commanding voice. "We need to stay on point here. Why did the witches betray us? What was there to gain?"

"It's simple…" Drew said. "People are more willing to believe someone is working toward good if that is the front they present. I have no doubt the Acta Sanctorum lied and deceived the witches in order to gain their support. The utter destruction of their coven is proof of that. Whatever promises were made were obviously not kept. Now, we can argue all night about what happened and why, but the fact still remains, it did, and now Lysander's crystal has been taken."

"Don't you think the 'why' is important, though?" I asked. "If the Acta Sanctorum was able to get to the witches, wouldn't it stand to reason that they could get to others close to us? What about other vampires or were-wolves?"

"They have what they want," Crystal said calmly. "Drew is right. How and why does not matter any longer. We must figure out how to proceed next."

"They have Lysander's crystal. Is there any way to track them down and get it back?" I asked.

"It could take weeks to track them down. We don't even know where to begin," Crystal's tone softened. "And… we may not have that long before it's too late."

"What do you mean?" I asked.

Crystal looked up to Drew. They exchanged worried glances as if having some silent, mental conversation. I looked over to see Zuri and Nicholas exchanging similar looks. Whatever it was they were about to say, it was something they'd all been keeping from me.

I glanced over my shoulder and watched Fallon for the same suspicious behavior, but she appeared as confused as I was.

After what felt like an awkward silent eternity, Drew finally spoke up. "We hoped we could avoid this. But we think that the crystal will not be able to hold Lysander forever."

My jaw dropped in shock. "What?"

Drew continued. "We've noticed for some time now that it had been getting weaker. The blood-red color would fade and so would the strength of Lysander's spirit. It was Ariana who helped us to understand what was happening. It was dying; and with it, so was Lysander's spirit. We've been trying everything to keep the crystal alive."

I stared at them in disbelief. Of all the things they could have said, I never expected something of this magnitude. "And you kept it from me all this time. The secret meetings, the backfiring potions and dead bodies in the basement…"

"We knew how you would take it. You've been so on edge lately, we didn't want to worry you any further."

I took a deep calming breath and blew it out slowly. As angry as I felt about being kept in the dark, I understood why. "So, how long do you think the crystal will last?"

Drew shrugged and leaned his head against Crystal's. "We don't know. A week… maybe more, maybe less."

"Then we really do need Santino's help. He has intimate knowledge about the Acta Sanctorum and how they operate. If anyone would know where they might be, it's going to be him."

Drew let out a sigh and looked to his mate. "She's right, love. We're going to have to work with him if we hope to save Lysander. Can you do that?"

"Fine," Crystal grudgingly agreed. "But I'll only deal with him when it's necessary to do what is needed to retrieve Lysander's crystal."

The look of sheer hatred on her face was impossible to miss. She snarled toward the hallway, where Santino had stood last.

Unhappy about it or not, at least she'd agreed, and that was as much as we could hope for with her. Crystal had never gotten over her anger toward Santino, not that I blamed her. After finding out he'd massacred an entire pack of werewolves out in Colorado — werewolves that had been as close as family to Crystal — I could see where her anger came from. It didn't matter whether Santino was working for our side or not.

"Fallon, please go and get Santino," Drew asked.

She nodded and stood.

Drew nuzzled in close to Crystal and whispered in her ear, "We'll get this sorted quickly. You won't have to deal much with him, okay?"

She nodded but didn't say a word.

Meanwhile, Fallon slipped off down the hallway to tell Santino we were ready for him, and Ariana began to stir. My own simmering anger began to boil as I saw the witch's eyes crack open. The fate of my Lysander hung in the balance, and it was all because of her coven.

Nicholas must have sensed my unease. Before I could get up from my seat and approach Ariana, he was at my side. "Don't be rash, Little Warrior." The words came out calm, but the warning look in his eyes said otherwise.

"We at least need to find out what she knows," I responded.

"We will… but not with force and anger. Wait until she has recovered and then we can question her."

Zuri, still close by, looked over her shoulder and saw Ariana was waking. "You got some explaining to do, sista'." Her tone was serious but lacked the anger I thought she should feel.

Ariana, groggy and disoriented, tried to sit up. She groaned as she pushed herself, favoring her right hand over her left. With deep breaths and a few painful gasps, she managed the task.

"You okay?" Zuri asked.

"No… I don't think I am," Ariana replied. "I think I broke something." She grasped her left hand and slowly wiggled her fingers and wrist, wincing with each small movement.

"Well, you're alive. That's more than can be said for the rest of your coven," I said without holding back my anger.

"What do you mean? Where are the others?

"Dead," I blurted the word out.

"They're… dead?" Ariana gasped. "All of them?"

As much as I wanted to hate her at that moment, I couldn't. She wasn't faking the shock, or the tears that began to stream down her face.

"We were ambushed," Zuri explained. "You're looking at all of the survivors, honey."

"Ambushed, but who would do that?" she sobbed.

"You mean to tell me you don't know what happened?" I narrowed my eyes as I looked down to meet hers.

She didn't shy away from my gaze, which I found extremely surprising. She knew the mental control we were capable of if necessary, and I took this as a sign she accepted my use of it.

I reached out with all of my power and delved deep into her mind. "Tell me the truth," I said slowly.

Her whole body shuddered. Her words came out in shaky gasps. "I... don't know ... anything."

"Let her be," Nicholas said harshly and grabbed me by the shoulders. "She's telling the truth."

I growled in frustration and blinked away the mental connection. He was right, though—I felt no deceit from Ariana, only fear. Whether that fear came from having five angry vampires staring down at her or the unknown depravity of the enemy who had attacked us, I couldn't tell. Neither satisfied my anger. I needed an outlet for it. I needed someone to blame and punish for what had happened. I punched a hole into the sheetrock wall.

"What are you planning to do with me?" Ariana asked, her voice still shaky.

Zuri put an arm around her. "Honey, we aren't gonna do anything to you. We're not like that."

"No. Nothing will happen to you," Nicholas sat down on a moss-green fabric-covered bench along the wall near the back windows. "But, since it appears your coven is at fault, you will help us in any way possible to fix the situation."

Ariana was quick to reply. "Anything. Of course."

Santino emerged from the room and stood in the hallway with his arms crossed. "I'm told you want me to stay now."

"It would appear we need to work together again," Nicholas responded.

"Yeah. Tell us everything you know. Where would the Saints take the crystal? Why do they want it? Who's running— "

"Calm down, girl. One thing at a time," Zuri said.

"Hey, after spending all this time in the dark, thanks to all your secrets, I think it's high time I was given the info."

"Alyssa, we told you… We didn't want to worry you," Crystal said, sounding a little annoyed.

Santino cleared his throat. "Standard procedure for the order would be to catalogue any unnatural artifact first, before sending it to Rome. If we are quick to act, we might be able to intercept it at one of their repositories."

"What are we waiting for, then?" I asked. "If you know where we should go, then let's get a move on."

"It's not so simple, girl," Santino snapped at me. "We can't just waltz in and take what we want. There's bound to be heightened security in place. We need a plan." He glanced over to Crystal. "And we need to assess our current injuries."

"I'll heal on my own," Crystal said.

"Only after the poison shrapnel had been removed," Santino replied.

"My mate can handle it." She squeezed Drew's hand. He looked down and nodded.

"Where is this repository, and have you been inside before?" Nicholas asked.

"Years ago, yes. It's in an old church," Santino said.

"Surprising," I said with a laugh, which earned me a dirty look from everyone in the room.

Santino let out an impatient sigh. "Below the chapel, in the crypt, there are various rooms used by the Acta Sanctorum. One such room is the artifact repository. All the local unnatural artifacts are stored there unless Rome has a particular interest in them. I would guess that the crystal will be held there until transport can be arranged."

"Wait, does that mean every city has a repository?" I asked.

"No. They are set up in major areas. Luckily for you, Boston happens to be where the local repository resides for the New England area."

That was a stroke of luck for sure.

"Being a church, and one currently occupied and in use, will pose some problem," Santino continued. "There will be civilians and clergy there… even during the evening hours. If indeed they were after the crystal as an item of interest, it will be under heavy guard. You can expect to see more soldiers on patrol."

"Would it be better to go in during the day?" I asked.

For the second time in only a few minutes, all eyes were on me as each person in the room gave me dirty looks.

"What I mean is, we have non-vampire friends who are not limited to night time, and may not be known to the Acta Sanctorum. Would it be easier to send them ahead of us to scout what they can?"

"Anyone you sent in there would be putting their life at risk," Santino said. "And I doubt you have any friends the Acta Sanctorum doesn't know about. They were meticulous in setting up this ambush. I can guarantee they've been keeping an eye on anyone you might be in acquaintance with. Even your human friend."

I crossed my arms and let out a desperate sigh. "Then we'll just have to go in with force." It seemed like we'd been backed into a corner that was impossible to get out of.

Nicholas approached me and put a hand on my shoulder. He looked down with what I assumed was meant to be a reassuring smile. "We'll get him back. We'll figure out a way. Try to relax."

10

Relaxing was the last thing on my to-do list. We spent the day trapped inside, helplessly waiting for the opportunity to retrieve Lysander's crystal. As night fell, Santino, Nicholas, Ariana, and I assembled and headed toward the old church. Drew decided to stay behind to watch over Crystal and Ian as they healed from their injuries. Zuri went back on her regular patrol, which was part of the duties of being a member of the Olde Town Pack.

None of the clan wanted me to go with the raiding party, but I wasn't taking "no" for an answer. If Lysander's crystal was in the old church, that's where I was going.

Ariana insisted she be allowed to go too. She demanded the opportunity to prove her innocence in our betrayal by offering her services, and magical knowledge, to help make our mission easier.

The evening felt unbearably cold. Perhaps it was the fact I hadn't fed since sharing blood with Ian, or that I was still not used to the New England winters. Whatever the reason, even through the layers of clothes I'd piled on, I felt like my whole body was slowly turning into a popsicle. I found myself moving slower and trailing behind the others.

"I'm not sure of what to expect when we get in there. You will listen to everything I say. If I say run, you run. You hear me?" Santino warned as we approached the old red-brick building with its pristine white steeple.

"Let's get on with it," Nicholas grunted. I could tell he wasn't pleased with having to take orders from Santino. Being a former Roman Legionary hadn't ever left him. Battle strategy and giving orders were his areas of expertise.

The place didn't give off the foreboding vibe it should have, given that the people inside were all bent on killing me and my kind. Wrought iron gates and low bushes surrounded the church. A heavy coating of snow covered them, reminding me of a Christmas-themed snow globe or a picture on a holiday greeting card.

Beyond the borders of the tiny churchyard and protective fence was the city. Narrow streets in all directions converged at the entrance, each of them housing three- and four-story brick row houses, shops, and commercial buildings. Along these narrow streets were tightly packed parked cars. Lamps dotted the thin sidewalks, casting small circles of light below, but leaving plenty of shadowy areas too. There were plenty of places for someone to hide.

"Wait," Ariana whispered as we edged along the silent street, our feet crunching on the snowy ground. She dug into her pocket and pulled out a few silver chains. On each chain was a pendant of twin crescent moons with a circle between them. She held them up to us in her gloved hands.

"This is a symbol of the goddess. Put these on, and she will protect us."

"No offense, but she didn't do much protecting last night, did she?" Nicholas said in his snarkier-than-thou voice.

"I'm trying to help," Ariana grumbled, and held out the chains.

While I felt much the same as Nicholas, untrusting of our witchy companion, I reached out and took one of the necklaces. "Better to be safe than sorry, I guess."

"Since when have you been concerned with safety, Little Warrior? Is someone beginning to grow up?" Nicholas asked.

I caught the hint of a genuine smile in his otherwise stony face. If I wasn't mistaken, it sounded like he'd attempted to praise me for my caution. However, as usual, it came out in a sarcastic and antagonistic way. I didn't bother to respond and risk ruining the moment.

Santino guided us around the building, which seemed surprisingly empty. "The chapel at the main entrance is small. It connects around back to the rectory and lower-level crypts. We'll want to enter on the other side."

I reached out with all of my senses but came up with nothing. Other than the smell of bums sleeping in the alley ways and the crisp breeze blowing through the bare tree branches, there was little sound or smell to indicate anything or anyone else was around. On the ground, the snow had been trampled so many times it would be impossible to locate specific footprints, not that I knew how to track. To all apparent senses, there seemed no danger. That's what I was afraid of.

"I thought you said there would be heightened security?" I whispered.

"There should be," Santino said gruffly. "This is very odd indeed."

"It's the things you can't see that you should worry about. There are many buildings around. Soldiers could be hidden inside," Nicholas said, his tone wary.

"He's right." Santino looked around in a small circle, then suddenly ducked and yanked Ariana down with him. "In the windows. Get down."

I crouched down low and slowly backed myself into a shadow created by the corner of a building. "Do you think they saw us?"

Nicholas put a finger to his lips as he hunched down beside me.

Santino turned to Ariana. "What magic can you do for us, witch?"

Ariana crinkled her nose at the way he said the word, but didn't respond with any anger in her voice. "What do you need, specifically?"

"Cover. We need to get to the back of the chapel undetected."

"Give me a minute and let me see what I can come up with." She dug into her coat pocket and pulled out a small moleskin notebook wrapped with a thick elastic band.

I exchanged worried glances with both Nicholas and Santino as Ariana thumbed through the pages.

"Got it," she said and dropped to the ground, sitting cross-legged in the snow. I really hoped her snow pants were waterproof. She set the small notebook open in front of her and began a low chant while holding her hands out, palms to the sky.

Minutes went by like this. Nothing seemed to be happening. I was never good at waiting. In fact, I hated it. I paced in front of Ariana, making sure to stay in the shadow of the building, letting out impatient sighs while she chanted away. Nicholas and Santino ignored me and focused, with hopeful expressions, all of their attention on Ariana. I paced so much that I had worn the snow into slush, and it no longer crunched under my feet. That's when I heard the first deep rumble. Thunder.

My head shot up. The sky became electrified with violently beautiful bursts of light that arced through the clouds. The low rumbles intensified into cymbal clashing sounds that shook the windows of the surrounding buildings.

Ariana wasn't shaken, though; she seemed almost in a trance of some kind. She continued to chant, holding her hands higher in the air, oblivious to what was happening.

The wind picked up, swirling all around us, and with it came a flurry of tiny white flakes.

I shivered as the temperature dropped, but I couldn't help the smile that erupted across my face. It was a brilliant plan. She'd called forth a small blizzard to conceal us as we approached. I made a mental note to thank her for that later.

"Let's move while we've got cover." Nicholas urged Santino and me on toward the church.

"What about Ariana?" I yelled over the now roaring wind. She seemed locked in her trance. I bent down and pressed on her shoulder, but she didn't respond. I shook her harder. "Ariana, we need to go now."

Still, she refused to respond. I looked up to the others and shrugged. "I don't know what to do. We can't just leave her here, though. She'll freeze to death."

The snowfall thickened and an icy blast of wind barreled into us, almost knocking me over. I tightened the pulls on the hood of my coat and zipped it up to my nose, but still the cold wind assaulted me. My eyeballs felt as if they might freeze in their sockets. Nicholas was right; we needed to move, now, before we all froze.

Nicholas bent down, picked up Ariana's small note-book, and tossed it at me. "Hold this." He reached out and shook her as I had. Just as before, Ariana failed to respond. He cocked his hand back and struck her across the face. I winced at the sound of the smack landing against her probably raw and frozen cheek. That seemed to get results, though. Ariana screamed, and her eyes shot open. A flood of anger flushed her face. Her cheek turned a brilliant shade of red. She spoke a phrase I couldn't quite understand, but it had a Latin edge to it. Then, suddenly, Nicholas was knocked back by an unseen force, onto his butt.

"Are we going to sit here and beat each other up, or are we going to head inside before we freeze to death?" Santino asked.

Nicholas stood and shook some of the caked on snow from his clothes. "I was trying to help. I'll be sure to refrain from that in the future."

"That hurt!" Ariana said angrily, then took and released a deep breath, and stood as well. "Sorry, I didn't mean—"

"Let's just get out of this cold," Nicholas said sharply.

I tried to nod in agreement, but my joints were so cold my neck felt stuck. We needed to find warmth soon, or we risked becoming statues in the churchyard.

The wind raged around us, swirling the falling snow so much that it was hard, even with my supernatural vision, to see two feet ahead of me. I had no doubt we were well covered from any human onlooker. Ariana's little spell was certainly working.

"Stay close," Santino managed to say over the rumbling wind.

Through the blizzard I saw the outline of his tan coat and navy pants. Using that as my guide, I headed toward him. As long as I kept him in my sight, I wouldn't lose him. I only hoped the other two were doing the same. I was afraid to chance losing sight of Santino in the moments it would take me to turn around and locate the others.

With my head tilted into the wind, I walked for what felt like miles, even though it was only the equivalent of crossing the street. The creak of the wrought iron bars told me we'd reached the gate. The church courtyard was small, and I counted twenty or so steps until I felt the hard brick exterior of the building. I kept it to my right, always following the tan coat of Santino in front of me as we made our way around the building.

When we reached a set of concrete steps, I nearly barreled into Santino.

"We're going to have to enter here." He spoke loudly enough to carry over the wind. "How long will this storm last?" he asked Ariana.

She shrugged. "There's no telling. I can invoke the magic of nature to begin the cycle, but it's not a light switch; I can't just shut it down at will. We may have an hour, we may have minutes. It's all up to the goddess."

"Longer is better at this point. It is providing excellent cover at the moment. If it lasts until we have finished, we may have a good chance to escape."

"Either way, we'll need some kind of distraction to get in, won't we?" I asked. "I doubt we'll just be able to wander inside."

"Thank you, Captain Obvious," Nicholas retorted. "Now, do you have anything helpful to add, or would you like to continue telling us things we already know?" He turned to Santino. "How many guards do you think they would have at this entrance?"

"Normally, only one. However, with the potential heightened security, they could have soldiers stationed throughout the halls."

"We've dealt with their guards before." Nicholas nodded at me.

We had done exactly that, only a couple of months prior, when we took out Quentin's operation. And from what I remembered of them, they hadn't been very well trained—just a bunch of fanatical guys with guns looking to shoot a vampire or two. The one in particular that I had let live hadn't even been smart enough to avoid looking me in the eyes.

"They are not always the best trained for the job," Santino agreed. "But they are armed and dangerous. A close-range shot will put you on your ass long enough for them to either run for help or try and finish the job."

"Finish the job" being to decapitate a vampire. Other than fire, it was the only way we could truly be killed. Our kind are very quick to heal.

"Well, if we stay out here, we'll turn into statues in this blizzard. I'll take my chances with a gun," I said through chattering teeth. "Let's distract them with a human." I looked at Ariana. "She can cause a commotion and claim sanctuary or something like that. Get their attention. While they're dealing with her, we attack."

"Not a bad idea, Little Warrior. I could go for a warm snack," Nicholas said.

Santino let out a sound like a growl.

"You can be all holier-than-thou about it if you want. If it's a case of me or them, I'm with Nicholas," I said. "And I need blood. The hotter, the better."

Ariana cringed. Sometimes I forget what it must be like for a human to hear us talk about our eating habits. "What about their guns?" she asked.

I shrugged. "Just hope we can disarm them before they can use them."

She grasped hold of her charm necklace and said a silent prayer, and then let out a worried breath. "Here goes. I'm trusting you all."

"Just like we trusted you," I said warningly. She might be on our side right now, but I still hadn't forgiven her coven for betraying us.

She scowled back at me, and then wrapped her scarf tightly around her mouth and nose so only her eyes were visible and pulled up the hood of her winter coat. Ariana took the steps one by one, slowly. Whether she was just being careful not to slip or she was too nervous, I couldn't tell. As she moved up, so did we, staying a few steps behind her, ready to pounce as soon as the door opened.

When she reached the top, she began furiously pounding on it. "Help! Help!" she screamed. "Please! You have to help me!"

Her loud cries were very convincing.

I heard the click of a lock and the creak of old wood. The door opened a fraction of an inch.

"Please. They're after me! I need sanctuary."

The wind still raged around us, but through the thick swirl of snow I saw the dark uniform of an Acta Sanctorum soldier. He spoke to Ariana so low, I couldn't pick up what he was saying.

She continued to play her part beautifully. She sobbed and hiccupped loudly, and then threw herself onto the door. "Please. Vampires. They're out there. They're going to kill me!"

The soldier finally opened up. He grabbed Ariana, shoved her inside, and stepped out, rifle in hand, to inspect.

That wasn't exactly the reception we were hoping for. I couldn't see far enough inside to tell if she was okay or not, nor could I tell how many more soldiers were inside waiting.

A gun discharged. The sound had come from the inside of the church. The soldier who had come out to inspect turned around before he got close enough to see us.

Anticipation had my heart pounding in my ears. I looked to Nicholas and mouthed the words, "What do we do?"

11

In the space of a second, Santino leapt up the stairs, tackled the soldier, and snapped his neck. Nicholas jumped into action and I followed close behind. We burst through the semi-opened door to find Ariana standing against the wall, unharmed, but trembling violently while holding up one of the soldier's rifles. A dead soldier, an older, heavyset man, lay at her feet with a hole in his chest. His blood pooled out onto the ground and slowly oozed its way to where Ariana was standing.

"He, he, he..." She couldn't seem to find the words. Ariana inched backwards to get out of the path of the blood, but could go nowhere with her back against the wall.

Nicholas took the rifle from her and strapped it over his shoulder. "Good job."

Ariana was in a state of shock. I guessed that she'd never had to kill a man before. That's not an easy thing to get over. I'd struggled with it myself too in the beginning. At times, I still had issues with it, but vampires almost always have to kill their prey.

"We have to move. I'm sure others heard the shot," Santino said.

I put my arm around Ariana. "C'mon. You have to hold it together right now. Can you do that?"

She trembled under my arm and squeaked out, "Okay."

"Good. You'll be fine. Stay close to me. I got your back." I helped her balance as she stepped over the pool of blood.

Santino waved us forward. He took a narrow hallway ahead of us. Nicholas watched our backs, taking up a spot in the rear.

As we moved, I picked up the putrid scent of death. Dry and dusty, it caught in the back of my throat, leaving a rancid taste of decay in my mouth. "Eww, what is that?" I whispered.

"Hush," Santino responded. "We're close to the crypts and the repository."

Another scent wafted toward me, accompanied by the thumping of heavy footsteps. "Incoming," I said.

A stairwell to our right vibrated as the footsteps became louder. Three, maybe four men were headed our way by the sound of their loud, heavy, quick footfalls.

I pulled Ariana with me against the wall just to the side of the staircase, while Nicholas and Santino flanked the bottom step, ready to pounce.

As soon as the first soldier reached the last step, Santino grabbed him, yanked him aside, and snapped his neck.

The speed and precision with which he moved was both awe-inspiring and a reminder why he had developed such a fearsome reputation.

The others were all too close to have time to stop, turn, and retreat. Nicholas grabbed the second. He bared his teeth and sunk them straight into the helpless man's neck. I let go of Ariana and lunged forward to grab the third, but there was one more I hadn't accounted for, and he was armed. In my momentary hesitation, seeing the additional soldier, he'd had time to fire his weapon.

The loud *bang* went off, and I felt the white-hot sting of metal race through my shoulder.

I bit back a cry as tears welled up in my eyes. The soldier in my grasp tried to struggle free; he threw me off balance, and I wobbled off the bottom step.

Another shot fired. That one, however, missed its mark.

Santino came to my aid, catching me before I fell over. He knocked me and the soldier still struggling to get out of my grip into the wall, and bounded up after the one shooting at us.

Pain quickly turned to anger. I locked on to the soldier still held loosely in my grip and bit down hard into his neck. His hot blood pumped into my mouth fast, aided by the frantic beating of his heart. Rich and soothing, it washed down my throat and warmed me to the core. The throbbing pain in my arm quickly stopped. I felt my torn skin mending itself and strength returning to my hand. I wrapped my arms around the dying soldier and squeezed as I sucked every last drop from his body. When I let him drop, he was no more than a husk.

I sighed in relief.

"Thirsty?" Nicholas taunted. "You've got a little something on your face."

"A little." I smirked and wiped my mouth.

Ariana went white as a ghost. She remained plastered against the wall where I'd left her. Her body shook with violent trembles. I took a step down to go soothe her, but she jerked backward away from me.

"It's okay, we're on the same team, remember?"

She held her goddess charm up as if it would defend her. "Stay back."

"I take it you've never actually seen a vampire feed before, have you?" I asked.

Santino stomped down the stairs. "We need to finish this up quickly. There were another two up there. I don't know how many more know we are here."

"Agreed. Let's not waste time," Nicholas said.

Ariana cowered into a corner, still holding up her charm necklace.

"If we leave you here, the Saints will get you. Like us or not, right now, we're your best option." I said, and held my hand out to her.

When she didn't immediately respond. I turned away. "Fine, your choice." I knew she would follow. I remembered Fallon's wary reaction to the first time she'd seen me feeding. I'll admit it can be a scary sight, but ultimately she knew we weren't the bad guys and, shaken as she was, Ariana would know that too.

I followed Santino and Nicholas down the stairwell. Ariana's soft steps creaking on the stairs confirmed that she was in fact following as I'd anticipated.

Below, the dank smell of decay was more prevalent. But there was something else. A warmth I hadn't felt in over a day. Lysander. His crystal was here. I sensed it, and smiled.

Nicholas turned to look at me with a relieved smile. "We're close."

A child vampire can always feel their maker's presence. Unlike the eerie, hair-raising, eyes-on-your-back feeling that accompanied a strange vampire, a master and fledgling connection was different. A maker's presence always held a calm and relaxing sensation. Nicholas and I had both been turned by Lysander and shared that connection with him.

At the bottom of the steps was a long corridor of what appeared to be old vaults. They must have been the crypts. To the end of the corridor was a heavy wooden door with a slot in the middle, set just about eye level.

We were spotted by the two men guarding the doors, and they opened fire. I backed up out of reflex and knocked into Ariana. She screamed as she toppled over onto the steps.

Bullets raced past me. I didn't want Ariana to get hurt. I could take a few bullets and heal; she, however, being human, might just bleed to death before we could get her help.

I dove on top of her. She kicked and screamed for me to get away.

"Shhhhh, I'm trying to help," I said angrily as she punched and kicked at me.

The shooting stopped at the same time Ariana began spitting out Latin-sounding curses at me, but unlike with Nicholas, they didn't seem to have any effect on me. I found it curious, but didn't want to stop and ask why. We had more important things to do.

I stood and turned to see Nicholas feeding on yet another soldier, while Santino bent over his dead soldier, removing weapons from his pockets.

"Why don't you feed?" I asked.

Santino turned to look at me. His wild gray and black mess of hair was wet with melted snow and perspiration; it clung to his scarred face, making him look like a monster. "You know I don't feed from humans."

"You need the blood as much as we do."

"I make my own choices. I'm not a savage who feeds on anything that crosses my path."

"Well, you could have at least saved him for me." Dead blood was no use to me. It turns bad so quickly. I needed fresh live blood from a pumping heart to sustain me.

"I'm not your caterer either," Santino grunted. He pocketed a handgun and a large serrated knife, and then stood and turned to face the wooden door. After trying the handle and finding it locked, he knocked three times.

"It's all right, Saul," Santino said confidently.

Saul? Who the heck is Saul? If he had a friend on the inside, why did we have to fight our way here? I wondered.

I heard the latch and watched the door creak open, just enough to see old wrinkled fingers wrap around the edge.

"Is that really you, old friend?" A shaky voice, withered with age, spoke from behind the door. "I'd heard you were killed."

"I'm well. But I'm afraid I'm not here for small talk." Santino spoke with such unfamiliar affection to this unseen man.

"You want the crystal, I take it," the old man said.

"Afraid so."

"Bad business these boys are getting into, mixing with the unnatural. 'Course, you know all about that, being what you are."

"Please let us have it. We'll cause you no trouble," Santino said.

The door opened all the way, and I could finally see the old man who'd hidden behind it. He looked frail, nothing more than sagging skin covering thin bones. A white lab coat hung from his shoulders like an old lady's cloak. The old man stood with a hunch, and I could see the bones of his shoulders underneath his coat despite the layers of clothes underneath.

"Won't do me much good to resist, now would it?" Saul said with a cough. "Those boys guarding me didn't slow you down. I'm not going to do any better."

"Saul, we've been friends for years. I would never dream of harming you."

I'd never seen Santino speak so kindly to anyone. It shocked me to the core. *Santino actually had a friend!*

The old man stepped aside and let us in. "I'll just take a walk now, and get some fresh air while you do whatever it is you're planning to do."

Santino smiled warmly. "Thank you, old friend."

I walked up behind Santino. "What if he's going to get reinforcements?"

"As slow as he walks, that will take some time." Santino smiled warmly, but not at me. He gazed out past the door to the fading shadow of his friend. "We should be well out of here before he comes back."

I looked around the room. It was deceptively large, with rows of shelves housing all manner of objects. At the end of each row was a placard with numbers written on it. I turned around and saw a desk on the opposite wall. Sets of file cabinets flanked it, and shelves filled with binders and folders lined the wall above.

"Where do we begin?" I asked.

Nicholas placed a hand on my shoulder. "Think. How would you locate his crystal?"

The warm presence was here in this room. I could feel it. I closed my eyes and took a deep cleansing breath. I let my mind and body relax and listened for the pull of Lysander's spirit.

There. Straight ahead.

I opened my eyes and was staring right at the desk. "There, I think." I took quick steps forward. The desk was a mess of papers and files. On top of those were what looked like some old scarves and a few decorative boxes. "It's got to be in one of those."

Nicholas and I rummaged through them, tossing aside the papers, cloth, and boxes in our wake.

"A little respect for Saul's work, please," Santino barked at us.

We'd torn through everything on the desk and still hadn't found the crystal. "It's here. I know it is. I can feel it."

"I can too." Nicholas widened his search, opening up the cabinets and knocking things down off the overhead shelves.

I turned around to see what Santino was up to and found him wandering up and down the aisles of catalogued items. Ariana, it seemed, had found something of interest. She held an old dusty book in her hands. Her eyes widened as she flipped through the pages.

"Check those lower drawers," Nicholas barked, snapping me out of my own thoughts.

I did as he asked. The lower desk drawers were locked, but a quick pull using my supernatural strength pried the faceplate off and I was able to gain access inside. I heard Santino behind me, grumbling about the destruction, but I didn't care. Inside the drawer, wrapped in newspaper, was the crystal. I felt the pulse of Lysander's energy the moment I touched it.

"Got it," I exclaimed and stood up triumphantly. It felt so good to hold on to it again. I zipped it up under my coat, and hugged it tightly to my chest. "Now let's get the hell out of here."

12

Our way out was much easier than the way in, though we did have to step over quite a few dead bodies to make it back to the door. I wasn't sure where Saul had disappeared to, but he was nowhere to be seen as we quickly made our way out.

The storm still raged outside, providing continual cover as we fled with the crystal and the old book Ariana had found. The thrill of our small victory helped us push through the cold, wind, and snow.

"How long did you say this storm was going to last?" I asked. It hurt to speak; my teeth chattered so hard they made my fangs pierce my wind-chapped lips. My already icy blood felt frozen in my veins.

"As long as the goddess wants it to." Ariana hugged the book she'd stolen to her chest and brushed past me as we loaded into the van and hurried back to Zuri's row house.

"Let's hope we have enough wood to stay warm until her majesty the goddess is finished," Nicholas said sarcastically. He rushed into the parlor and began stacking logs in the fireplace. It wasn't long before he had a roaring fire going.

I shucked off my coat, wrapped Lysander's crystal in it, laid it on the couch, and then took a good seat right in front of the hearth.

Ariana grabbed a spot on a chaise longue to the side of the fireplace. Book in hand, she sat slowly perusing the pages.

Fire had never felt so good. I sat in front of it, luxuriating in the heated glow as it warmed my skin, my aching muscles, and my stiff bones. Warmth was such a delicious feeling after being chilled straight to the core. "I can now safely say I know what defrosting meat feels like. And it's good!"

Nicholas let out a hearty laugh—the first I'd heard from him in a long time. "Careful. You get any closer, you'll learn what roasting meat feels like."

"Ask me if I care at this point." The heat felt so good I almost wanted to stick my hand in the fire just to absorb more of it. But, knowing better, I stood and stretched, and then walked back to the couch and picked up the crystal. Immediately, I felt the pulse of Lysander's warmth, but there was something else too. A sense of worry and foreboding. I looked down to inspect it and saw again the clear tip. Not even a day had gone by and it was already draining. It seemed to be happening faster and faster.

"How long did you say he could last in here?" I couldn't hide the worry in my voice.

Concern played across Nicholas's face. His eyes softened as he too gazed upon the crystal. "We don't know," he said somberly.

Ariana looked up. "This tome is filled with ancient magic." Her eyes sparkled with awe. She held up the book in her hand. "These pages are covered with so many wonderful spells, the likes of which I haven't ever run across before. It's fascinating. I'm certain I can find something in here."

"But how long will that take? And how much are you going to charge us?" I said with a mixture of anger and worry. Witches never did anything for free.

"I'm in your debt," she said with a frown. "Instead of leaving me to the Saints or killing me yourselves, you spared me after my coven betrayed you. All I ask is that once I've done my duty, you never call upon me again."

"Had enough vampire business, have you?" Nicholas asked, the snark returning to his voice.

"Werewolf too," she added quickly. "You all lead bloody and violent lives. I just want to be left in peace to practice my magic."

"Can't speak for the wolves, but we'll let you off the hook if you save Lysander."

Nicholas gave me a warning look, like I had spoken out of turn or promised something beyond our ability to give. But he didn't speak his thoughts out loud. I didn't care what I had to promise. All I wanted was my Lysander back. Then we could return home and live our lives in peace.

"I'll do my best," Ariana said. "But I'll need a little time to decipher some of these spells, and access to ingredients. I'll have to make a trip back to the coven house for supplies."

"You'll leave the book with us for safekeeping while you're gone," I blurted out, not bothering to check what Nicholas thought. "For insurance purposes, I mean."

Nicholas smirked at me. "When did you become the shrewd negotiator?" He turned to Ariana. "She's right, though. Because of your coven's betrayal, we still have reason to distrust you, so the book stays with us while you collect your supplies."

"Fair enough. I'll need some protection as well. If my high priestess had dealings with the Acta Sanctorum, then they will most certainly know where our coven kept their things."

"That is something you will have to request from the wolves. If they agree, they can escort her during the day when it is safest," Santino said. I'd almost forgotten he was there.

He stood like a guard in the foyer, as if waiting for someone to barge in through the front door. He hadn't even bothered to come warm his hands by the fire. Such strange behavior; but then again, I was glad to have him on alert. His reputation for being an undefeated warrior and hunter made me feel much safer with the Acta Sanctorum so close at hand.

"This is all well and good, but is there anything we can do for Lysander now? I can feel his weakness, and that makes me worry." I hugged the crystal to my chest.

"Blood is the only thing that has helped in the past." Ariana stood and set the book aside. She walked to the door leading to the basement, opened it, and disappeared down into the darkness. A moment later she returned carrying a small tan ceramic saucer and what appeared to be a ceremonial dagger. It was beautiful, with a carved wooden handle with silver accents depicting the various elements surrounding a woman whose hands were lifted upward. The double-edged blade had a mirror finish and smooth sharp edges. Ariana laid the saucer on the coffee table in the center of the room.

"The crystal please," she said and looked directly at me. Thankfully, now there was no fear in her eyes.

I breathed a sigh of relief for that. There was nothing worse than calming down a scared human who's worried, for no reason, that you're going to kill them. I didn't enjoy that with Fallon, and I would not with Ariana either.

I joined her and knelt at the table, then handed the crystal to her.

She placed it in the center of the ceramic saucer, standing it on its wider end with the point upwards. "Hold out your wrist, please."

I did so without hesitation. The knife's edge was very sharp. I barely felt the slice as she opened my veins. Blood pooled to the surface of my skin and drizzled down my arms. She twisted my wrist, positioning it over the over the saucer, allowing my blood to fall on the crystal.

To my astonishment, as soon as it touched the stone, it disappeared as if it had been soaked up by a sponge.

Shock widened my eyes, and I stared down transfixed by what I'd seen. As my blood drained out and was soaked into the crystal, I felt the pulse of Lysander's energy strengthen. It was as if he were really drinking the blood and taking the energy from me. I suppose he was, but just to see it disappear into the crystal made it such an abstract concept.

My wound healed quickly, but the crystal had not filled up. "How much blood does he need?" I asked.

"That's been the problem we've run into. He can drain a human and still need more." Nicholas stepped up to the table and knelt. He held his wrist in offering to Ariana. "Vampire blood goes much farther. We've all been pitching in."

She cut into his wrist, and again I watched as the blood was absorbed right into the crystal.

"I can't believe you all kept this from me. All those weeks," I said with astonishment rather than the anger I'd previously had.

"We didn't want you worrying any more than you already were." Nicholas looked down on me with mournful eyes.

"I'm a big girl. I'd have rather known than been kept in the dark. But thanks for the concern. Your heart was in the right place." I smiled at him, a genuine and happy smile. No matter how much shit he gave me, I knew Nicholas really cared, and that meant a lot to me.

An awkward silence fell across the room. Nicholas cleared his throat and turned to Santino. "Care to add a few pints to the cause?"

Santino grumbled something about wasting time, but he too knelt down next to the table and offered his wrist.

After the three of us had shared what we could spare, the crystal appeared more red, but it still had not filled all the way to the top.

"Does this mean Lysander is getting weaker?" I asked.

"There's no way to know. We've never seen a crystal prison before." Nicholas looked to Santino. "Have you ever come across such a relic?"

"I'm afraid not. The only unnatural prison we've ever heard rumor of was the Pandora's Box. But, you all know how that one works." He turned to look at me. "Where would that be, anyway?"

"Safe," Nicholas said with a note of finality.

"Good," Santino replied with equal tone.

Nicholas stood and brushed his hands off on his jeans. "Well, while you girls rest up and stay warm by the fire, Santino and I will head back to the preserve and get the others. They should be ready to go by now."

Santino stood and headed toward the front door. He peered through a curtain covered window next to it as if looking for someone or something. "I don't think it is safe to leave the girls here. Nor is it safe to bring the others back and work from this house while the Acta Sanctorum is actively pursuing us."

"And where should we work from? This is our home… for now," Nicholas replied.

"We are defenseless in the daylight," Santino said matter-of-factly. "All it would take is for the Acta Sanctorum to find this home and wait till daylight to torch it. Where would you all go then? Will you run out into the street to be shot by their soldiers, or stay and burn in the basement?"

He had a good point. I'd forgotten how ruthless the Saints could be in their methods when hunting my kind.

"And where do you suggest we go?" I asked.

"Back to the wolves."

"They're not our guard dogs," Nicholas said.

"Yeah, and if you didn't already know, this is their city, not ours," I added. "We don't order them around. It works the other way here."

"You claim to be part of their pack. You've already asked for their protection once." Santino crossed his arms and leaned into the doorframe between the parlor and the foyer. "Has that need for protection ended yet, or does your enemy still bear a threat against you?"

Nicholas sighed and shook his head. "Connor's not going to be happy with us if we bring the Acta Sanctorum down on him and his pack." He sounded as if he'd resigned himself to another fight with the pack leader.

The last time we had to convince the wolves to help us, it had taken Nicholas going toe-to-toe with the leader of the Olde Town Pack to prove his point.

"So, we hide out with the wolves. Then what? Wait for the Acta Sanctorum to attack them?" I asked. "We'd be bringing another fight to their front door."

"You've already involved them," Santino said. "They are a part of this now. Their level of involvement from this point forward will have to be decided when we return to the preserve. First you should secure your place with them. We need to leave this house and do it quickly while we have the cover of the blizzard. The longer we sit here, the better chance the enemy has of catching up to us."

It seemed we had no choice. I only hoped that Connor and the rest of the Olde Town pack would be accommodating.

13

Reluctantly, we left the shelter and warmth of the house and headed back toward the wildlife preserve that served as the home base for the Olde Town pack. The wind and snow had let up, but what had already fallen made it nearly impossible to drive through at any decent speed. I was thankful that Santino had decided to take the wheel. I had no patience for gridlock, detours, or navigating around blocked streets, and that was all you could expect after a storm of that magnitude.

It took us nearly four hours, and when we finally made it to the preserve, it was close to dawn.

Not surprisingly, Fallon was awake and waiting for us. She rushed to greet us at the door. "Oh, thank God you're all right. Did you get it?"

I held up Lysander's crystal triumphantly and smiled. "Piece of cake."

"Liar," she laughed, and pulled me into a hug. "But I'm glad you're safe!"

"I'll be a frozen vampire-sicle if I don't get out of this cold though." The snow had stopped, but it still felt like minus fifty degrees outside. The van's heater hadn't been much help either during the drive. It had barely kept us above freezing.

"Get inside where it's warm," Nicholas said gruffly and pushed his way past us into the main building.

I didn't need to be told twice, and practically stumbled over the threshold to get into the delicious heat. Not quite as nice as sitting next to a roaring fire, but central heating was still better than nothing. I zipped the crystal back into my coat and rubbed my hands to restart circulation as I looked around the deserted lobby.

Everyone else must have been sleeping, even the rest of my clan. It was pretty late in the evening—or early in the morning, depending on how you chose to look at it. And I had to admit, the thought of lying down in a nice soft bed was pretty appealing as well.

"Quite a storm tonight, and it came out of nowhere," Fallon said. She too looked a bit exhausted. Her eyelids drooped a little, and she struggled to stifle a yawn. "We were really worried about you guys."

"You can thank our witchy friend for that," I said, and shot a quick smile at Ariana. "She's got way more power than we anticipated. She practically buried the city in snow."

Ariana smiled sheepishly. "I'm just happy the goddess listened to my plea."

"I'd say she listened. It was all over the news. The weatherman was completely stumped. He said he'd never seen a cold front move so quickly in his life." Fallon covered her mouth as she yawned again. "When we didn't hear from you, we assumed the worst."

"The storm provided excellent cover. It kept our movements well hidden," Santino said with a nod of approval toward Ariana. He stomped out his boots on the mat by the door and walked to join us in the center of the room.

"How are the rest of the group?" Nicholas asked.

Fallon locked the glass front doors. "Drew and Crystal are fine. They're sleeping in cabin 12. Ian is having a hard time. His wounds are better, but his arm and his leg…"

"I'll bet he's a wreck," I said somberly. I couldn't imagine what eternity would be like missing an arm and a leg. At least we lived in a time where prosthetics were available.

"Yeah, a wreck… that's putting it mildly." Her tone matched my own. Fallon didn't care much for Ian as a person, but even she had to feel bad for the wounds he'd sustained.

"It's hard to be the ladies' man when you're only half a man," Nicholas added.

I wanted to laugh, but chose not to out of respect for the injured. He was right though; Ian's life would never be the same.

"We'll check on him in the evening. It's nearly dawn, and I'm exhausted," I said.

Santino cleared his throat. "We're going to need shelter." He looked around at all the windows and glass doors in the main building. "Even with the cloud cover, I don't want to take any chances of sunburn."

"Relax. We've set aside places for you all." Fallon walked us toward the back set of glass doors. "Alyssa and Nicholas, sorry, but you'll have to room together. With the full moon, most of the pack is here. Take cabin 6." She handed me a keychain with a small silver key.

"No problem." I shrugged and looked at Nicholas. "Rock, paper, scissors for the bed?"

He scrunched up his face in confusion. It was always fun picking on the older vampires. As much as they made progress to fit in, the little nuances of growing up in this century escaped them.

"Never mind." I laughed, and Fallon giggled too.

"Ariana," she continued, and handed her a key as well. "You can have cabin 1. That's the closest one to the doors. And Santino, sorry to have to do this, but Connor has requested you remain in the main building under watch. We have a sun proof room here you can use."

Santino grimaced but did not argue. No doubt he knew how futile it would be if he tried. He was lucky Connor had agreed to let him stay at all.

"Speaking of Connor, where is he?" Nicholas asked. "We have some business to discuss."

"Sleeping at the moment, which is where I'll be too once I get you settled in. He, Aiden, and Brady have asked that you all meet with them immediately upon waking tonight."

Nicholas nodded. "Sounds like both sides have much to discuss."

"You may not like what they have to say," Fallon said, her tone suddenly taking on a serious note.

I didn't like the sound of that, nor did I like the fact that we'd have to wait until sunset to find out what she meant. Fallon was my best friend and normally told me everything. For her to be so short about this really worried me.

"The same can be said for what news we're bringing," Nicholas responded. "But that will have to happen later, after a good day of rest."

"Yes, get some rest. You guys look like you need it." Fallon opened the back door for us.

Again we faced the biting cold of the outdoors. I shivered and hugged myself for the walk down to the cabin.

Fallon said a quick goodnight and then turned to Santino. "I'm really sorry, but you'll have to come with me. I'll show you where you're staying tonight."

"Thank you," Santino said with no hint of anger. "Please, lead the way."

As the door closed behind us, I looked back to see Fallon walking with Santino down the long corridor. I hoped, for all of our sakes, that nothing bad happened while we took our daytime rest.

***

Though I was completely exhausted, I barely slept at all during the day. I watched light creeping in through the sides of the blackout curtains as the clouds disappeared and the sun came out to melt the snow. I hated being trapped inside that little cabin. The curse of not being able to handle the sunlight was the most bothersome part of being a vampire. I felt helpless and restless. While the rest of the world went about their day, I could only sit and stare at the walls.

Just like the one I'd stayed in before, the cabin was a simple one room structure; a place to lay your head for the night. Very much like a studio apartment, there was a kitchenette on one wall. To the back, there was a closet and toilet room flanking a queen-sized bed. And in the center of the room, a seating space with a threadbare couch. For warmth, since there was no heater in the cabin, there was a fireplace stocked with lots of wood.

I spent many of my restless hours maintaining the lit fire and listening to the snap and crackle from the flames. Though the sun was out, the biting cold was still there. I hated the cold. I vowed that when all was said and done, and I had my Lysander back, I'd go home to my warm desert and never complain of the summer heat again.

As I tried to stave off the cold, pacing around the small cabin, my mind wandered between what had happened with the Acta Sanctorum and what could be happening to Santino back in the main building. The wolves had every reason to hate and distrust him, and the fact that he was currently helping us couldn't sway that opinion. I only hoped my vouching for him was enough to keep him safe. But even then, I was putting my own life on the line, hoping that he didn't do anything stupid. One small thing could set the wolves off and should a fight ensue, it might mean the death of us both.

My boots clomped with each step I took as I circled around the worn-out couch.

"Go to sleep," Nicholas moaned through his pillow. He pulled the sheets and blanket up over his head.

I couldn't stop walking. I had to do something with my nervous energy. "I can't. I'm too anxious. When is sunset?"

"Never if you keep up this noise," he grumbled, and then sat up in bed. "Can you at least do something quiet to pass the time? Read, think, anything that doesn't involve stomping around like an elephant."

I purposely stomped harder as I took my last two steps toward the couch and then flopped down on the cushions. "Sorry, some of us are worried. You wouldn't understand that concept, but when you care for other people, and they are in danger, it keeps you from things like sleep."

"Is that what you think? I'm some uncaring ogre?" He narrowed his eyes at me. "You should know better than that by now."

"Well, I don't see you acting like you care. Look at you, snoring away while who knows what is being decided by the wolves. They could have killed Santino by now. They could decide we're not worth having around either. Maybe they'll turn us in to the Acta Sanctorum next."

"Alyssa, listen to yourself. You're talking crazy. The wolves would never be so stupid as to deal with the Saints. And just because I am not wearing a track into the wood floor over our situation doesn't mean I have no feelings on the matter. I don't particularly like Santino, but nothing can be done about him at the moment. If anything, saving my strength for when it is needed is the best way for me to care."

Male logic. I do nothing because I care. I huffed.

"Who do you think is going to have to go toe-to-toe with Connor? You, Little Warrior? Do you think you could take on the Alpha if need be?"

"Who says it will come to that?" I said stubbornly, crossing my arms in front of my chest.

He stared down at me, as if determined to make his point, but softened his tone. "These are wolves, Alyssa. They only understand strength. If I have to flex my muscles to get them to listen to us, I'd best do it well fed and rested, don't you think?"

I didn't want to admit it, but he was right. Nicholas was always right, as much as it annoyed me.

"But doesn't it bother you at all that they put us into this situation? I mean, why couldn't Santino stay with us?"

"First of all, *they* didn't put us in this position." He pointed an accusatory finger at me. "You did, by coming here. Then you vouched for Santino."

"But—"

"Honorable as your intentions were, you dragged the wolves into this. They have their own ways of doing things, and while we're under their rule, we must follow their laws."

I groaned in frustration. It aggravated me how calm he was about the whole thing.

"The wolves won't do anything until after we've met with them. Connor's an ass, but he's a good and just leader." He tossed one of the pillows at me. "Nothing will happen if you get a few hours of sleep."

"I hope you're right," I said reluctantly, and settled down on the couch in front of the fire.

"I'm always right," he chuckled. "Now go to sleep."

14

Immediately upon waking, Nicholas and I left the cabin and headed toward Connor's office. The door had been left open, and inside we found Drew and Crystal waiting.

Crystal appeared to be back to her old smiling self. She'd been leaning against one of the many bookshelves that lined the walls, but as I entered she pushed away and stepped confidently toward me.

I rushed forward and threw my arms around her. "You're all right!" I was glad to see she wasn't limping anymore. Her leg had looked pretty bad the night before.

"The same can be said for you too. I'm so sorry I couldn't go with you guys. But I needed to heal."

"Don't even think about it. Besides, Ariana and her magic really came in handy."

"So I heard." She pulled back and smiled so wide I could see the tips of her fangs.

"Yes. I'd have liked to see Ariana in action." Drew put away the book he'd been thumbing through. He hugged me and then gave Nicholas a friendly pat on the back. "Good to see everyone back in one piece."

"There's still trouble ahead, though," Nicholas said in almost a whisper.

"More than you know," Drew replied quietly. "The wolves are not happy."

"I expected as much," Nicholas said with a curt nod.

"How's Ian? Where is he?" I asked.

Crystal's smile faltered. "We'll go talk to him later."

Before I could say anything else, Connor marched in. His mouth was set in a solid line. Anger surrounded him like a cloak. He shot us a menacing glance as he passed me on his way to his large desk. Aiden and his brother Brady followed in Connor's wake. I sensed the same animosity from them as well. That set the hairs on the back of my neck standing straight up and quickened my pulse.

Both brothers held onto thick chains like leashes. Attached at the end of those heavy chains, clanking as he entered from the hallway, was Santino. He seemed sluggish and was barely able to move his legs to walk. He'd been bound and gagged. His scarred face was swollen with yellowing bruises. Where he wasn't bruised, his skin was ashen and clung to his bones. Knowing how fast vampires heal told me these wounds were recent, and worse than that, Santino must have been bled out to make him weaker.

How could they do that to him? Anger and rage began to boil inside of me. "Let him go," I shouted before I realized what I was saying and who I was speaking to.

"Excuse me?" Connor said. He lowered himself onto his chair and folded his hands neatly on the desk.

Nicholas was right—I couldn't challenge Connor to a fight, and that would be the only way he'd let me get away with shouting. No matter how angry I was, I knew if I wanted them to listen, I should try the nice approach.

I cleared my throat and attempted to sound as calm and businesslike as possible. "Sorry. What I meant to say was, why is he in chains? I vouched for him, for his safety and ours. Your son Aiden accepted my word and assured me all was well."

Neither Brady nor Aiden acknowledged me or what I had to say. They silently went about attaching the ends of the chains to the wall next to the desk, then pulled them tight, strapping Santino to the wall. Santino made no effort to struggle. I'd seen him break through chains before. Why wasn't he trying to get out of them now? Had they really weakened him that much?

Connor looked down at his gold wrist watch, and then smoothed a hand through his hair. "Let's try and wrap this up quickly. I have a hunt to get to with my younger wolves." He was all business. His eyes trailed up to meet mine. "Alyssa, you've done me a service and saved my life. For that I am grateful, and I'm happy to honor you and yours as members of the pack. But this man." His calm voice hardened. He jabbed his finger at Santino. "This … *Saint*," he spat the word. "He's killed more of my kind than I could possibly count. His life is not yours to vouch for."

I wanted to say something in protest but couldn't find the words. I wished Lysander was there with us. Diplomacy was his thing. He always knew the right way to mellow out a situation. I turned to Nicholas, eyeing him, silently pleading for help.

"What is to be done with him?" Nicholas' tone gave no hint as to how he felt about what Connor had said.

Connor returned to the calm, businesslike tone he'd used previously. "He'll be set out at dawn to burn in the sun as punishment for his crimes against our kind. If he survives the day, what remains of him will be cast into the bonfire before our final moonlight hunt."

My breath caught in my throat. I glanced up at Santino. He struggled against the chains, rattling them, but they did not give. In his current condition, he was just too weak.

"Silence, vampire, or I will silence you myself," Connor growled the words.

My heart pounded in my chest. I balled up my fist in anger and opened my mouth to speak, but before I could make a sound, Nicholas beat me to it.

"Sounds like a fitting punishment, but I can't let you kill him just yet."

"What do you mean, 'just yet?'" I blurted the words out.

"Quiet," Nicholas snapped at me. He turned his attention back to Connor. "This vampire, Saint, whatever he is, has information that is invaluable to us. He can help us."

"Really?" Connor's eyebrow quirked up. "What kind of information?"

"The Acta Sanctorum is active again in Boston. Santino knows how they operate as well as where they operate. Since they obviously know about all of us here, we'll need him to help us prepare for any attack they might bring."

"Why they are active is the bigger question." He stared down his nose at Nicholas. "How is it they know about… us? We are careful here. We do not bring attention to ourselves."

Brady cleared his throat. "Wasn't it Alyssa who brought the problem to our den?"

My jaw dropped. I was outraged that he would dare to blame me like that.

"She's a member of this pack," Aiden said with a growl. "That is all that matters."

At least he had some sense, though I had a feeling he only cared for me as far as Fallon was concerned. Either way, I was glad to hear him speak in my defense.

"Honorary member," Brady said with a snort. "And she's brought nothing but problems to our pack."

"We had no choice but to come to you when the witches sold us out to the Saints. We're supposed to be part of this pack. That means we help each other out, like family." The anger inside of me threatened to boil over. "Besides, these problems would have found you anyway, without my help. The Acta Sanctorum are killers of our kind. Unnatural creatures. All of us, not just vampires, not just werewolves. If they hadn't found you today, they'd have found you tomorrow or the next day. Don't blame me because they finally showed up on your doorstep."

"If you're to place blame, you have to look to all of us, not just to Alyssa." Drew stepped up to my side.

"Exactly. We're family. That means we're all in this together." Crystal joined me as well.

Connor held up his hands in peace. "No one is laying blame… at this time. Both of my sons do bring up valid points though. Since you have arrived, there have been more problems. If it is deemed that you are the cause of these problems, it will be dealt with; but not until we have taken care of the issues with the Acta Sanctorum."

His words surprised me, but gave me hope. We needed the werewolves and the witches as much as we needed Santino. If we could all work together, we might just pull off the impossible and get rid of the threat of the Acta Sanctorum. At least what remained of them in the U.S.

"So, does this mean you're willing to help us fight against the Saints?" Nicholas asked.

"It seems we have no choice," Connor said with an impatient sigh. He looked down at his watch again, then pressed his palms into the desk, pushing himself up.

"And what of Santino?" I asked. I wasn't letting up that easily.

"His fate is in our hands," he said sternly.

"He's of no help to us in this condition. Look at him. He can barely stand."

"I'm not convinced that he is an asset to our cause. My wolves can handle whatever the Saints bring."

"We thought so too. Until we saw what happened to Ian," Drew said. He moved to the doorway to block Connor from leaving.

Connor growled as he came face to face with Drew. I was never more thankful for Drew's stature. He stood a full head taller than the Alpha and had the bulk to fill in the doorframe. Connor, a formidable man and wolf, seemed somehow less intimidating standing next to Drew.

"They ripped a vampire apart," Drew said poignantly. "If they could take down one of ours from a distance, think of what they can do to your pack. Silver weapons would hurt your wolves, would they not?"

Drew may not have liked Santino, but he made a great argument to keep him alive. Connor had to listen to reason where his pack was concerned.

Nicholas approached Connor from behind. He whispered in the Alpha's ear, but I could still hear his words. "I have no love for this killer either, but he can be useful to us alive. Spare him for a little longer. When we're done, have your way with him."

Those words ruined the moment. *What an asshole.* I couldn't believe what I was hearing. "What's wrong with you all?" I shouted, and I didn't care who heard me or who I was going to piss off. Crystal grabbed my arm as if to stop me. "No," I shot back at her as I pulled out of her grip. "I'd expect as much from you. You've hated Santino from day one. But you," I turned to Nicholas." I thought better of you. And you as well, Drew."

I stormed over and tried to push Nicholas out of the way to get better access to Connor. "You're all no better than he is, but at least Santino is trying to do the right thing. All you care about is getting rid of a problem. I thought your kind were more honorable than that." I stared up into Connor's eyes. I knew better. Never try to stare down a wolf. It's a sign of aggression and dominance.

"Hush, child," he growled at me. I heard the echoing growls from Aiden and Brady as well, but they didn't approach. They shouldn't either, that much I knew about werewolf politics. A challenge made to one wolf must be answered by that wolf only.

Either way, it was stupid of me to try to challenge the leader of the pack. At that moment though, it didn't matter. Rage had taken over and I wasn't backing down. "No," I growled right back at him. "I will not hush. You will let him go. He's under my protection. I vouched for him."

"Alyssa, enough," Nicholas yelled at me.

I felt his hand on my shoulder and shrugged it away. "Stay out of this." I maintained eye contact with Connor, not blinking, not looking anywhere else but his eyes.

 Connor's rumbling growls became louder. His lip curled, revealing his own set of sharp teeth. Not fangs like mine, but certainly sharper than a human's. He turned his whole body and towered over me. Still, I maintained eye contact. The eyes are the windows to the soul, and for a vampire, they act as the doormat to the mind. I'd never tried to make a connection with a wolf before. I wasn't even sure it was possible, but it was worth a try. I reached out through my eyes and into his. Connor's mind was black. Not empty, but dark and hidden. I couldn't penetrate through the thick veil he held there.

"Your mind games will not work on me, child," Connor taunted.

Around me, I heard the protest and continued growls and grumbles of the others, but kept my focus on Connor.

"No game. I'll do what it takes to make you let Santino go. He's mine to judge," I said, putting as much menace in my voice as I could.

I focused too hard on his eyes and didn't see the swing of his arm as it came around and made contact with my cheek.

Flames of pain erupted across my face. The sting radiated through my bones. I jerked sideways and let out a hiss.

A foot swept my leg before I could recover and sent me crashing down to the floor.

I hit the ground and instinctively rolled up to my hands and knees.

"You want the vampire's life. Earn it," Connor said as he swung his foot forward, aiming for my ribs.

I caught him mid-kick and twisted his leg. He spun in time to avoid toppling over and ran into Drew, who caught him.

"Leave Alyssa alone. She's young and rash."

Connor pushed away from Drew and faced me again. "If she's old enough to make a challenge, then she's old enough to face the consequences."

I stood and readied myself for his next attack. "You broke your word. Your pack offered sanctuary and protection to us all, Santino included. If you're not willing to keep your word, then someone should challenge you. A leader should have honor and integrity."

"What do you know of honor?" Connor lunged forward and tackled me. Together we fell. I hit the ground with him on top, and all the air rushed out of my lungs. Before I could even think to fight back, he landed a hard punch across my cheek.

Spots appeared in my vision. Pain throbbed through my jaw. Loud ringing drowned out the sounds of the room, but through all of it, I could still make out the rage in Connor's face above me. He pressed his knee into my chest and cocked back for another punch.

I struggled to get the words out. "I know when you make a promise, you follow through with it. That's honor. Whether it was you or your son who said it, we were assured protection by the Olde Town pack."

Before he could land the punch, I jerked sideways, throwing him off balance, and kicked up my leg, hooking it around his neck. With my thigh, I pushed his head down as I twisted and rolled away, bringing myself back to hands and knees. He tumbled aside, and we both scrambled at the same time to get to our feet and face each other again.

Our eyes locked, but I still wasn't going to back down from his menacing stare. "I don't want to fight you, Connor. I'm only asking that you do the right thing here."

He sidestepped slowly and I did the same, matching his pace, anticipating his next move.

Around us, Drew, Crystal, Nicholas, Aiden, and Brady stood at opposing corners. They all looked ready to fight if called.

Tension in the room ran so thick you could choke on it.

Connor lunged again, and this time I was prepared. I stepped out of the way, but held my arm out and caught him in the neck. Tightening my grip, I clamped down on his windpipe and pushed with all my might, shoving him backwards. His arms swung violently. He raked at my face with one hand while trying to pry my hand free with the other.

I slammed him into the wall.

"Enough," he choked out the word.

I immediately let go and backed away.

He massaged his neck with his right hand and caught his breath. "Do what you like with the vampire."

Once he had regained composure, he smoothed back his hair, straightened his collar, and walked out of the room.

Confused, I looked to Nicholas, then Aiden, and back again. No one else seemed to understand what was happening either.

"Well, you heard the man. Let Santino go," I said.

"Do it yourself," Brady said and tossed a small ring of keys at me. Without another word he left the room.

Aiden looked at me with mixture of confusion and admiration. "This isn't over, you know."

"I wasn't trying to start anything. I just wanted what was promised."

"I understand, but every action has a consequence." He clapped me on the shoulder and followed his brother out into the hallway.

"Little Warrior indeed," Nicholas laughed. "When I asked you if you would challenge the Alpha earlier, I was only joking. You didn't have to do it to prove anything."

"I wasn't doing it to prove anything to you either," I said coldly. I took the keys, walked over to Santino, and began unlocking his chains. "I can't believe you all are so willing to send him to his death after all he's done for us."

Crystal crossed her arms and turned away with a huff.

"Who said we would have actually done it?" Nicholas asked. "Sometimes it's best to bargain for the moment and work out the other details later."

I hadn't really considered that option. But still, if that was his plan, he should have let us know. "With that attitude, how is anyone to know what side you're on?" I grumbled.

"Who cares about sides as long as you know how to play the game. We had the wolves ready to fight along with us. Now, after your Little Warrior act, they might not be so friendly. You just made their leader look like a pussy." He snickered as he said the last word.

"That wasn't my intention."

"Intention or not, that's what you did. We got Santino back, but it's going to take some major ass kissing to put the wolves back in our good graces. I hope you're up for the challenge."

15

I left Nicholas and Drew to attend to Santino's wounds and sought solace with Fallon. She'd been keeping Ariana company and also helping her to go through the ancient book we'd recovered from the Acta Sanctorum's repository.

Word of the fight with Connor must have traveled fast because the moment I entered the cabin, I was met with an icy stare that rivaled the cold winds blowing outside.

"I guess you've heard." I shrugged my coat off and tossed it on the rack next to the door.

Fallon shook her head and chewed on her lip as if she was biting back the words she so desperately wanted to say.

I didn't need to be able to read her mind to know what she was thinking. She was pissed that I'd made her boyfriend and his father look bad. I couldn't understand why everyone was so mad at me. Sure Santino was a monster, but so were we all, in our own way. And since we'd worked with him back in Vegas, he'd been our ally. It wasn't right to let him be beaten and abused by the wolves.

Anger flared up again inside of me as Fallon watched my every move like a lioness waiting to pounce. How dare she judge too! She was supposed to be my best friend. She was supposed to support me. "If you're expecting any kind of apology, you can kiss my ass."

Ariana, it seemed, was too preoccupied to pay attention to my entrance or the anger in my voice.

Fallon, on the other hand, narrowed her eyes at me. "You can be so selfish at times, you know that, Lyssa?"

Rage had me balling my hands into fists, ready to fight. "Oh? So that was me being selfish, standing up for another member of our group?"

"Technically, he's not a member of *our* group," she said with emphasis. "But you, however, are a member... of this pack."

My heart pounded in my ears. "So I'm supposed to just let a friend die because that's what the pack demands?" I threw my hands up in frustration and paced the small cabin, walking circles around Fallon and Ariana who were sitting on the couch.

Ariana was ignoring my angry huffing and puffing. She had buried herself nose-deep in the book, staring at it like a child who'd found a favorite cartoon and would not be moved.

"No. That's not what anyone is saying," Fallon lowered her voice. I sensed fear in the room, and it was coming from Fallon's direction. "It's just how you went about it. There might have been a better way to save Santino."

Angry or not, I would never hurt Fallon. The fact that I smelled her fear made me pause and take a calming breath.

"Well, now you sound like the others." I stopped in front of her and put my hands on my hips. "Look, I'm not going to be the bad guy here for trying to do the right thing."

"That's not what I'm saying—"

"I get it. You have to defend the pack now that you're officially Aiden's girl. Fine. But don't lecture me on my methods. You've known me for long enough to know—"

"I think I found the answer," Ariana said, effectively shutting me up. She looked up from her book and confusion washed across her face. "Hey, Alyssa, you okay?"

"Fine, just fine!" I said with a sigh. "What answer?"

Ariana shook her head at me and set the book down on her lap. "There's mention here of a soulstone. It was said this stone could safely contain a spirit, reanimate corpses, or bind someone's soul to it."

"Why would anyone want to do that?" I asked.

Ariana bit her lip, hesitating before she spoke. "Necromancy, bodysnatching, creating minions, that sort of thing."

"What?" The thought of those things repulsed me. "You mean there were people who actually did that sort of thing?"

She let out a heavy breath. "Not all magic is used for good. Necromancy isn't a common practice, but to some, that branch of magic is very enticing. Think about it—to be able to control life and death. That's a lot of power to wield."

I shuddered. The thought of controlling death brought up images of animated corpses. Even as a vampire, that stuff gave me the creeps.

Ariana continued, "It says here the elements needed to create the soulstone are blood, fire, a willing sacrifice, and the full moon."

"And that's just what we had the night you sealed the Pandora's Box," Fallon said, with a hint of amazement in her voice.

"Exactly. When I threw the stone into the blaze, I must have inadvertently made it a soulstone. When Lysander's spirit left his body, it was pulled into the stone."

"But you said the stone should safely be able to hold the spirit. Why then is his stone getting weaker?" I asked.

She shrugged. "I don't know. Maybe ours isn't a true soulstone. Or maybe because it's a vampire's soul, it has a different effect. Magic is variable. Sometimes the slightest change in ingredients or words can have drastic effects. Either way, this is the best lead we've gotten in weeks."

Fallon and I both nodded. I smiled, feeling that little spark of hope return. If she was right, we might be able to get him back.

"So, does that book tell you how to get the soul out?" I asked.

"There's a spell in here. It doesn't look too difficult." She flipped forward a few pages. "We might even attempt it tonight if you'd like. I was able to pick up some general items at home during the day." Before I could say anything, she jumped in. "Brady escorted me."

I was too happy to care about the details of how or where she got her supplies. I just wanted my Lysander back. "What are we waiting for then? Let's do it."

"Where is the crystal?" she asked.

"Tucked safe and sound in my cabin."

"Go get it and meet me in the lobby with the others."

***

"While the wolves are out on their final hunt of the full moon revelry, we can set up space in the open lobby," Ariana said, as she consulted her book for the necessary supplies.

I set the crystal inside my coat and laid it safely on the reception desk while I went about helping to set up.

Crystal pushed chairs away from the center of the room, creating a wide open space. She'd found two sawhorses in the store room and set them up in the center.

Ariana drew a pentagram in white chalk on the ground.

When all had been set in place, Ariana directed Nicholas and Drew to bring out Lysander's coffin and lay it across the sawhorses.

Ariana then handed Fallon and me five inch-long black pillar candles and told us to place them at each of the five points of the star. She followed us placing smaller purple and gold candles at various points within the pentagram.

Crystal followed behind Ariana and lit each of the candles.

With the help of Nicholas and Drew, Ariana opened the lid of the coffin and turned it sideways so she could set items on it like a table.

I couldn't help but stop and take a peek inside the coffin. Lysander looked like death. I had to stop myself from tearing up, and took a deep calming breath. This would work. It had to work. I couldn't bear to see Lysander like this any longer. Before the emotions overwhelmed me, I returned to my task of arranging the candles for the ceremony.

On top of the makeshift table Ariana placed herbs inside a medium-sized black cauldron. Next to the cauldron she drew a circle in salt. Then she reached around her neck and removed her goddess pendant. "You'll want to take off any protective talismans if you have any." She set the pendant inside the circle of salt and began to dig around in the bag she'd brought for other supplies. In separate dishes she laid out various herbs and incense, and then lit them.

Instantly, the cavernous room was filled with pungent smoke. I did not recognize any of the herbs or their smells, but they reminded me of death.

"I'll need the crystal," Ariana said to me after she'd finished setting up her altar.

I unwrapped it from my coat and hugged it tightly to my chest. "See you very soon, honey," I whispered to the crystal, and then handed it to her.

"You're still wearing the pendant I gave you," she said to me. "That's a protective talisman. You'll need to take it off for now. We don't want anything inhibiting the magic from working."

"Sorry." I'd completely forgotten about it. I reached around, unclasped it, and handed it to her.

She placed the pendant in the circle of salt with hers and took Lysander's crystal from me. Gingerly, as if she feared breaking it, Ariana set the crystal down, with its point facing the ceiling, inside the cauldron.

She consulted her book once more and then laid it on the makeshift table. "I'll also need some of his blood." Ariana looked into the coffin and scratched her head. "Does he have any left?" She pulled out the same ceremonial knife I'd seen used before and picked up Lysander's wrist. She made a quick slice across, but nothing came out.

Confidence turned into confusion. She frowned and looked up to us for an answer.

"We cannot produce our own blood," Drew said matter-of-factly.

"But, without *his* blood, the spell will not work.

"I have *his* blood, as does Alyssa," Nicholas said. "We are of his direct bloodline. Will that work?"

"There is no guarantee. As I said before, spells can be affected by not having the proper ingredients."

"This is the best we can offer," Nicholas said.

That caused my anxiety level to spike. *Why did everything have to be so complicated?*

Ariana sighed and waved us forward. "It's better than nothing."

I offered my wrist first. She sliced it quickly and cleanly, but the sudden sting made me hiss. Ariana held my wrist over the cauldron and allowed the blood to flow into it until my wound healed over itself. As before, the stone seemed to soak up the blood like a sponge, but this time some remained, coating the herbs at the bottom of the cauldron.

Nicholas went second, and again Ariana repeated the process, holding his wrist over the cauldron until it healed. "Is that it?" he asked, rubbing the spot where his wound had healed.

"Yes, I think so." She consulted her book again. "Please, everyone take a spot next to the five candles."

We did as instructed. Ariana pulled a jar from her purse and sprinkled the contents into the cauldron; then she lit a match and tossed it inside. A small explosion shook the stone, but it remained upright. Smoke began to billow out from the cauldron and sink back down into the coffin.

Ariana took the tip of the knife and poked her index finger. "As the channel of this magic, my blood will help aid the connection." She rubbed the small bead of blood on the tip of the crystal and started a chant. I couldn't understand the words she was saying—they sounded foreign or old, with a bit of a Spanish flair.

Smoke from the incense surrounded us like a thick blanket, choking out any fresh air that might remain. Though I didn't need to breathe, it bothered me to avoid it, but as I inhaled, my head began to swim. Whatever herbs she was burning had a drug-like effect. I could only imagine how the humans, Fallon and Ariana, must be reacting.

Something was definitely happening. The lights flickered and went out, leaving only the candles to illuminate the room. The gentle twinkling of each flame only added to the dreamy and drug-induced feeling that was taking over.

"Please work, please work, please work," I mumbled to myself and crossed my fingers behind my back like a child does for good luck.

Ariana's chanting grew louder and louder, echoing around the room. As she spoke, the air became electrified. My heart sped with anticipation. The crystal began to glow. It took on a hazy white halo. The deep red color inside lightened to an orangy-amber. Within the crystal, it looked like liquid was swirling into a mini tornado.

A smile crept across my face. "Come back to me, baby."

Still chanting, Ariana picked up the crystal. She held it up in the air as she circled around the coffin toward Lysander's head. The crystal's glow reflected off the waxy skin of my unconscious mate.

Ariana lowered her arms and pointed the crystal tip down, between Lysander's eyes. The swirling liquid inside of the crystal moved faster, spinning into a perfect funnel-shaped cyclone that pointed its energy toward the tip.

"Arise," she commanded loudly.

Lysander's whole body jolted as if hit by an electric shock.

I sucked in a breath and held it in anticipation. My eyes were glued to his body, hoping, praying…

"Lysander, arise," she commanded, and again touched the crystal to his head. His body twitched, and this time with a loud moan erupting from his chest, his eyes fluttered open.

At first, his pale blue-gray eyes held shock and confusion. He looked around the room, finally setting on my face; then I felt his fear. "Help me," Lysander rasped. "I'm not alone in here." And just as quickly as he spoke, his eyes closed and his body went limp.

16

The thick, enveloping smoke began to dissipate on its own, as if someone had opened a door and sucked it right out of the back of the room. But none of the doors had been opened.

I shook my head to help clear away the remaining haze. Lights flickered on around us. The crystal fell from Ariana's hand, and I gasped as it tumbled into the coffin.

Ariana sank to the ground.

Lysander had again become motionless, looking as if he were sleeping. If I hadn't known better, I would have thought nothing had happened. But I'd seen him move, heard him speak. Something had definitely happened. *But why didn't it work? What went wrong, and why did Lysander say he wasn't alone?* Somewhere, deep down, I feared we might have just lost our shot at saving him. Whatever was with him in that crystal might never let him go. A tear welled in the corner of my eye. I fought back against the feelings of despair, unwilling to give up just yet.

Ariana clutched her head in her hands and let out a groggy moan on the floor. I rushed to her aid along with Fallon.

"Are you all right?" I asked.

Her head shot up, and her eyes, filled with an unusual fire, locked onto mine. A wave of pure hatred rolled off her. It crashed into me with such force I felt my own anger surging to meet it.

"Get away from me, death bringer!" she spat the words out. Then, her voice deepened. Ariana said something else. I couldn't quite make out the words. She sounded strange, as if someone else were speaking through her. The next thing I knew, a shock like a bolt of electricity hit me. Suddenly, I was on the other side of the room, my head colliding with the wall.

"What the fuck?" Stars danced in my vision. My ears rang and the back of my head throbbed where it had struck the wall.

Across the room, Ariana sat up and scowled as she looked around at the other vampires surrounding her.

Fallon was still at her side. "Why did you do that?" she asked.

"Vampires. Death bringers. You have no power over me. I am the true master of death." Ariana turned her head toward Fallon. "Get behind me. I'll protect you from these murderers."

The rest of the clan froze in their spots and exchanged confused glances as if trying to determine the best way to handle the situation.

"They're our friends." Worry tinged Fallon's voice. "Don't you remember?"

"You're friends with these leeches?" Ariana eyed Fallon suspiciously.

"So are you," she replied back.

Confusion played across Ariana's face. Her lips quivered, and for a brief moment her eyes rolled backwards in their sockets.

Nicholas must have caught her momentary lapse. He bent down to Fallon and Ariana. "She doesn't remember." He reached out a hand toward the fallen witch. Instantly, the confusion on her face turned to a scowl.

"Do you know who I am?" Nicholas asked.

Ariana's eyebrow quirked. She lifted her hand and pointed a finger at Nicholas.

"You might want to back away." Fallon warned. "She's not in her right mind." Fallon held tight to Ariana's arm, pulled her hand down, and whispered in her ear. "It's okay. Take it easy. We're all friends here."

Ariana refused to take her eyes off Nicholas. She looked dangerous, as if she were a frightened animal, backed into a corner, ready to fight for its life.

Nicholas stood and backed away slowly, around to the other side of the coffin. He hunted for the book. "Something went wrong with that spell. We need to know what's going on. Necromancy is dark magic. There is no telling what effect using it has had on our witch."

"What does a death bringer know of magic?" Ariana spat out the words.

Nicholas returned her anger with his own. "My mate was once a witch before she joined me in this life. I know plenty." He turned to me and I saw the pain etched on his face as he mentioned Rozaline. "She should have never messed with this dark magic. Just once was enough to poison her mind."

Fallon helped Ariana to her feet and guided her to a bench along the wall. "Come sit down over here."

"My necklace," Ariana moaned, and for that brief moment, she sounded like herself again. "I need it. Protection... from evil."

"I got it," I said, and grabbed both hers and the one she'd lent to me and hurried toward her.

Ariana's eyes focused on me as I approached. The confusion returned as well as the anger. She opened her mouth and uttered another curse. I winced, expecting more pain and another trip across the room to crash into the wall, but this time it had no effect. I looked down at my hands, seeing the goddess pendants there on their silver chains, and it hit me.

"These things really do help. Quick, have her put this on." I tossed the necklace to Fallon and then clasped the other around my neck again.

As soon as the necklace was around Ariana's neck, fear left her eyes. Her hand fell from her head, and she gazed around the room as if seeing it for the first time. "What are you all sitting around here for? Let's get on with the spell."

"The spell didn't work, and you lost it." I continued my approach toward her, safe now in the knowledge she wasn't going to curse me again. "Don't you remember?"

"Lost it?" She shot me a curious look. "We haven't done anything yet."

"Look around. The candles have been lit for a while now. There's smoke in the cauldron. The incense is almost out. Don't you remember anything that happened?"

She shook her head.

"You called me a death bringer. Sent me flying across the room. You snarled at Nicholas. Should I continue?"

"I don't remember any of that. Last thing I did was…" She peered around the room curiously. "You might be right. I do remember something. I pricked my finger and touched the crystal."

"Do you remember anything else? You were pretty out of it until I gave you back your necklace."

Her hand shot up to her neck. "The necklace gives protection from evil."

"But you said magic is not good or evil, it's how it is used that makes the difference."

"Power over death is not a good thing, I don't care who says otherwise," Nicholas responded before Ariana could say another word. "Be careful the magic does not poison your mind to the point you can't recover."

"That is not the only thing we need to worry about," Crystal said.

"I'll say. What did Lysander mean by 'I'm not alone'?" I asked.

"Is that what he said?" Ariana asked. "From what you describe, there must have been some other presence here. I wish I knew what happened."

"At this point, 'not alone' could mean anything." Drew bent over the coffin as if inspecting the contents. He reached out and took hold of the crystal. "But, at the very least, there is good news. The crystal appears undamaged."

I joined them around the coffin. "Yes, at least it looks okay. When Ariana dropped it, I was worried."

"Lysander said *he*, not *we*, were not alone. That makes me think the crystal holds another secret or soul. What else would be in there with him? And if that is the case, is that why he can't get out?" Crystal asked.

I had a suspicion of what else might be in there, but I didn't dare mention it. There had been only one other entity around when Lysander had been pulled into the crystal. And if he was the thing trapped inside with Lysander, there was nothing, save for the Pandora 's Box, to keep him at bay.

Aniketos, the first vampire. Unconquerable and uncontrollable. All of our problems had started when we accidentally opened his prison and set him loose on the world.

"Soulstones were only meant to hold one spirit at a time. I doubt another would fit," Ariana said.

Nicholas thumbed through the pages of the book. "But, you yourself admit to not being familiar with this kind of magic. Let's say something else is in there with him. Could that be why the crystal keeps fading?"

"It's entirely possible, yes," Ariana responded, her tone hinting at worry.

"Whatever is inside, we have to isolate it from Lysander and get him out safely," I said, hoping to push the others away from the same conclusion I had drawn. "He can't last forever in there, and he needs our help. You heard him."

"What if we are not able to isolate Lysander from the thing inside the crystal with him?" Nicholas looked at Lysander's unconscious form and let out a deep sigh.

"We just have to keep trying," I said, with determination.

"Not here, you won't," Connor's voice boomed from the open front door. His sudden appearance startled me. I had assumed we had more time. They were supposed to be out hunting.

The last remnants of smoke billowed out behind him as he held open the glass doors. Clothed in only a pair of pants and thick coat that appeared to have been hastily buttoned, he stared at us with contempt. "You've ruined yet another full moon for us."

Behind him, Aiden and Brady looked in on us and shook their heads. Connor, though in his human form, bared his teeth menacingly at us. He eyed the room and the mess we'd made. A rumbling growl vibrated in his chest. The veins in his forearm protruded, and I could see his thundering pulse underneath. He was mad, to say the least.

Connor stepped inside and let the door swing behind him. "This is the final straw. I've been as patient with you as I can be. But you." He jabbed an accusatory finger at me. "You bring nothing but trouble wherever you go. You've disrespected me among my kind. And now, while we are out celebrating the full moon, I hear you dare to defile our home with dark magic. I want you all off my land. Tonight!"

Who had told him what we were up to? We'd only just come up with this plan. And why was I the one being blamed for it all?

I opened my mouth to respond, but before I could utter a word, a hand wrapped around my mouth.

"If that is your wish, we'll be gone before dawn," Nicholas said calmly.

"If you're not, you will be destroyed." Connor turned on his heel and headed toward his office, down the hallway.

"Live to fight another day." Nicholas released his hand from my mouth. "We have no time to argue with him tonight. Let's go now and make peace another time."

For once, I didn't want to argue with him. I looked to Fallon, but she avoided eye contact with me. Something told me she might have been the one to let slip our plan. "Are you coming with us?"

She bit her lip and hugged herself. Covered or not, I heard the guilty racing of her heart. I knew what that meant. "Fine, stay. See if you can talk some sense into Aiden while you're at it." I hoped it didn't come out as snarky as it sounded in my head. I couldn't really be mad at her for letting her boyfriend know what we were doing. It's not like we meant to do any harm by it. And the wolves up to this point had been very supportive of our efforts to release Lysander from the soulstone.

"Save the sweet goodbyes for later," Nicholas barked at me. "Go get Santino and get to the van. We need to leave now if we want to make it to the city before dawn."

I glanced back at Fallon. "Call me if you make any progress."

She half smiled at me. It wasn't very reassuring. "I'll do my best. Just try to stay safe."

I tried to stay positive. It might work to our advantage to have her stay behind. Aiden was the second in command, and she had his ear.

17

Crammed into the van, we drove away from the wolf preserve. For miles we sat in silence, no one daring to say the thing that had to be on all of our minds. It was Santino who chose to put our fears into words. "We won't be safe at Zuri's house. You can be sure the Acta Sanctorum knows of its location. We could have been followed when we recovered the crystal."

His words rang true and sent a shiver of fear down my spine that chilled me more than the winter ever could. We'd be sitting ducks come daytime.

"Where else can we go?" We were on the run with no safe place to hide from the sun. And worst of all, our allies were either mad at us or already dead. Things couldn't look much bleaker, could they? I didn't dare tempt fate and utter those words aloud.

"We'll do as we've done before," Nicholas said calmly, though his hands were wrapped tight around the steering wheel. "We will hide in plain sight. Wait out the day in some populated but indoor place, and then return to Zuri's house come nightfall."

Ariana cleared her throat and turned around from the front passenger seat to face us. "You can stay at my place if you don't mind being cramped. I rent the second floor of a triple-decker in Dorchester."

I wasn't quite sure what exactly a triple-decker was, but anything was better than having to stay out in the open all day. We'd done that once before and it wasn't much fun.

"Are you sure the Acta Sanctorum has not gained knowledge of your home?" Santino asked.

"I told you before, I didn't have any dealings with them. Mysti had to have set everything up, and she never knew where we lived. When it came to coven meetings, she called us to join with her."

"There is no guarantee they haven't learned of your home though simple traces." Santino turned to look out of the window. "The Saints are resourceful."

With Ian out of commission and no better solutions, this sounded like our best option. "We might as well do it," I said. "What other choices do we have?"

Crystal crossed her arms and leaned back into her seat. "I don't see any other choice either."

"We'll all take turns keeping watch. The Acta Sanctorum is ruthless, but I doubt they would burn down other God-fearing humans' houses to get to us. We should be okay for one day," Drew added, attempting to sound comforting.

"I don't know how many God-fearing people there are in Dorchester," Ariana said hesitantly. "It can be a pretty rough neighborhood, but if the thought of it keeps my house off the arson list, great." She finished with a nervous laugh.

"We'd better warn Zuri as well not to go home. She's been out on patrol this whole time. She's probably unaware of what's been going on," I said in a strained voice. "She should still be safe with the wolves; they're not mad at her or Ian, just us."

"Yes. For a few days at least," Nicholas agreed. "The wolves should keep them safe."

We drove slowly through the snow and slush with Ariana as our guide until we reached her home. Under the soft glow of the streetlamps, the house looked large and majestic: a beautiful three-story heather-gray clapboard building filled with windows. Large L-shaped porches wrapped around one corner of the building. Painted in a stark white, they created a striking accent.

We parked in the back on a concrete slab shared between two of these large three-story homes. It appeared to have been recently shoveled.

"So this is a triple-decker?" I asked.

"Yeah, you don't have these in Vegas?" Ariana responded.

"We have apartments."

"We have those too, but these buildings are more common around here. Follow me."

We walked toward a small concrete set of steps at the back of the building. Ariana fumbled with her set of keys while the overhead light flickered and threatened to go out. Once she'd located the right one, she opened the back door and revealed a tiny, two person wide hallway. Directly ahead of us was the front door of the building. To my left appeared to be someone's front door, with a large peep hole in the center. To the right was a narrow set of stairs. We took the steps single file up to the second floor. Our footfalls echoed in the tight passage; mixed with the groaning of the wood, we sounded like an invading army.

So much for going in unnoticed. We could wake the dead with all the noise.

Ariana didn't seem to care. She pushed forward, up the stairs to the second floor landing. "Here we are. Home sweet home." She unlocked the only door on this floor, an ancient wooden thing with a large peep hole in the center.

Inside, the air was thick with rich herbal scents, and I spotted a few incense holders that could have been the source. Shiny hardwood floors met richly painted walls of sage and twilight. A large flat-panel television had been mounted to one wall. Below it sat an entertainment credenza filled with DVDs of all kinds. A small altar had been set on top of the credenza. Sitting on a neatly folded blue cloth with the goddess symbol atop it was a miniature cauldron with pentagrams emblazoned on its side. Flanking the cauldron were two small candle holders with small thin green candles inside. Next to the right candle sat a cobalt blue glass goblet. Around the room in every corner sat potted plants, probably herbs she used for her witchcraft.

"Make yourselves comfortable," she said as she headed into the kitchen, "I'll be right out in a minute."

"What about Lysander's coffin?" I asked. "We can't just leave it out there in the van all night."

Nicholas took one look back down the stairwell. "I'm not sure we'll be able to get it up the stairs."

Drew shook his head. He heaved a sigh and looked at me with sorrowful eyes. "He may be safer down there in the van. If we need to make a quick escape, trying to carry around a coffin would slow us all down."

I didn't like what I was hearing. My voice shook as I spoke. "But what if someone breaks into the van? Or if the Saints do find us?"

Nicholas put a hand on my shoulder. "This is not the perfect situation, but we have to work with what we have. Drew and I will secure the van and cover up the coffin before dawn. We'll all take turns keeping watch during the day. That's just going to have to be good enough for now."

"But, Lysander—"

"Is like a brother to me," Nicholas spoke in a carefully controlled tone. "I won't see any harm come to him, okay?"

As much as I didn't want to, I had to trust Nicholas. He could be a jerk most times, but he really did have our best interests at heart. And if he felt that we'd be okay for one night, he was probably right.

"Fine." I crossed my arms, hugging myself, as if that would help keep my anxiety in check. "But if we end up staying longer, we have to come up with a better solution."

"Agreed." Nicholas smiled at me.

I turned and walked away, wandering around the room. My nervous energy was going to get the better of me again. I had a feeling I'd spend another day wide awake. "I guess you can give me first shift."

Ariana had one small shelf of books that had been filled with magic-related texts; books like *The Solo Practitioner*, *Crystal Healing*, *Elemental Craft*, and *Moon Magick*. Small statues served as bookends. I was admiring the tiny green figurine of what looked like a wolf when Ariana came back out into the living room carrying dark sheets.

"I thought you might want some coverings on the window, to help with the sunlight. It's not much, but these should help."

"That's really thoughtful of you," I said, wondering if she was making up for the little episode back at the wolf preserve.

She handed me some thumbtacks and the end of a black sheet. Together we pinned them to the edges of each of the three windows in the front.

"Nice place you've got here," Crystal said, collapsing onto the overstuffed microfiber couch in the living room. Drew joined her.

"Thanks." Ariana beamed at them. She gave off a definite sense of pride in her home. "I've tried to make the most of it. These older places have a lot of character, but the upkeep is tremendous."

Santino cleared his throat. I looked over to see him standing like a sentry, guarding the front door. "The time for small talk is later. We should assign shifts now so that some of you can get rest."

I continued my pacing, unable to stand still from nervous energy. "I already said I'd take first shift. I'm not going to be sleeping anytime soon."

"I'll stay up too," Crystal added.

Ariana finished pinning another sheet to a small window in the kitchen. "I'd like to study the book some more. I want to find out what might have gone wrong with the spell."

"We'll need more than women to guard us," Santino said curtly.

"Excuse me?" I glared at him. "You're really going to play the sexist card here?"

"If the women want to take first shift, that's perfectly fine." Nicholas stalked over to Santino. "They're more than capable of keeping watch for a few hours."

"And if we are attacked?" The menace in Santino's voice was unmistakable, but he avoided looking at any of us *women*.

"They will alert us." Nicholas matched his tone.

"Every second is key in an attack. The women are not—"

"You might want to consider your words carefully," Nicholas said through clenched teeth. "If not for Alyssa, you wouldn't be here. She took on Connor to keep your sorry ass alive. And she's the youngest of these women. Show some respect."

It was odd to hear such approval coming from Nicholas, but I really appreciated it. *I might just have to rethink all those times I called him an asshole or a jerk.*

"So be it," Santino said dismissively. "Let the women take the first shift."

Nicholas nodded curtly, and then turned to me and whispered, "Don't fuck it up and make me look bad, Little Warrior."

Perhaps I was too hasty in taking back the jerk comments. "Thanks," I said with a slight groan.

Ariana showed Nicholas, Drew, and Santino to a room where they could rest and then returned to the living room.

"I have a theory," she said, but there was hesitation in her voice.

"Okay?" I sat at the edge of the couch waiting for the bad news.

Ariana grabbed the book from the coffee table. She flipped through the pages, finding the one with the soulstone on it, and showed it to us.

"When one is created, it acts like a vacuum and pulls in the nearest soul it can find."

"Right. Lysander's soul was sucked in. We know that already."

"But he's not alone," Ariana said poignantly. "Those were the words you said he spoke."

I knew where she was going with this, but I didn't dare say it aloud. And I didn't have to. Crystal had come to the same conclusion.

"Aniketos," she said.

"Yes. That would mean the Pandora's Box is empty."

My heart momentarily stopped. I'd thought of it as a possibility, but hearing it spoken aloud made it all that much more true. After all of our hard work, all the sacrifice, the loss of life, we might not have defeated the bloodthirsty spirit of Aniketos. The Pandora's Box had been our only hope. He was unconquerable, being a true immortal, born of the gods themselves. Only the magical cage of the Pandora's Box had been strong enough to keep his spirit locked inside. If he was locked in the crystal with Lysander, it was no wonder it was fading so fast. And as it faded, Lysander's spirit grew weaker. I felt our bond, the connection we shared as master and fledgling, fading.

"What happens then, if we let the crystal fade?" I asked, praying that my deepest fear, Lysander's death, would not be the solution.

"I wish I could say. The book is hazy on the details. Most spirits bound to a stone are preserved, not used up. If his spirit is exhausted, it could strengthen Aniketos, and he might be strong enough to break free of the crystal himself."

Used up. Those words sounded so dirty. It was as if his soul were equal to a piece of tissue that once used could be discarded without a second thought. No. Lysander wouldn't be treated like that.

"He cannot be allowed to break free of the crystal." Crystal's brow furrowed. "It seems we may need to plead our case to Connor, at the very least, to retrieve the box. That's the only thing we know of that can hold Aniketos safely inside."

"The box that's buried under how many feet of concrete?" I didn't try to hide the hopelessness in my voice. It was uncertain if the wolves would continue to be our allies, and they were the ones who kept watch over the Pandora's Box.

"All we can do is try." I could tell Ariana was trying to sound positive, but the effect was lost on me.

"Let's say we do get the box; what then?" I asked.

"We try to summon out the spirits again. Both of them this time," Ariana said, with added emphasis. "And then recreate the ritual to put Aniketos back in the box."

"Simple as that," I said sarcastically.

"Obviously not, but that's the best plan we've got." Annoyance began to overtake Ariana's positive tone. "Sorry." I let out a deep breath and slumped in my seat. "I shouldn't be getting snippy with you. I know you're giving us all you've got. It just feels so hopeless."

Crystal put her arm around me. "We're all hoping for the best, but we need to prepare ourselves in case things don't work out."

Tears welled in the corners of my eyes. I wasn't ready to face the possibility that we might fail. I didn't want to say goodbye to Lysander forever. But if Ariana was right and his spirit would eventually be used up, it would unleash the worst kind of evil back into the world. Many more would die. Lysander had willingly sacrificed himself, in the hopes of trapping Aniketos, so that we would survive. I couldn't let that act go to waste because I wanted my boyfriend back.

I sniffled a little and wiped my eyes. "You're right. We need to make peace with the wolves, and get the box back."

18

I tried to call Fallon multiple times during the day, but she didn't answer. Finally, as desperation set in, I decided to leave her messages explaining our situation, what we thought might be happening with the crystal, and the fact that the Pandora's Box would need to be unearthed. I thoughts surely those would grab her attention, but she didn't respond to any of my calls nor return even a text message in response to the information I'd given her.

Was she mad, or was something going on? We'd had our fights in the past, and sure, there were plenty of times where we avoided talking for a few days, but this was too important to ignore. No! I couldn't believe that she'd be so petty as to let a guy come between us. She was much more mature than that.

After making one more attempt to contact her, I threw my cell phone down in frustration. "Something is seriously wrong. We have to go back to the wolf preserve."

"That would be suicide," Drew said. "You saw how angry Connor was with us. No. We cannot go back until we know for sure it is safe."

"That's the point. I don't think it is safe. I think the wolves are in trouble. Fallon would never ignore me for something this important. I don't care how angry at me she is."

One of Drew's eyebrows arched sharply. "You're willing to put the lives of six people at risk over a hunch?"

I didn't like his tone. "I know my friend. This isn't a hunch. Something happened up there."

"Why don't we try the others, Zuri or Ian, before we jump to any conclusions?" Crystal suggested. "Wake Ariana and have her call."

She'd fallen asleep a few hours earlier, after we'd explained everything to the men taking the second watch. Though we were all exhausted, neither Crystal nor I got any sleep during the day. I walked to Ariana's bedroom, just down a small hallway, and knocked a few times on her door.

A moment later a bleary-eyed Ariana greeted me.

I didn't wait for her to speak. "Do you have Zuri or Ian's cell numbers?"

She stared at me for a moment as if she didn't know who I was, and then blinked a few times. "Phone's on the counter in the kitchen. Gimme a few to splash some water on my face and I'll be out in a minute."

I didn't think we'd get very far with calling the other vampires. Under normal circumstances, they'd be sleeping at this point, like we should've been doing. The sun was hidden behind a thick layer of clouds, but we were still at least an hour from sunset. My gut instincts were screaming, *Something is wrong!*

I returned to the living room and spotted Ariana's phone lying on the edge of the counter in the kitchen. "She'll be out in a minute," I said to the group as I made my way toward the small brick-style phone. It had a full keyboard instead of just number keys making it look like a mini computer compared to my little flip phone. I fumbled with the buttons, trying to locate her address book, and ended up calling Aiden by fortunate mistake.

His phone rang through to voicemail just as Fallon's had. "Aiden, it's Lyssa. I'm worried. Fallon hasn't answered her phone all day, and we have some important information that concerns everyone. Please call us back either on Ariana's phone or mine. You know the numbers. Thanks."

I turned and walked back into the living room. "Aiden isn't answering either. I'm telling you guys, something is wrong. We need to go back there and see for ourselves."

"Alyssa might be right," Santino stood and walked to the window to peek out of the makeshift curtains. He squinted, but didn't shy away from the fading light of day. "Think about it. The full moon is over. There's less protection at the wolf preserve. Many of the pack members would have gone home, leaving only a few. Those that remain might be weary from the nights of hunting and merrymaking. That would be an excellent time for any enemy to mount a strike against them."

The cold and calculated way he spoke told me he'd been involved in plots like this. It was easy to forget what kind of a monster he'd been before he changed sides. I wondered how many times he'd hunted down others, like myself or the wolves. "That's just the kind of ruthless behavior the Acta Sanctorum is known for having. Hit them while they're weak," I said, slamming my fist into my palm. "You know better than most, don't you?"

"Precisely." Santino nodded.

"If you both are correct, then we too would be walking into a trap if we chose to go back there," Drew added somberly.

"Yes, but our friends are in there. We can't turn a blind eye to their needs," Crystal said. She turned to me and let out a sigh. "And, showing our willingness to help them in their time of need would go far to repair our strained relationship."

"Yeah, I did sort of bring the problem to their doorstep. The least we can do is help with damage control."

"You're assuming we have anyone to help at all," Nicholas said curtly. "No one's answering. What if no one is alive?"

I closed my eyes, took a deep breath, and pushed aside thoughts of seeing my friends dead. "I'd hate to think that was true."

"Wolves are resourceful," Santino chimed in. "If for nothing else, I have to give them credit for their ability to adapt and overcome deadly situations."

Though he spoke respectfully, I caught the hint of anger behind his voice. I knew he was not fond of the wolves, especially after what they had done to him. In all honesty, he had probably done worse to their kind, but the fact that he was still working toward helping us, and them, truly solidified in my mind that he was on our side and wanted to make up for past transgressions.

"I hope you're right," I said.

Santino's voice softened. "Even when I was sent in to take care of the pack in Colorado, I couldn't guarantee I had taken them all out. They're crafty and have many places to hide. The Saints may have gotten a good majority of them—"

I sucked in a breath and winced at hearing that.

"—but you can bet there are still some out there. And they will need help if they're being hunted." For the first time ever, I saw Crystal look directly at Santino without appearing as if she wanted to rip his throat out.

"Good to know," she said. "Let's get a move on then, shall we?"

Ariana appeared in the living room, looking much more awake and put together than she had when I'd woken her. "Where are we going now?"

"You're staying here," I said. "The rest of us are going back to the wolves to help hunt down the Saints."

"Can't I go with you?"

"Too dangerous," Nicholas said.

"What about being left alone here, isn't that dangerous too?"

"Good point. Someone should stay behind with you. Alyssa?" Nicholas said.

"No, Fallon is out there. I need to find her. I'm going."

"I'll stay and protect her," Crystal said. "I can help with research too. Maybe while you are all gone, we can find a better solution to Lysander's problem, and maybe separate the spirits in the stone."

"Perfect!" I was glad she volunteered and happy she at least sounded like there was still hope of saving Lysander too.

"We've got good cloud coverage," Santino said. "We can probably get on the road now if we wanted to. It would help to get a jumpstart on things. I doubt the Saints would expect a counter attack so soon, especially from vampires."

"What are we waiting for, then?" I headed toward the door.

19

Just as full darkness was descending on the forest, we pulled into a small clearing and parked the van. I recognized it as the same spot where the witches had held their moonlight ceremony.

"Why are we stopping here?" I asked.

Santino pushed open the driver's side door. "This is far enough away for us to park but close enough to the wolf preserve that we can reach it on foot."

My feet crunched in the snow as I stepped out of the van. Thankfully, it wasn't snowing any longer, but the crispness of the air was still biting enough to be uncomfortable. I zipped my coat up high enough to cover my mouth and pulled the faux-fur-lined hood tight over my head.

"We all stick together, you hear?" Santino ordered. He too tightened his coat against the biting cold.

Knowing his past history, I wasn't one to argue. You didn't get the respected fear of being the Acta Sanctorum's most notorious hunter without being good at what you do. But I wondered if the others' egos would clash.

Nicholas and Drew silently exited the van as well.

"You sure it's smart to leave the van unprotected like this?" I asked.

"We've got no choice. There was too much daylight when we left to attempt bringing Lysander's coffin up to the apartment," Nicholas responded. He turned to Santino. "We can't leave the vehicle to sit unprotected for too long."

I was glad to see Nicholas looking out for Lysander, but I still felt uncomfortable leaving him unprotected with the Saints roaming the forest.

"Understood," Santino said with no hint of argument. "We will scout the area and if all is clear, we can return and drive it to a better spot. But for now, this spot is safe. It is well hidden, and no one is expecting us."

"Let's get moving then." Drew closed the van door.

Santino closed his eyes and turned his head up to the sky. I'd seen Nicholas do this before. He sniffed the air like a bloodhound, and then crouched down and touched the frigid earth, as if searching for any clue as to which way to go.

"Follow me." Santino didn't wait for us to respond; he took off running.

I followed along with the other two.

Santino was fast. I found it hard to keep up. He darted in between trees and bounded over small bushes and fallen logs with ease. Meanwhile, I had to catch myself from slipping and sliding on icy patches of ground and try to avoid the low hanging tree branches clawing at my face.

He stopped suddenly, and I almost barreled straight into him. He held a hand up in a very military fashion, and I could only assume he meant for us to stand where we were.

Nicholas, it seemed, understood his signal. He nodded and waited while Santino took small, silent steps away from us.

The scent of blood wafted to my nose. Not human blood, though. This had a deeper, richer smell. It was earthy; the scent of werewolf blood. Though I knew it was the smell of our fallen pack members, the fact I hadn't hunted in so long made it hard to ignore. The tantalizing scent tugged at my self control, and I had to fight the urge not to wander off after it. Elder vampires could hold out longer than I could, but even Drew looked tempted by the blood too. We all should have found a way to hunt before we'd come here.

"Wonder what's taking Santino so long. What's going on?" I whispered.

"Shh." Drew shot me an angry glare. "Can't you smell that? I think he's found something."

I mouthed the word "Sorry."

Nicholas shook his head at me. Drew turned his attention in the direction Santino had walked. The same direction the scent of blood was coming from.

We stood in silence for what felt like forever, waiting, watching, hoping for something to happen. I hoped the source of the blood wasn't one of our close friends. Then, just as my patience was wearing thin, Santino emerged from the darkness carrying a limp body in his arms.

"The Saints were here," he said solemnly and set the dead man at our feet. "There are more body parts back there. This one is the only intact corpse."

Through the matted hair and battle-worn face I recognized the dead man. My heart momentarily stopped and all of the air rushed out of my lungs.

"No," I choked the word out. "Connor."

His body was covered in the same series of wounds that Ian and Crystal had been given, but wolves don't heal as fast as vampires do. He'd stood no chance against those mines.

Even though his blood called out to my inner beast, tears welled in my eyes. I never held a grudge against Connor. I respected him. We might have had our differences, but he was a good leader. Even when he kicked us off of his land, I knew, deep down, he was just doing it to protect his people. If only he'd let us stay, we could have helped to defend them.

My sadness quickly turned to worry. Fallon had remained at the preserve, as well as Ian. Zuri too would have most likely come back here when she got our message not to return home.

"What about the others?" I said, trying to keep my voice low; but panic still showed through. "Santino said there were other body parts lying out there in the woods. What if one of those were... No. I'm not going to entertain that thought. We have to find the others... alive. And make those Acta Sanctorum pieces of shit pay for what they did here."

"We'll get them back, Little Warrior," Nicholas said, though his tone didn't sound very convincing.

"We must be careful," Santino said. "There are bound to be other traps. Whether they have been sprang or not, we don't know."

"What do we do about the body?" Drew asked with a heavy sigh.

Nicholas shrugged. "We do not have the luxury of time to deal with him right now. We'll have to come back for him later."

"He deserves a proper burial," I said.

"Agreed." Nicholas nodded. "That he does. And we will come back for him." He gently folded Connor's arms across his chest and dragged the body to rest between a small group of pine trees.

"Keep your eyes alert. Look for small red flashing lights. Those indicate RF triggers for these claymore mines. They also emit the scent of blood, as a way of attracting their prey. It will be hard, but you must ignore it." Santino looked directly at me. "You should have fed before we left."

"I'll be fine," I grumbled. "I have more important things to hunt tonight." I planned on taking my vengeance out on those Acta Sanctorum pieces of shit.

"Good. Keep that mind frame. There may be more Saints lurking around. Depending on how long ago they attacked, they might still be searching for stragglers. We don't have time for you to stop for a snack. Break their necks and move on."

They deserved more than a quick death for what they had done here. I would make some of them pay. But I knew it would do me no good to argue with Santino about it. I gave a quick nod. "Lead on."

Santino began heading toward the wolf preserve, walking cautiously, peering in each direction.

Drew followed next.

Nicholas clapped me on the shoulder as he passed by. "Don't worry, we'll get our revenge."

I felt my own resolve strengthen hearing Nicholas say that.

We walked for what felt like miles with the scent of blood teasing our noses. Some of it I recognized as werewolf, and some was human. I could only imagine the extent of the battle we'd missed.

The closer we came to the wolf preserve, though, the less blood and carnage we found. That gave me some comfort. I hoped that the wolves, even if they'd lost, had been able to keep the sanctuary safe.

We approached with caution, but Santino stopped us before we could break through the tree line. All the lights inside the building were on, but I saw no movement.

In the distance, I heard a rumbling like a large truck, but nothing else to indicate anyone was there.

"It's a trap," Santino said. "We're meant to think it is all clear."

"Create a false sense of security, that's dirty," Drew said.

"Nothing is considered dirty when you are cleansing the world of evil unnatural creatures," Santino said.

"You really bought into all that crap, didn't you?" I asked, keeping my voice at a whisper.

"I was never taught to look for the good in creatures like ourselves," Santino said.

And if I wasn't mistaken, he actually sounded like he might feel some sorrow for the way he had thought about our kind. Now wasn't the time to rub it in, though.

"So what do we do?" I asked.

Santino looked around. "Circle around the perimeter. See if we can sniff out any survivors. And take out any Saints you can find."

"Let's split up," Nicholas said. "Santino, you with me. Drew, you with Alyssa."

Drew and I exchanged glances and nodded.

"If anything should go wrong, run back toward the van." Nicholas directed the statement at me. "And keep your eyes peeled for traps."

"Got it," I said.

Drew and I took off, heading east toward the cabins behind the main building. We moved at a jogger's pace, darting in between trees, making sure not to stray beyond the tree line. I kept a lookout for any signs of strange lights and listened for any other sounds of movement.

A click, barely audible over the crunching of my feet in the snow, caught my attention. "Get down," I whispered. I grabbed hold of Drew's coat and yanked him down as hard as I could.

Moments later three shots were fired in rapid succession. I felt the break of wind over my head as they sailed past.

Drew rolled on the ground until he butted up against a tree and then sat up against it. Lifting a finger to his lips, he instructed me to follow, cocking his head to the side.

I nodded and rolled just as he had to the large tree trunk.

Silently, we waited and listened to the sounds of the forest. Thankful for my enhanced hearing, I was able to pick up the softest of footprints. The gentle crunch of the snow added just enough sound, and I could tell someone was heading in our direction.

Drew edged himself up to a standing position, keeping his back firmly against the trunk of the tree. He motioned with his hand for me to do the same.

The footsteps came closer. There was more than one. They kept in step with each other, but I heard the slight delay on the second step. I held up two fingers to Drew and he nodded. He must have come to the same conclusion as I had.

My heart pounded in anticipation as the steps came close enough to us that they had to be just on the other side of the tree where we were standing. I closed my eyes, took a deep breath, and slowly let it out, trying to calm myself.

Drew tapped me on the shoulder. I opened my eyes. With his hand up he counted backwards.

Three.

Two.

One.

We jumped out on opposite sides of the tree trunk. Each of us grabbed hold of a soldier. I took hold of my soldier and twisted the man's neck with blinding speed until I heard the satisfying crunch of his bones. Before either of the soldiers could comprehend what was happening, they were dead. I'd have loved to sample their blood, and savor giving them a slow torturous death for what they'd done to my friends, but Santino was right, we had to do this quickly and move on. There were bound to be more where they'd come from.

I left the soldier in a lump on the ground, and Drew and I resumed our search of the perimeter.

Ahead of us, I saw the flash of a light, but not a red one. This one was larger and white in color. I tapped Drew on the shoulder and tilted my head toward it. "Let's check that out."

"Could be a trap."

"Or it could be someone stumbling around in the dark. Either way, they're going to attract the Saints. Better we get to them first, right?"

"Good point." He smiled at me. "Lead on."

As fast as I could, I took off toward the white light. The scent of blood hit my nose as we came closer. Then the light disappeared. I stopped in my tracks.

Was this another trap?

The smell of blood was definitely from a werewolf. I recognized the richness and earthy nature of it immediately. Waiting to see if the light would flash again, I stood still. Drew came up next to me. His nose crinkled as he took in a big breath.

"Fresh blood," he whispered. "Someone is or was recently hurt."

"Do we chance it?" I asked, suddenly worried about walking into a new kind of trap.

Then, I heard the soft whimper. Someone was hurt, and they close. I took a few tentative steps forward. The ground suddenly sloped downward. I caught myself before falling flat on my face, but not before uttering a loud "Oof."

"Alyssa?" I heard the weak voice of Fallon call out to me.

20

I turned around, instantly spotting the reason I'd tripped. The uneven ground had created a shelf, and a few downed trees covered the area making a small shelter big enough for a person to hide inside.

I was glad for my enhanced vision; it allowed me to see better in the dark. Peering closer into the small cave-like space I recognized Fallon and let out a sigh of relief. Most mortals would have missed her hiding back there. *Thank God she's alive!* "You okay?" I whispered.

"I'm fine," she called back from behind the snow-covered branches. Her words were followed by the light whimper of an animal coming from her direction too. "Aiden's with me too."

The smell of blood, thick and musky, was coming from her direction. But it wasn't human blood. Aiden was hurt. "Is he all right?"

"No." She reached up, holding something long and slender in her hand. I registered what it was, just before she flicked it on and sent light blaring in my direction.

"No flashlights," I said a little louder than I wanted to. Not only would they affect my night vision, but the light might alert unwanted visitors.

"Sorry. I can't see very well," she whispered back, and the frantic tone she spoke in told me all I needed to know. Aiden was hurt really bad.

"Don't worry. I see well enough for the both of us." I looked up toward Drew. "I've found them."

"Get them, and let's get out of here," Drew's whispered so low I was probably the only one who heard it "I'll keep watch."

He didn't need to tell me twice. I didn't want to linger any longer than we needed. There could be more soldiers scouring the woods.

I peered back into the small cave-like shelter. Fallon was sitting with her back to the trees while Aiden, the dark gray wolf, rested next to her, his head buried between his paws.

I crouched down, eye level with her. "What happened?"

"They came out of nowhere. One minute we were cleaning up the mess in the reception hall, and the next, windows were shattering and men with assault rifles were coming in after us. Connor called all of the remaining wolves to help, but with most already gone home, we were outnumbered."

We never should have left. "Are you sure you're okay?"

"I'm all right, but Aiden's really hurt." Fallon ran her hands through the large wolf's fur. Aiden whimpered, a pathetic and pitiful sound. When she pulled her hand away it was coated in blood. "He took some of that shrapnel. He's got these wounds everywhere."

That accounted for the blood I'd smelled. It teased my nose with its earthy scent, but the danger of our situation helped me keep my internal beast in check.

"C'mon. Let's move," Drew called down from above me. "Can they walk?"

"We've got to get you two to safety; there are more of those guys out there. We ran into a couple just a few minutes ago."

"I know," her voice faltered. "I heard the shots."

"Can you get Aiden to stand?"

"I can try." Fallon stood and bend over in front of Aiden. "Come on, Babe," she said tenderly.

The large wolf groaned and pushed up on to all fours. He wobbled a little and leaned against Fallon's body for support. I'd never seen Aiden so weak. It wasn't a good sign. Werewolves, no matter how hurt, always showed their strength, especially dominant ones like Aiden. Weakness was something other potential dominant males took advantage of.

Blood dripped from his matted fur to the moist dirt below. Aiden lowered his head as if in shame for his injuries.

"He's not going to make it very far. Not if he's losing all that blood," I said cautiously. I didn't want to scare Fallon any more than she already was. Werewolves don't heal as fast as vampires do, and as weak as he was showing us he was, he wouldn't last much longer without some kind of medical attention, or at the very least first aid.

I called up to Drew. "We can't move Aiden just yet; he's bleeding all over the place. Can you keep watch?"

"Whatever you're going to do, you'd better do it quick." Frustration edged his voice. "It's not safe out here in the open."

"I know." I didn't want to hang around either, but I felt if we tried to move Aiden in this condition, he'd die of blood loss. "Trust me, Drew, we've got no other choice right now. I'll hurry."

He sighed, though whether from exasperation or worry I didn't know. "Okay."

I turned to Fallon. "This is going to probably hurt him a lot, but the only way I can try to save him is to stop his bleeding. To do that, I need him to transform back to human form."

"Do you think it will work?" she asked, and I saw the utter desperation in her eyes.

"Yeah, it will," I lied. I knew nothing about werewolf anatomy. I hoped the transformation would push the poisoned shrapnel out. It was a guess and a fifty-fifty shot at best, but I didn't see any other way. If we didn't do anything, he would probably die.

"Then do it." As long as Fallon had known me, she could always tell when I was lying. It was a testament to her anxiety that she'd accepted the lie now.

I grabbed Aiden by the muzzle and looked him in the eyes. "This is really going to hurt. But no matter what, you have to be silent. We can't alert anyone else that we're here. I need you to take your human form."

The large gray wolf snorted and sat back on his hind legs. He turned his snout up toward Fallon.

"I'm here for you. You can do this," she said in her most reassuring voice. She ran her hands along the sides of his muzzle and looked him in the eye.

Aiden nodded and let out one final snort. The air around us became electrified. Fur slowly began to fall from the wolf's body. He let out small strained whimpers and yelps as his body began to contort. Each movement was accompanied by a popping and cracking sound. His muzzle shortened, his paws grew, and his body gradually began to look human. Whimpers and moans became strangled grunts. He twisted and contorted through the change. Where fur had been, blood now coated his naked skin. I could see a large patch of wounds on his back, but thankfully, they didn't cover his entire body. That was a good sign. If I could take care of that localized area, he just might make it.

When Aiden had completed his transformation, he passed out and collapsed on the ground.

"Quickly pull him in close. He needs body heat," I said with a shiver of my own. It may not have been snowing at that moment, but the temperature was still hovering around freezing. "It looks like most of the wounds are on his back. Turn him so I have easy access."

Though he wasn't conscious, his body shook violently. I hoped it was just a reaction to the cold and not the poison working through his system.

Fallon couldn't lift Aiden to position him so I bent down and hooked my arms under his and lifted him to his knees. "Let him rest against you. Just try to keep him warm and quiet."

She nodded and wrapped her arms around the upper portion of his back. Anxiety widened her eyes. "Just do whatever it is you have to do."

I bent down to inspect the wounds. Some were trickling blood, while others looked as if they were bulging with shrapnel sitting just below the skin.

So much for hoping the transformation would take care of this part.

I knew the mixture of my blood and saliva would work to stem the flow of his blood. I'd done it once before and saved Connor's life, but this time it wouldn't be so simple. I had to be sure the wounds were clean of the poison and the bits of metal before I sealed them; otherwise, I might make things worse.

The smell of his blood was intoxicating. I remembered too the rich taste of werewolf blood. It had been hard to stop myself the last time I'd sampled it.

Focus. I found the worst of the bleeding wounds and bent to take a sip. Unlike what I was expecting, I could taste a sharp, metallic taint. It ruined the flavor for me, which I found helpful. Without the temptation to drink deeply and take in all of his life-giving blood, I'd have a much easier time of doing my job. I sucked harder at the wound, while Aiden's body shook and convulsed underneath me.

It took a few moments and a lot of pressure, but soon, a nasty bit of metal rose to the surface. I gently grasped it with my teeth. I tasted the poison in his blood.

Fallon covered his mouth with her hand to stifle the pain-filled noises he made as I pulled out the tiny bit of sharp metal and spat it to the ground.

"Hurry," Drew said frantically. "I hear someone coming."

My heart pounded anxiously. There were still more bits to remove and many more wounds to seal.

Above us, I heard a scuffle and the sounds of Drew fighting with someone or something.

I worked at a feverish pace, losing all pretense of being gentle as I attempted to yank out another bit of poisoned metal from his back. Aiden's body twitched and shivered beneath me. I spat each tiny piece I removed to the ground as I hurried to get them all before we were attacked.

The scuffle above us silenced. I listened carefully as I continued to work, hoping to hear Drew say he was okay, but the only thing I heard were the unconscious grunts and moans Aiden was making.

After repeating the process several more times, I felt safe in the knowledge that I had removed the remaining bits. I pierced my tongue with my fang and lapped at the wounds on Aiden's back, making sure to spread my healing saliva and blood all over to close the wounds.

I pulled back and wiped my face, knowing I was still leaving bloody smears behind. "He's not bleeding anymore."

"He's not conscious either." Fallon looked worried.

I listened for a moment and confirmed that his heart was still beating. "He might need some time before he comes around. He lost a lot of blood."

"Drew," I called. *Please still be up there.* I hadn't heard a sound since he'd warned us of someone approaching.

Seconds went by without a sound.

Fallon and I exchanged worried glances.

"I'm here," Drew called back, panting and out of breath. "There were two of them, hiding in the trees. I got them though."

"I'm glad you're all right. But we've still got some problems down here. Aiden's not going to be able to move. He's out cold. We need to get him back to the van."

"Understood. We can't linger here any longer. Do you know the way?" Drew responded.

"I think I can find it. Let's pull back and regroup there."

"Good idea," he said. "I'll meet up with the others and let them know. Use your cell phone and let me know when you've reached the van."

"Will do." I pulled off my coat and wrapped it around Aiden, and then dug my arms under him and lifted him off Fallon's lap. "Let's go."

I didn't have to tell her twice. She was up in a flash and right behind me.

Running though the dark forest, we attempted to make our way back to the van as quietly and as quickly as we could. Determination to get us where we needed helped fuel me, and I was able to spot landmarks and footprints from our way in, making the trip back a much easier journey.

The added spur of the icy cold weather, freezing the blood in my veins, pushed me to run faster; but Fallon, being human, would never have kept up. Reluctantly, I had to limit my speed.

Aiden rested limply in my arms, occasionally letting out a grunt or a moan, but remained unconscious.

In the distance, I heard the long high-pitched call of a wolf. "Did you hear that?" I asked.

Howling, no matter how distant, was a comforting sound. That meant others had escaped the Acta Sanctorum's raid. And we'd need all the resources we could muster to fight back.

"Yes. Before we scattered, Connor tried to call back the pack."

He was a damn good leader. A twinge of pain tugged at my heart. *Was all of this really a result of our bringing the Acta Sanctorum so close to their borders, or would they have eventually attacked anyway?*

"We need to find a way to signal them. Get them to re-group with us at the van. If there are enough of us, we might be able to retake the wolf preserve."

"How do we alert them and not the Saints?"

"Your guess is as good as mine. Let's get Aiden to safety and we can figure it out."

When we finally reached the van and shut ourselves inside, I inspected Aiden's wounds again. Thankfully, they'd all formed scabs and appeared to be healing with no sign of infection. "I think he's going to be all right." I pulled one of the blankets off Lysander's coffin and wrapped it around Aiden's naked body.

"Thank you for saving him. Even after… you know."

"Like I would let your man die?" I said trying to sound as nonchalant about it as possible. Then the thought occurred to me. With Connor's death, Aiden was now the leader of the pack—assuming no one stepped up to challenge him.

"Still… thank you." She pulled me into a hug, squeezing me as tightly as she could.

"Don't thank me yet. We still have a lot left to fix. We need to figure out how to call the rest of the pack. We need to take back the preserve, and unearth the Pandora's Box."

She pulled back, shock widening her eyes. "Do the Saints know about the box? And what's inside?"

"That's the other thing. We don't think there is anything inside. The spirit we meant to put back might be hiding out in the same crystal that Lysander is trapped in."

"So you're saying—"

"We buried an empty box. The Saints know about it and the wolves, and that's why they took over the preserve… yes."

"If Connor had known all this, he would have never sent you away or let the rest of the pack go home after the full moon."

"About Connor…"

She gasped and covered her mouth. "Oh no. He—"

"Didn't make it." I didn't like being so blunt about it and wished I'd found a nicer way to break the news. "That leaves your man in charge." I glanced down to Aiden.

"Or Brady. Aiden is in no shape to do anything."

"Do you know where Brady is?"

"No. Connor ordered all the women to scatter and the men to transform and fight. I took off into the woods and got lost. Aiden found me just before I sprang one of those traps. He pushed me to the ground. When it was all clear, we tried to make our way back, but his back was pretty badly hurt and he was bleeding everywhere. I haven't seen anyone until you and Drew."

I'd momentarily forgotten that the others were still out there and I was supposed to send them a message when we'd gotten to the van safely. If I could get a message to them and they ran into one of the wolves, they could pass our plan along. I dug into my pocket and pulled out my phone. I texted to Drew and Nicholas both, "We're safe. Tell all wolves to regroup at van. Make a howling chain."

"A howling chain?" Fallon scrunched up her face in confusion.

"What else am I going to call it? That's how they communicate, right? They pass messages along when they howl."

"I guess. How will we know if it worked?"

I shrugged. "Listen for someone to howl."

Aiden, still unconscious, twitched and almost fell out of his seat.

Fallon rewrapped the blanket around him and snuggled as close to him as the space allowed. "He's going to freeze to death if we don't find something warmer to cover him with."

"He needs his fur coat back. Once he wakes, try to get him to transform."

"What if he's not healthy enough to transform?"

"Honestly, I don't know. Wolves are different than vampires. We just need blood. I have no idea what will heal them. We need a wolf here."

"But that would be dangerous. If Connor is dead and Aiden is too weak to take over, there might be a power struggle." The worry had returned to Fallon's voice.

"Do you really think that, with all of this going on, someone would want to challenge an injured wolf?"

Fallon pursed her lips, as if trying to hold back what she wanted to say.

"Well. I'm not letting anyone attack a defenseless man, wolf or not. We have more important things to deal with."

"Wolves can be pretty vicious when it comes to power and leadership."

"And I can be just as vicious in protecting those who cannot do it themselves."

"As frustrating as you can be sometimes, Alyssa, I'm glad you're so recklessly loyal."

I smiled. "Not sure if that was a compliment or not, but I'll take it."

Another wolf howl pierced the night. It was a long and deep call that reminded me of a rallying cry. A moment later, another howl followed, then another. I smiled with relief and said a silent thank you to modern technology. "I think our message got through."

21

Aiden stirred from his unconsciousness. He groaned, and his eyes slowly opened.

Fallon perked up, smiling the second she saw the life returning to Aiden's face. "It's all right, Baby. We're here with you. You're safe."

All around us, sounds of the wolves' howling grew more frequent and closer. I felt comforted knowing they were on their way. Aiden looked as if he wanted to join in the rallying cry. His muscles strained as he tried to move.

"Don't get up," I said, pushing Aiden back into the chair. "You've still got a lot of healing to do."

He mumbled something, but I couldn't understand him. I assumed it was his dominant wolf side grumbling about being told what to do. I smiled at that thought. If it was true, then it was a good sign—meaning he was on the mend.

I gave him the quick rundown of our situation and told him we were waiting to regroup with the others.

"With my father… Connor gone… it falls to me to lead." Aiden strained to get the words out. "Or Brady."

"We know." I tried to sound sympathetic. Aiden was in a bad position, losing his father and potentially being too injured to join in the upcoming battle. For a wolf of his status, he was in a very vulnerable position. "You're in no condition to fight, and as soon as you have the strength, you need to change to avoid freezing to death."

Fallon sat on his lap and snuggled in closer as if she was trying to smother him with her body. "You just worry about staying warm and healing, okay?"

A cold prickling tingle crept up the back of my neck. "Someone's here," I whispered, welcoming the tell-tale sensation of another vampire approaching.

"Who?" Fallon eyed me nervously.

"Don't know. But it has to be one of us. I'll go out and check. You keep him warm, and get him ready to change."

She nodded stiffly.

I eased the door open, and peeked through the crack before stepping out of the van.

It seemed the night had turned colder, or perhaps I had just gotten used to the lukewarm atmosphere in the van. I shivered and pulled my coat closed as the breeze blew past me, bringing with it the smell of death and blood. Normally, I'd savor the smell of hot, rich blood, but not now. Knowing it originated from the Saints' ridiculous quest to rid the world of unnatural creatures made me want to find each and every one of them and feast on them. They needed to pay for their crimes against my kind, and I would see to it that they would pay.

The tingling sensation intensified. I felt as if eyes were on the back of my neck, watching me. I turned.

Santino was there, silently stalking forward. I let out a huge breath.

"Where is Nicholas?" I whispered feeling both relieved and worried seeing only him.

"Shhh," he said and continued his silent approach.

Confused, I turned around, half expecting to see someone coming up behind me. But there was nothing there.

I caught a whiff of something else on the breeze. It wasn't blood. Musky sweat maybe, heightened by adrenaline. I couldn't quite place it. "What's going on?" I whispered again.

In a flash, Santino shot past me. He was a blur of motion, too fast for even my vampire vision to process. A moment later, I heard the satisfying crack of a neck being snapped.

Santino returned with a rifle in hand. "You were being hunted. You should learn to be quiet."

"Looks like I owe you now," I nodded, feeling a little embarrassed but very appreciative that he had my back. If he hadn't been there, that Saint might have attacked us in the van. Aiden was already weak, and Fallon... a human might not have survived.

He grunted in acceptance and handed me the rifle. "The others are coming."

"Fallon and Aiden are inside." I gave him the quick summary of our plan, but when I got to the part about needing Brady to take leadership, he scowled.

"Brady is in the hands of the Saints. I saw them. They know about the box. He's being tortured for the location."

My breath hitched in my chest. *Poor Brady. They'll kill him no matter what he tells them.*

"Nicholas and Drew are working to gather the remaining wolves and clear away any traps between the preserve and our path."

Another wolf howled, this time much closer.

"I wish they wouldn't do that," Santino said. "They're giving away their positions."

"How else are they going to communicate?"

"That was always their downfall." His voice held no emotion, a reminder that he was a cold-blooded killer.

"Just remember whose side you're on," I said angrily.

"I was just stating a fact. And you of all should know where my loyalties lie."

"Like I said before. Don't fuck me over." I may have vouched for him, but in the back of my mind there would always be some small remembrance of him playing for Team Vampire Hunter.

"If the wolves give away their position, and they are heading toward us, then our position is compromised as well," he said matter-of-factly.

"We're damned if we do and damned if we don't right now. All we can do is remain on alert. We can't coordinate an attack without the wolves. We just don't have the manpower."

Santino clenched his jaw. I sensed he had more to say but decided it wasn't worth arguing. "Then I'll start patrolling the area."

Before he could turn and walk away, two wolves appeared to our left. Both were large. One had splotches of light gray and white fur around its muzzle and at the ends of its paws. The other was solid white, the only hint of color was it's dark eyes. Both wolves hunched down and bared their teeth at us.

I held my hands up in surrender to assure them that we were on the same side. "Thank you two for coming so quickly."

The white wolf stood and walked toward me. He sniffed at my ankles and then looked up. I could see the recognition in his eyes and in a very dog-like manner, he wagged his tail.

Good boy. I smiled at him.

The other wolf sat back on his hind legs and turned to face the van.

"Aiden is inside," I said, knowing wolves would understand me even if they couldn't speak themselves. "He's hurt but alive." I tried to sound reassuring.

The white wolf whimpered and trotted over to the door.

"Let him rest until it is time," I said, putting authority into my voice. Wolves respect authority; I hoped that would be enough to prevent them from pressing the matter. I wasn't sure how fast Aiden would heal, and with him so weak I didn't want any struggles for power.

The wolf growled at me.

I narrowed my gaze and locked eyes with the wolf. "We need everyone working together tonight if we plan to retake the preserve, understand?"

The wolf snorted but made no attempt at further aggression. It walked back over to the other wolf and sat down.

Waiting was unbearable. Slowly, more wolves trickled in. They created their own circle around the van, leaving me alone for the most part.

Santino patrolled the area, looking for traps and roving Saints. I watch as he circled the perimeter.

Things were quiet—too quiet. It was the calm before the inevitable storm, but I took no comfort from it, only anxiety. My mind kept racing, wondering what was going on back at the preserve. I hadn't heard any new messages from the guys. I wondered about the fate of Ian, who would have been trapped by the daylight and his own injuries. No one had heard from Zuri in days. I knew the longer we waited to move, the more damage the Saints could have done, but I didn't want to start the attack without Nicholas or Drew, who hadn't returned yet.

What if the Saints got the information out of Brady and killed him? What if we were wrong about Aniketos being in the box and the Saints open it again? What if...

A rustling in the bushes had me gasping for breath. I'd been so caught up in my own thoughts and worries I failed to recognize the tell-tale prickling on the back of my neck that signaled another vampire's approach.

Seeing Drew and Nicholas was like having a giant weight yanked off my shoulders. I rushed up to them and threw my arms around them both. "I was so worried."

"Calm down. This is no way for a Little Warrior to act." I heard the amusement in Nicholas's voice, but it didn't show on his stony face.

"We need to move quickly," Drew said. "We tried to alert as many wolves as we could and clear away any traps we could find, but the Saints still have the preserve."

"They were moving in construction equipment last we checked," Nicholas added.

"That must mean Brady gave up the information about the Pandora's Box." If he did that, he might no longer be alive. My conscience nagged at me, like a little voice saying *I told you so*. "I knew we shouldn't have waited so long to retaliate."

"We don't know anything for sure," Nicholas said, his tone warning. "Either way, we need to strike back hard and fast. Where is Santino?"

I looked over my shoulders. "He's been patrolling."

"And Aiden?" Nicholas asked.

"In the van with Fallon," I said. "He's hurt pretty bad. I won't let any wolf in there to start a war for dominance."

The wolves had remained in a tight circle around the van. None of them had broken ranks to come join in our conversation yet.

Nicholas's eyebrow quirked up. He gave me an approving nod. "Good plan. Aiden's in good hands. Now for the attack. What are our assets?"

I looked around. "We have about fifteen wolves here and four vampires, ready to fight."

"What about weapons?" Drew asked.

I held up the rifle I'd had strapped across my shoulder. "Just this, and I was planning to give it to Fallon when we left."

"That doesn't leave us much to fight with." Nicholas clenched his jaw and let out a frustrated growl. "We fight with what we've got, then."

"How many Saints are we looking at?" I asked.

Drew's face was grim. He shrugged. "Unknown. They've got the main building. There is no telling how many of them are holed up inside. And there are still more patrolling the forest."

"Are any of them vampires?" I asked, remembering that until we had destroyed Santino's group, there had been other vampires employed in the ranks of the Acta Sanctorum.

Nicholas shook his head. "I haven't felt any new vampires. I did sense someone in the building when I passed by. Maybe Ian or Zuri, but no new threats."

I held on to a small hope that Ian was still alive. He may have been an arrogant pervert, but no one deserved to die at the hands of the Acta Sanctorum.

Nicholas walked over to the van and faced the wolves. "Let's rally the troops. I'll lead the charge," he said. "We have a clear path back to the preserve with no traps."

The van door slid open. "No. I will lead the charge." Aiden stepped out, wincing slightly as he moved. The blanket was wrapped around his waist, hiding some of the scabs on his backside.

The rest of the wolves surrounding the van immediately sat at attention. Fifteen pairs of eyes zeroed in on him.

"Our leader is gone," Aiden began. "Slain at the hands of these monsters who hide behind religion. They've taken our land, our homes, and our family."

Growls and grunts rumbled through the assembled wolves. A few looked in my direction and snarled.

Aiden continued. "Some of you blame the vampires." He turned walked a few short steps toward me. I watched him wobble a bit, probably still a little woozy from blood loss. I met him halfway, placing an arm around his shoulder as a sign of unity, while hoping to offer him some support so he would not reveal to his pack how injured he really was.

"I don't blame them," Aiden continued. I saw the look of thanks in his eyes. He leaned in, resting his body against mine. "These vampires are just as much a part of this pack as we are. All of us, werewolves, witches, and vampires... we're all persecuted by the Saints. And we must work together if we hope to have a chance to fight back."

"We're prepared to fight," Nicholas said. He joined us and stood next to Aiden.

"Will you join us?" Drew asked. He too took a spot next us and faced the pack of wolves.

Santino reappeared as well, walking around the back of the van. "I once believed as the Saints did, that all creatures like us were evil. Now I know the truth. You may hate me for my crimes, but I am here, and willing to help make amends."

"Together we fight and take back what is ours!" Aiden said triumphantly.

The wolves responded with yips and barks. They jumped to their feet, excited and ready to charge into battle.

I turned and looked back at Fallon. "Hold the fort here, okay?"

"How will I know when it's safe?" she asked.

I handed her the rifle. "We'll get you when it's all clear."

Aiden bent to the ground and dropped the blanket that had been covering him. "Follow me," he said, and quickly transformed back into his wolf form.

22

We tore into the forest, racing toward a fight we had an unknown chance of winning. Aiden, though injured, loped ahead of us as if he had never been hurt. A dark gray blur, he led the pack at a pace that even I had trouble keeping up with.

The sight of him moving swiftly through the trees and bounding over rocks and brush was inspiring. He was a true leader, just like Connor had been. I had a feeling that if we survived the night, he'd make his father proud.

As we neared the preserve, Aiden let out a few short barks and the wolves dispersed, fanning out in a wide arc.

"Alyssa—with me," Nicholas called. "We're going to take the back."

I veered left toward Nicholas. To my right I spotted Santino and Drew heading in the other direction. "Good luck, you guys," I whispered and continued on, following Nicholas to the back of the main building.

In the distance, I heard the sounds of gunfire and wolves yelping. My heart began racing, imaging what horrible things could be going on, but no matter how much I wanted to veer off and check on them, I needed to stay with Nicholas. Together we were a deadly team; individually, we'd be target practice.

We stayed within the tree line as we surveyed the area. A few soldiers stood around casually talking, rifles in hand, while another patrolled in a circle around some large construction equipment. Anger and anticipation fueled the beast inside of me. I hadn't really fed in a long while, and the prospect of sinking my fangs into the neck of one of those Saints had me chomping at the bit to attack.

Nicholas reached out and grabbed my shoulder. "You ready, Little Warrior? You're looking a little pale."

I sucked in a breath and tried to calm my racing heart. "I'm ready."

A large truck outfitted with a jackhammer sat idling close to the back door of the main building. Next to it, another large excavating truck, run by a withered old man, was busy digging a hole into the frozen earth.

"Saul?" I wondered aloud. "Is he planning on digging up the entire preserve?"

Three other large holes disfigured the place where the wolves held their moonlight bonfire ceremonies.

"Brady's sending them on a wild goose chase," I whispered to Nicholas. "They'll be digging all night."

I glanced around, hoping to see a sign of our lost werewolf friend, but he was nowhere to be seen.

"Brady can only hold them off for so long. And they will tear up every inch of this wildlife preserve to find what they are looking for," he replied gravely. "By my count there are five men here, but there could be more."

"Divide and conquer?" I asked, ready to attack and hoping I'd have a chance to taste fresh blood.

"Exactly." He smirked. "You take the one on patrol. Then stop the man in the truck. I'll get the small group on the other side."

"Got it." I nodded.

"Be as quiet as you can." He held his fingers to his lips.

I snuck away from Nicholas and prowled silently through the trees after the lone soldier on patrol. He walked in a wide circle around the two construction trucks. I attempted to gauge the course his path would take. If I was lucky, he'd come close enough to the tree line. If he did that, I could pull him away with no one seeing.

As with many of the other soldiers we'd run into in the past, this one was young, maybe just out of high school.

Probably easier to manipulate the younger they are. So sad.

Closer and closer he came toward me. The monster inside of me called out, begging me to take his neck, not just break it quickly.

Young and firm, and full of hot blood.

I could just imagine the strength of his heart, pounding, flooding my mouth with his blood. I hadn't fed in so long that the temptation of it was a torturous thought.

My heart pounded as I watched his steps. Each crunch of his boot in the snow matched the beating of my heart.

Maybe just a sip.

The construction truck backfired, startling the soldier. He lifted his rifle and shot blindly into the trees. All thoughts of blood and a quick meal went out the window at that point. I sprang to action, leaping from my hidden spot in the trees, and dove at the soldier's body. The force of impact as I collided with him caused him to fire one more shot, but he was dead before his body came to rest on the ground. I'd snapped his neck, damn near tearing it off as we fell.

I looked up quickly, hoping to see Nicholas, but the construction truck blocked my path. The man inside, whom I recognized as Saul, spotted me. Our eyes met. My heart thundered. One word from him and the soldiers that Nicholas was stalking could be alerted.

Strangely, he didn't make any effort to raise an alarm. Confusion held me frozen in place. Something was off about that man. Twice now, he simply stepped aside or ignored our actions as if he didn't care about the outcome.

Was he just trying to save his own skin, or was he—like Santino—one of the few who had chosen to forsake the ways of the Acta Sanctorum?

The break of wind as a bullet raced over my head snapped me out of my thoughts and back into reality. Saul may not want a fight with us, but there were plenty of other soldiers out for blood.

I turned and spied out of the corner of my eye a dark figure crouching behind a pile of logs. "Oh no you don't," I whispered and took off before the sniper could set up his shot.

As fast as I was, the wolf that came up behind him was faster. Large jaws opened wide, revealing long slick teeth ready to strike their killing blow. With a graceful leap into the air, the wolf sailed into the sniper and bit down as he collided with the soldier's shoulder. The large beast jerked his head sideways, using his momentum to throw the soldier to the ground in a deadly pirouette. Even though he had stolen my kill, I had to appreciate the might and power this werewolf had. The soldier never stood a chance. Even after

I heard the first crack as his neck snapped, the wolf remained, jaws clamped shut into the soft flesh of his enemy. He shook the dead man in violent spasms of jerks and twists.

When satisfied he'd killed his prey, the wolf turned to me. His white muzzle had been stained with blood. If wolves could smile, I'd say this one was, clearly proud of the kill he'd just made.

"Thanks," I said and gave a quick nod.

The wolf took off again. I turned on my heel to do the same, but in that short amount of time the entire area had erupted into an all-out war zone. Shots were being fired from every direction; some of them flew dangerously close to me. I ducked down behind the wood pile for cover. Wolves had launched their attack, and a few were tearing apart dead bodies littering the ground while others were attacking any soldier they came across. A few, unfortunately, were lying dead or dying on the ground.

I looked back toward the construction equipment. Saul was no longer sitting in the driver's seat, but I could see a body crouching low behind it. My intuition nagged at me to go investigate, but with the battle raging all around, I knew I should be hunting down all of the snipers and killing any soldier I could find. Still though, the mystery behind Saul and the way he acted piqued my interest too much.

Looking left and right through the chaos, I spotted various wolves fighting in full fury. One had clamped his jaws onto a soldier. He viciously shook his head, killing his prey. He looked up, and I swear I saw him smile. Blood dripped from his fangs from the many kills. Wolves were definitely adept killers when they needed to be. I was grateful they weren't hunting me.

I spotted Nicholas. Two bodies lay at his feet, and he held a third in his arms. The soldier pounded on Nicholas's back, trying to break free from the deadly grip. Nicholas would not be budged. His teeth were sunk deep into the soldier's neck as he fed from him.

All around me shots rang out. Gun powder hung in the air. The battle was far from over. Still, I needed to solve the mystery behind Saul.

I sprinted toward him.

Saul was crouched even further down behind the large tire of the construction truck. His wide eyes peered out at me from behind the shaking hands attempting to shield his face. "Mercy," he said weakly, his voice barely audible over the noises of the battle surrounding us. If I hadn't been a vampire I'd never have heard the word.

I locked eyes with him. "Why? Give me one good reason not to rip your throat out!"

"I mean you no harm." He balled up, making himself appear smaller and frailer than he had when we'd last met.

"Of course not. You're not in a position to harm me now, but you work for them." I cast an angry glance over my shoulder to the fight. Thankfully, no one was paying any attention to us.

"They pay me, yes. They let me research, yes. But I'm not one of them."

His pathetic voice tugged at my heart. There was true fear there. I could smell the tang of it emanating from him as well as see it in the depths of his eyes. But fear is no indicator of innocence.

"Why are you here, then?"

"The box. I have to see it for myself. It would be the pinnacle of my life's work to know it exists, to touch it and hold it."

"If you knew anything about it, you'd know no human can resist opening it," I scoffed.

"But you know as well as I do that it is empty."

How does he know?

"That crystal holds the evil within it, doesn't it?" he asked, but it sounded more like a statement of fact to me.

"We don't know that for sure," I said cautiously, wondering just how much he knew about the crystal and the box.

"You know it as well as I do. And you know the crystal is dying. We have to find the box and put things right."

"You say you're not one of them, but you'd allow the slaughter of an entire pack of wolves to get at the box?" Anger welled up again.

"The evil that resides inside would kill more than this pack of wolves if it's left to roam free. I can't allow that." I caught the hint of sorrow in his voice. "But I did not kill the wolf or the vampire here. I spared them. I told the soldiers they had to hold them for questioning until I found the box."

I searched his face for any sign of deceit, but found only fear. "Show me. Now!" I practically shouted the words.

"They are close." He nodded and pointed with a shaky finger toward the cabins that dotted the area behind the main preserve building.

Part of me wondered how much I should trust this man, while the other part of me desperately wanted to know that my friends were all right. It was a risk I'd have to take. If there was even the slightest amount of truth to his words, he could help us put things right with the crystal, Pandora's Box, and maybe even Lysander.

"I hope I can trust you," I said anxiously.

23

Being old and frail, Saul was in no condition to sprint across the battlefield, past the soldiers, wolves and vampires, so I scooped him up into my arms and took off running toward the cabins.

With all the fighting going on around, I couldn't tell which group had the upper hand. As I swerved past one pair battling it out, I almost tripped over another. Neither of them, thankfully, paid me any attention.

Flashes of bright light went off in my peripheral vision, followed by the loud mournful howl of wolves. A thunder of rapid gunfire assaulted my ears, but the bullets weren't coming my way. My heart beat a drumroll as I continued on. I pressed on into the battlefield and ducked my head as if it would give me any protection, while Saul clung to me for dear life.

Everything around us was in utter chaos. I stopped behind the stacked wood again and tried to get my bearings. Crossing the battlefield directly was going to get us killed. I needed to retreat to the forest for cover and come around from a different side. With a new plan in mind, I took off again.

"Which cabin?" I asked as we passed into the forest.

"One of the closer ones, I think."

"You mean you don't know exactly where they are," I growled the words. There were many cabins on the wolf preserve. We didn't have time to search them all.

"Keeping prisoners is not my job." Saul's voice hinted his annoyance. "I did what I could to spare them, but beyond that I had no control over what the soldiers did with them. I only have so much power in the organization."

I bit back my frustration. He had managed to buy them time and for that I was grateful. I kept running through the forest, hoping to use the trees as cover as I made my way around the outskirts of the battle and approached the cabins.

"Your friends will be heavily guarded," Saul said to me as we came within eyesight of the first few cabins.

Thank you, Captain Obvious, I thought but didn't dare say out loud. There was no use venting my anger on him. I needed to save that for the soldiers.

Sure enough, there was a noticeable presence of soldiers surrounding cabin number three. That made my job a lot easier.

I set Saul down and surveyed the area. Two men stood at the door, holding assault rifles. Another appeared to be patrolling around the small cabin. He too was armed. To the left I spotted a fourth soldier, having a smoke break.

He'll be first.

"Use me as a hostage if you need to," Saul offered. "I am somewhat important to the organization."

"Sorry to burst your bubble, Saul, but everyone in the Acta Sanctorum is expendable. These bastards would just shoot you if it meant hitting me too. You stay here. I need you alive."

"I see." He seemed surprised by my words, or maybe by the blunt way I'd said them. "What's your plan, then?"

"I'm working on that."

The sound of gunfire still rang out in the distance, but the soldiers guarding the cabin paid it no attention.

"I need some kind of distraction," I mumbled to myself.

"If you can get me a weapon, I can try and pick off one or two of the soldiers," Saul offered eagerly.

I looked at him crossed-eyed. "You'd be willing to kill one of your own?"

"You're going to kill them anyway; I'd just be wounding them a little for you." His gaze darted to the soldiers quickly and then back to me.

I shook my head, utterly confused. "You Acta Sanctorum guys have a weird sense of morality. I guess your God doesn't blame you for being an accomplice, he only cares who deals the death blow."

Saul shrugged. "Something like that."

"See what I mean? Your group treat everyone as expendable."

He pursed his lips. I was right.

"Better than nothing." I shrugged and quickly changed back to the matter at hand. "I'm going to swing around back and grab the smoker over there. When he's down, I'll bring back the rifle."

He nodded, and I took off running again.

I trotted to the next closest cabin, watching as the soldier on patrol made his round. When he wandered out of sight around the corner of the cabin, I made my move. As fast as my legs could carry me, I barreled toward the soldier who'd been enjoying his final cigarette. I connected with him just as he was stamping the smoking butt into the wet ground. He let out an "Ooof," but before any other sound could escape his lips I covered his mouth with my hand and sank my teeth into his neck.

The heat from his blood coursed through my veins, strengthening me, warming me. I hadn't fed in too long, and I needed this, though I knew I couldn't savor it for long. I drained him quickly, squeezing his body and slurping down his blood as fast as his heart could pump it. When at last his heart failed, I pulled him back into the cover of trees and relieved him of his gun.

True to his word, so far, Saul had remained hidden in the trees, waiting for me.

"You've got a little something on your cheek," he said with a cringe.

No doubt in my haste to feed I'd been a little sloppy.

I wiped my cheek quickly and tossed him the gun. "Get used to that; there will be a lot more blood before the night is over."

He gave me a curt nod and lifted his rifle to inspect it.

"I'm going after the one on patrol next. You work on the two standing guard at the door. And try not to get shot, okay?"

"I'm not much of a marksman," he said, fidgeting with the gun, "but I'll do what I can."

"I don't need you to be a sharp shooter. Just distract them long enough for me to kill them." I turned my gaze back to the soldier, watching for the right time to make my move.

"Yes ma'am." Saul's voice shook a little.

"And try not to shoot me in the process."

I didn't wait for his response. The soldier on patrol had just rounded the corner of the cabin again. His back was toward me, a perfect time to charge. I took off again at full speed.

Behind me I heard a shot; and then yelling from the other soldiers.

No time for seconds, no matter how thirsty I was, I had to kill this one quick.

As soon as I caught up to the soldier, I snapped his neck and then turned on my heel. Instantly, I spotted one of the two soldiers who'd been guarding the door. He was heading toward the forest, gun in hand. He sprayed a wide arc of bullets blindly into the trees.

I hoped Saul was quick enough to duck behind something.

Sprinting again, I ran after the charging soldier. Renewed by the blood I'd drunk, I was able to put on a little more speed and quickly caught my prey. His neck too snapped easily under my grip, but his death was so unsatisfying. I wanted to deliver a slow and painful death to at least one of these Acta Sanctorum bastards.

There was only one soldier remaining. I turned around and found him lying on the ground cradling his knee in his arms.

"You can come out now, Saul," I called and headed toward the wounded soldier.

This one I can make suffer!

His eyes locked on to me as I approached. He knew his death was imminent. "Do it quickly please," he said with no hint of fear, only pain in his voice.

"Where are my friends?" I sneered and stared down at him with all the malice I could muster.

He refused to answer.

Stupid man. I'll deal with you in a moment.

I stepped over him and picked up the rifle lying at his back. I reached out and touched the handle on the door, pausing for a moment to sense if there might be anyone else nearby. I heard Saul approaching and the sounds of the battle still going on in the distance, but nothing else.

"Kill me," the soldier whimpered again, but I ignored his plea. He wasn't getting off that easy. And, if my friends were inside, they would need blood to help heal. Dead blood was of no use to a vampire.

I opened the door slowly. Inside, in a large steel cage, was a wolf. *Brady.* A little bloody, he looked like he'd been through some ordeal, but he was alert and paced in his cage.

Next to Brady, lying as if dead on the couch, was Ian, a large wooden stake jutted out from his chest.

Bastards.

I tossed the gun aside and ran to Ian's side. "Please be okay. Please!"

Wooden stakes by themselves aren't deadly, but enough damage to the heart could be. Vampires can only regenerate so much. His heartbeat was faint but still there. I said a silent thank you. Ian's chest was coated in blood, but the stake had not gone through his heart. It looked as if they had just wanted him paralyzed, not dead.

The wolf Brady growled at me as he continued to pace inside of his cage.

"I'll get you in a second," I said, and then turned to Saul who was just entering the cabin. "Drag that asshole soldier over here."

The look on his face said he'd rather not, but Saul made no attempt to argue with me. He heaved a sigh and turned around.

I knelt down in front of Ian. With both hands, I grasped hold of the stake and yanked it sharply out of his chest.

Saul attempted to drag the soldier, but his old body just didn't have the strength. "Move," I shouted as I jumped up and stormed over to the soldier. He may not have looked frightened before, but now his eyes showed their true feelings.

"Kill me quickly," he pleaded.

"You don't deserve that luxury," I snarled, and bent down to grab him by the scruff of his coat. With a rough jerk, I sent him across the floor.

I turned to Saul. "Look away if it will bother you."

"Why don't I try to find the key to the cage?" he said nervously.

"Good idea." I knelt down between Ian and the soldier and pushed up the sleeve of my coat. I bit into my wrist, and as soon as the blood pooled to the surface of my skin, I placed it over Ian's mouth. As injured as he was, he'd need a lot of blood to heal properly. I hoped giving him a little of mine would speed things up. It took a few painfully quiet moments before Ian swallowed. I let out a small sigh of relief. His lips began to move over my wrist, and gently he began to suckle. Confident that he was able to feed on his own, I turned my attention to the soldier. I'd need to replace the blood Ian was taking.

The fear in the soldier's wide eyes told me he knew what was coming. He whimpered and began to beg and plead for a quick death. He attempted to profess innocence and said, "I was only following orders."

That enraged me further. He had a choice. He didn't have to be a Saint. I reached out with my free arm and pulled him up close to me. "Don't give me any of that 'following orders' crap. Own up to what you've done. Go out with a little dignity," I said.

The soldier took a deep breath, closed his eyes, and turned his head, revealing his neck to me.

"That's better. Go out like a man." Quick as a viper, I latched on to the pulsing artery in his neck, ripping it open with my teeth. His blood bathed my tongue, rushed down my throat, and sent a tingling rush of ecstasy through my body.

I barely registered the drain at my wrist as I indulged in the soldier's rich warm blood. I took him slowly, leisurely, more for the pleasure it gave me than the punishment I'd wanted to give. These last few days meals had been fast and unsatisfying at best. Now that I had the few moments to spare, I wanted to enjoy them.

And his heart was strong, this soldier's. It pounded out a steady rhythm of life-giving blood, as if it would never run out.

The minutes ticked by and still he had more to give, and I took it all.

"Found them," I heard Saul's voice behind me, and it pulled me from my revelry. Instantly, I was reminded of the danger still at hand.

I pulled my wrist free from Ian's mouth and quickly slurped up the last drops of blood I could from the soldier.

When I stood up, Saul was already working with a key ring to unlock the cage where Brady had sat patiently waiting.

I wiped my face and looked Brady in the eye. "It's a war zone out there. Be ready for a fight."

The wolf snorted and pawed at the door of the cage.

Saul worked the lock, and as soon as he yanked it off and opened the door, Brady lunged, knocking the old man to the ground. He placed his large paw down on Saul's windpipe and bared his teeth menacingly.

"Wait, Brady! He's helping us. We're all friends here."

The wolf turned to me and growled.

"Okay. Maybe 'friends' was the wrong word. But he's on our side. He's an ally. You want to kill him, you'll have to kill me too." I hated having to vouch for Acta Sanctorum members, but it seemed that was my lot in life. Saul, just like Santino before him, had earned my trust, and I'd be damned if I'd let them get killed by the wolves. If anyone was going to do the killing, it would be me—if they turned out to be traitors.

Brady eyed me. He snarled and snorted, as if contemplating what to do, or maybe in wolf language he was trying to say something. I couldn't really tell.

"We have bigger issues to deal with. Leave the old man to me and go help the pack."

24

Brady ran off out the cabin, but not before issuing a few growls and snaps of his jaw at both Saul and me.

"Thank you," Saul said to me, his voice cracking under the strain.

"Don't thank me yet. You're not safe until this whole mess is taken care of."

"Understood." He nodded, stood up, and closed the front door.

I turned to Ian. His eyes began to flutter open. It was a good sign. "Don't try to move, Ian. You're badly hurt."

"This day just keeps getting better and better." He shifted his weight, and with his one arm attempted to push himself to sitting. Too weak, however, he fell back against the couch cushions.

"I told you not to try to get up, you big idiot."

He groaned in frustration.

"Quit trying to be Mr. Macho Man. Save your strength. You need to heal."

The corner of his lip quirked up. He stretched his arm and folded it behind his head. "Are you going to be my sexy nurse and take care of me?"

I ignored the comment. "Was anyone else besides Brady with you? Have you heard from Zuri at all?"

Ian shook his head, and his face became serious. "She didn't report back after her shift. I assumed she went home."

My jaw tightened. I shook my head. *Dammit, I wish someone had gotten ahold of her.* "She shouldn't have gone back there. We tried to talk to her but she never answered her phone, so we left her a message telling her not to go home. What if they—"

"Zuri's a smart girl with many friends. She probably went to a safe house."

"Well, I hope you're right." I looked to Saul. "Do you know anything about Zuri?"

He shrugged. "Sorry, no. Our objective was to take the preserve and locate the box."

That gave me some relief. Maybe she wasn't on the hit list.

Ian glanced up, and his eyes locked on Saul as if he had just at that moment realized he was there. "Did you bring me a snack, Alyssa?" He licked his lips.

I rolled my eyes. "You just had a snack, Ian. Besides, Saul's helping us, so don't get any funny ideas."

"Helping… He's the one who did this to us." Anger overtook the playfulness that had been in Ian's voice. "He's one of those Saints."

"Look. I know he's one of the bad guys. It's complicated, I guess, but he knows about the box and the crystal. We need him… for now."

Saul visibly paled. His eyes grew large in their sockets. He gulped and slowly edged backward, butting up against the door.

"Don't get any funny ideas. I'm stronger and faster than you, old man. Be smart and continue to prove whose side you're on, and things will work out."

Ian tried to sit up again, groaning as he pushed himself. "I need blood."

"I know, but we're on limited supply at the moment. You're just going to have to deal with it for now." The phone in my pocket buzzed. I'd almost forgotten it was there. I pulled it out and found a message from Nicholas.

"You okay Lil Warrior?"

Seeing that made me smile. Not only was he okay, but the fact that he had time to type out a message meant the battle must be slowing down and going in our favor.

"I think we can safely hole up here for a little while. I'm letting the others know what's going on." I quickly typed out, *"I'm good. Found Ian and Brady. Cabin 3. Need blood."*

"More sitting and waiting." Ian let out a sigh. "I feel so useless."

"Deal with it."

"You could help me deal with it." He waggled an eyebrow at me.

"Seriously? We're in the middle of a war, and that's what you're thinking about?" I laughed sarcastically. "Well, you can't be too bad off if you're still trying to flirt."

My phone buzzed again. I checked the message. *"Be there as soon as we can."*

"Hey, it's all I got left." Ian beamed one of his brilliant smiles at me. "You could consider it stress relief."

"You just don't know when to quit, do you?" I let out an exasperated sigh.

A cold prickling sensation crept up the back of my neck. Ian must have felt it too. His smile quickly faded and his eyes jumped toward the door.

"Saul, get back," I said as I walked to the door. "Have that gun ready to fire too, just in case."

I hoped it was Drew; I knew it was too soon to be Nicholas. Either way, it was better to be cautious.

Saul did as he was told, and with shaking hands aimed his rifle at the door.

Slowly, I turned the handle and opened it. On the other side stood Santino, and for the second time this evening, his wild mane and battle-scarred face was a welcome sight.

"You going to let me in?" he said wearily. "Or should I just stand here like a target and wait for one of the Saints to come finish me off?

I yanked the door the rest of the way open. "Get in."

He lumbered inside, favoring his right leg, but otherwise looking uninjured.

"How's it looking out there?" I asked, hoping for some good news.

"We've taken a beating, but we're not losing." He glanced over to Saul, standing in the corner. "Glad to see you here, old friend." Then he turned to me his eyebrow quirking up ever-so-slightly. "You've spared him?"

"Seems he's a lot like you. I'm letting him live, for now."

Santino's face brightened. "I'm only going to say this once, and if you tell anyone else I'll deny it. But—you're the reason I turned away from the order. You may be young, and rash, and naïve…"

I opened my mouth to protest. Santino held up his hand as if to say, *Let me finish.*

"And don't know when to shut that mouth of yours. But your heart is in the right place. You've always been willing to let people have the benefit of doubt. You don't kill arbitrarily. And if abominations like us can still hold on to some of that goodness, then we're not all the monsters the Acta Sanctorum makes us out to be."

"Thanks… I think." It was a bit of a backhanded compliment, but that was probably the best I could hope for from him.

"What's the plan?" Santino asked.

"We regroup here when the battle is over. Saul is going to help us with the crystal and the box."

"Then I'll stand guard outside," Santino said. He turned and limped back to the door.

"You sure you're okay for guard duty?"

"Don't worry about me," he said proudly. "Even with my injuries, I'm still the best warrior of our little bunch."

I didn't feel like arguing. "At least take the rifle." I turned to Saul and cocked my head sideways.

He took the hint and tossed the rifle at Santino.

"Try not to get killed," I said.

Santino caught the rifle, grunted in approval, and walked back outside.

"And you." I pointed at Saul. "Tell me everything you know about the box, and the crystal."

"What do I do?" Ian asked.

"Just lay there and look pretty," I quipped.

He groaned. "Is this my lot in life now? I'm just a pretty ornament?"

"For the moment, yes. You need rest. We'll let you know when we need you for something important."

Saul came to sit on the chair by the fireplace. "You probably already know as much as I do about the stone itself. And you already know about the box and what used to reside inside it. What seems to have happened, and this is just a working theory, is that the stone took in both spirits at the same time. When that happened, they merged, in a sense. The crystal, now a soulstone, cannot handle that much power inside for too long."

"Yes, we already know all of that. What I need to know is how to get Lysander out."

"I don't think it will be as simple as that."

"I understand that."

"I don't think you do. That stone is holding a lot of power inside. Too much. It will eventually break down. When that happens, it may release the spirits inside, or it may just drain them both until they no longer exist. We really cannot guess at this point what might happen. The only thing we know for sure is that they—Lysander and Aniketos—cannot remain in there forever. I feel the only safe way to dispose of the crystal is to put it inside the box. If we seal the crystal inside, we can safely seal both spirits forever."

That was not what I wanted to hear. "There has to be another way. I... we need to get Lysander out safely first."

Saul's eyebrows knitted in confusion. He put a finger to his lips as if contemplating what to say.

"We cannot trap them both in the box for eternity!" I found myself almost shouting in desperation.

"But the Pandora's Box will safely hold both of them. In the legends, the original box held all the evil in the world inside. We'd never have to worry about Aniketos getting out again."

"Yeah and Lysander too! He isn't some evil. He's my mate." I balled my fists in anger. "We can't condemn him. We have to try to separate the spirits."

"Here we go again," Ian sighed.

I snarled at him. "You stay out of this."

"Alyssa, he sacrificed himself to save us, to save you. He knew there would be consequences. If all it takes is putting the damn crystal inside the box and shutting it, I say we do it. Case closed. The world is right once again." Ian rubbed his hands together in the air as if washing them of this whole mess.

Desperation weighed heavily on my shoulders. I felt as if I was the only one who cared enough not to give up. "We have to at least try to save him. That's all I'm asking for. If it doesn't work, then I give up. But please, don't just take the easy road out."

Saul leaned forward and placed a hand on my shoulder. "As much as you've trusted me and gone out on a limb, I think I'm obligated to help. I don't know what we can do, and I'm not saying that we'll find a way to make it work, but we'll try, okay?"

I nodded, unable to speak. My throat had swollen with emotion.

"But if we're to have any chance of success," Saul added. "I'm going to need that book your witch stole from my office."

25

Time passed in a blur of small events. Nicholas and Drew eventually made their appearance at the cabin, bringing with them a few dying soldiers to help feed Ian and get him on the road to recovery.

"You never cease to surprise me, Little Warrior." Nicholas gave me a hearty pat on the back.

"You say that like you have some hidden meaning." I eyed him suspiciously.

"Well… when you disappeared like that, I had a feeling I'd be mopping up your remains."

"Don't sound so disappointed," I chuckled.

"Hey, I'm just glad I won't have to explain to Sleeping Beauty why his woman wasn't there to give him his wake-up kiss."

I perked up hearing his optimism. "So, you think we have a chance then."

"Hold on there, Sparky." Nicholas held up his hands. "I never said that. But if we do manage to save Lysander, I'm glad you'll be there."

"There is still a big *if* there," I said.

"We'll just have to see what we can do. Have some patience."

"I hate waiting," I groaned.

"Have faith then." Nicholas laughed. "Keep an eye on Saul. I'll take care of Ian. He needs to get up and moving. Get the blood flowing."

Wolves began to show their snouts as well. They passed the cabin in small groups but made no attempt to enter. I felt a sense of relief each time I saw them wander by. That, and the lack of gunfire in the distance, were clear signs that we had won against the Acta Sanctorum—at least for the moment.

Saul, though, seemed to grow more worried by the moment. Not that I blamed him, being an Acta Sanctorum lackey. He shrank down into the chair where he sat, making himself as small as could be, as if that could hide him from the wolves. The smell of his fear was a potent odor that any predator would recognize. And it played with my own inner beast.

"Relax," I said. "I've got your back. As long as you don't do anything stupid, you'll be fine."

A very exhausted wolf-Aiden accompanied by a naked Brady in his human form appeared at the door to the cabin.

"The perimeter is secured." Though he stood in front of us stark naked and covered in blood, Brady spoke in a very businesslike tone. "You can join us back in the main building now if you like."

In an effort not to look at Brady, I glanced down at Aiden. His fur was matted with blood, he panted heavily, and his tongue lolled out to the side as if he had just finished a long hard run and needed water.

"How is he?" I asked, still avoiding looking at Brady's firm naked body.

"He's fine," Brady said sharply.

"He's hurt and needs rest," I retorted. "What of the others? Will they give him any trouble?"

Brady's voice softened. "What does this matter to you?"

I glanced up for just a moment and saw his head slightly sideways, a very animal-like movement indicating curiosity.

"With Connor gone, I don't want anyone challenging him while he's weak," I said, putting a little authority into my voice.

"He's not weak. He is the new leader of this pack." Brady's tone regained its former sharpness. "And as his second, I'll be sure anyone who thinks to bring challenge is made aware of this."

I smiled. That was exactly what I wanted to hear. I'd worried Brady might try to take the title himself, but it seemed he was content with his place in the line of succession.

Aiden looked up to his brother and let out a short burst of whines and grunts. If I didn't know any better, I'd say he was trying to talk.

Brady nodded and looked back at me. "Where is Fallon?"

"I've tried to call her but haven't received any response—"

Brady cut me off. "That's probably because she doesn't have her phone."

"Yeah, I thought of that a little too late. I could have kicked myself for not making sure of that before we took off. It was stupid to leave her like that all alone in the woods. Santino and Drew set off after her a few moments ago. They seemed pretty confident that she was safe, though, since we were the ones bringing the battle to the Saints."

Without another word, Aiden turned and bolted off into the forest. I didn't need to be told where he was going.

"He really loves that girl," Brady said matter-of-factly.

"I know." I sighed. "She's in love with him too."

"If she hopes to keep him though, she'll have to become one of us. An Alpha must have a mate he can have children with."

I grimaced. Fallon was pretty adamant about staying human. "That's something they'll have to work out."

"As her friend, you should let her know."

It was hard to speak to Brady without looking at him. But I didn't want to look at him standing there, naked. Especially not while having a discussion about my best friend having his brother's puppies, or whatever they call werewolf babies. "Later. Now is not the time for this. We still have more work to do."

His eyebrow crooked up sharply. "What work? The Acta Sanctorum is gone. We've won."

"One cell, sure, but there are many more around the world. And that's not our only problem." I looked up and quickly met his eyes. "We still have the issue of the crystal and the Pandora's Box."

Brady folded his arms in front of his chest. "The box is safely buried."

"The box is empty."

His jaw dropped, and for a few moments Brady stood in stunned silence.

Saul tentatively came forward. "It's true." His voice shook with fear. "The crystal that holds your friend's spirit is also inhabited by another. It is our belief that this second entity is the one that belongs in the box."

"Why is *he* still alive?" Brady snarled.

"Because he knows things. He can help us put the box and the crystal right again."

His eyes narrowed and he shot angry glances at both Saul and me. "You have a soft spot for these religious nutjobs, don't you?"

"No, I just don't believe in killing people solely based on affiliation. He's a person, like you and me. And he's been helpful."

Brady shook his head. "He's one of them. There is no other distinction."

"Look, we can argue this all night, or we can put it aside until we've dealt with the important issues. I don't know about you, but I'm done fighting for one night."

"Fine." Brady huffed. "Join me and the others back at the main building. I need to get back and help with the cleanup efforts."

"Okay. I'll be there in a few."

Brady turned sharply and stalked away.

I placed a call to Crystal and Ariana to let them know to come back and to bring the book and any witchcraft supplies they could as well.

After filling him in on the details, Nicholas helped Ian hobble to the main building.

I wasn't too sure how well Saul would be received by the others, so I instructed him to follow very close to me.

The place, though filled with broken glass, had been largely spared from any real damage. It seemed the goal had been to find the box, and when it was learned that it did not reside inside, the Saints moved their ransacking out to the bonfire area. I wondered if they knew how close they had been to finding the box.

Brady and another woman were handing out bandages, towels, and clothes to the injured and wounded. Of the original fifteen or so we saw before we made the charge, only a handful remained. Most of them remained in their wolf forms, licking their wounds clean. It was a somber sight that broke my heart. The Acta Sanctorum had practically wiped out yet another wolf pack, and for what reason? Hatred, desire for powerful artifacts, just because? Silently I vowed, no matter what the outcome was with Lysander, once we were done here, it would be time to take down the Acta Sanctorum once and for all. If that meant going to Rome, to their home office, so be it.

"Tell us what we can do to help," I said to Brady, and knelt down next to one of the injured wolves, the same white and gray wolf that had helped me back by the wood pile.

Saul stood behind me. "Please, let me help as well."

"Her injuries are pretty bad. Can you stop the bleeding?" Brady responded to me.

The wolf looked up at me and whimpered. A large gash ran the length of her belly and blood oozed out onto the ground. Normally that would tempt me, but not now. The smell did not call to my inner beast. Sympathy and affection were much stronger forces working within me. I wasn't about to let another pack member die.

I looked the wolf in the eyes and spoke in the most commanding voice I could. "This will hurt, but I need you to turn back into your human form, so I can help close the wound."

"You sure you are up for this?" Brady asked cautiously as he came up beside me.

"As a member of this pack, I'm part of this family, am I not? I'd never do anything to hurt my family."

"Do what you can, then." He held out a first aid kit.

"I won't need the bandages; my methods are a bit different, but should work just as well."

He smiled. "Go ahead, then. And when you're done with her, come help the others."

Saul reached out and took the first aid kit from Brady. "I swear to you I am not your enemy. Let me help here."

Brady eyed him silently for a few moments. The room became so quiet I could hear the beating of my heart. Injured or not, it wouldn't take much for Brady to snap Saul's neck.

"Please," Saul said with no hint of animosity.

Brady turned sharply. "Follow me."

I let out a breath I hadn't realized I'd been holding.

Saul shot me a quizzical look.

"That's probably the best response you could hope for," I said. "Now go. Follow and be helpful. There are lots of wounded to attend to."

Saul gulped, gave a quick nod, and fell in step with Brady. I turned my attention to the wolf who was in the process of changing back to her human form. "Let's get you fixed up."

26

Fallon pushed open what remained of the shattered glass front door. Behind her, looking beaten, bruised, and exhausted, were Santino, Aiden, and Drew.

Aiden, naked in his human form, looked the worst of the group. His body was covered in dark purple bruises and scabs, but though he looked like death, he walked straight and tall up the steps behind Drew, helping to carry Lysander's coffin.

My heart skipped a beat. I never thought I'd be so happy to see that long pine box. Silently, I thanked God that everyone was safe, and turned my attention to Fallon.

I ran over and pulled her into a tight bear hug. "I'm such a stupid idiot, leaving you out there with no way to communicate. I was so worried about you. I'm so happy you're okay!"

"I won't be if you keep squeezing me like that." She choked out the words, but I could hear the smile in her voice.

"Sorry." I let her go and took a step back. "I can't help it. I was so worried about you. Please forgive me. I completely spaced the fact that your phone was missing. I should have never left you alone out there. I'm a horrible friend. Can you ever forgive me?"

"Quit rambling, Lyssa." She held up her hand to stop me. "It's fine. Everything's good. Honestly, I was more worried for you guys." She looked around the room, her face fluctuating between curiosity and grief. "Looks like quite a battle took place."

"Yeah. You can say that again." All happiness left my voice as I turned and glanced around the destruction and wreckage in the room.

There were still a few injured pack members nursing their wounds. Saul was helping to bandage one man's chest. He had a large gash across it from shoulder to belly button.

Aiden walked over to his injured pack member and knelt down before him. "You fought bravely tonight, and you, as well as the rest who came back, will be honored for your services here."

Aiden was truly meant to be a leader. I knew he would be a good one. And I hoped Fallon would remain at his side. They were good together, even if she wanted to remain a human.

I turned back to look at Fallon. Her eyes were darting all over the destruction in the room.

"It was touch and go for a bit. Those Saints fight dirty," I said.

Her jaw tightened. "I can see that. How many are left?"

"Of the pack members who returned to fight, we have less than ten. Ian is still pretty bad off." I nodded my head toward Ian, passed out in the corner of the room. Nicholas sat at his side, looking just as weak and tired. "Zuri is still unaccounted for, but the rest of the clan is okay."

"At least it wasn't a complete loss." Though Fallon spoke solemnly, there was relief in her tired eyes. "The fireworks I saw in the distance looked pretty scary. I seriously thought I'd come back to find you all dead."

"We were lucky, as outnumbered as we were."

"What about the Saints? Are they all gone?" she asked.

Drew and Santino set Lysander's coffin down on the ground in the center of the room.

"The Saints will never truly be gone," Santino said.

There was an air of certainty in the way he said that, and it sent a chill down my spine. We'd dealt with them too many times, and it always ended the same way, with unnecessary death and destruction. The Saints were like cockroaches—no matter how many we got rid of, there were always more infesting our lives.

"But," he continued, snapping me from my thoughts. "I think it is safe to say we crippled their operations out here. Now all that remains is to destroy their local repository."

Saul, who had been wandering around the room helping to tend to the injured, gasped. "Destroy? No. Please do not do this! My life's work is in there."

Santino walked toward his friend. "You knew that was how it would have to end." He knelt down eye-level with Saul. "I will let you retrieve what you can before I do it."

The two men stared at each other for a silent moment before Saul let out a breath and nodded. "I guess I should be thankful for that." Pain edged his voice.

He really did care for all of those artifacts that had been stored there.

Drew drummed his fingers on top of Lysander's coffin, drawing our attention. "Once we have finished our work here, I will join you in the destruction of the repository."

The ghost of a smile crept across Santino's face. "I'd be honored."

"Count me in as well," I added. "It would be nice to take some aggression out on the Saints, and destroy one of their buildings for a change."

Fallon cleared her throat, and turned our attention to the long pine box. "Have we figured out what to do about him yet?" she asked.

I didn't need her to clarify who "him" was. I knew she was talking about Lysander.

"We might have," I said, trying to sound hopeful, though I knew we were still working with a long shot. "Saul seems to think we need the Pandora's Box to help. Brady's out back with a few of the healthier wolves digging it up. Crystal and Ariana are on their way from the city with supplies and the book of spells. Between Ariana and Saul"—I smiled at the old man—"we might have a solution."

Saul did not return my smile. I wondered briefly if he was sad for the destruction of the repository or worried about our solution to the crystal issue and its potential impact on his own survival. That worry was in the back of my mind.

What if it didn't work? What if it did more harm than good? What if we lost Lysander's spirit forever?

Fallon must have recognized my stressed expression. She reached up and squeezed my shoulder. "If there is anything I can do to help, let me know."

Her tone, while kind, was not as reassuring as I'd hoped. I guessed that she too felt we were grasping at straws for an answer.

I couldn't let this worry weigh me down. I had to try to remain hopeful. *This would work. It just had to.* I needed to get Lysander back.

"For now, just help with clean-up and first aid," I said, trying to banish the fear from my voice.

"I'm on it." She rolled up her sleeves and walked to the corner to grab a broom.

***

The rest of the night passed by uneventfully with clean-up and organization. Locating the box took longer than anyone had anticipated. Then there were still layers of concrete to get through before they could reach it. When the wolves had buried it, they'd made sure it would not be easily unearthed. The box had yet to be retrieved by the time I had to take shelter from the morning sun.

The members of my clan, as well as Santino and Ian, all took shelter in one cabin and waited out the day in quiet anticipation. I tried to sleep, listening to the sound of the construction equipment as it banged and drilled and rumbled in the distance.

The moment the sun dipped enough behind the horizon for it to be safe to venture outside, I left the cabin.

The construction equipment sat idle, and the silence allowed me to hear my footsteps crunch the snow. I hoped this was a good sign.

I spotted a small crowd gathered at the back of the building.

"Hands off," I heard Aiden commanding.

I broke into a sprint and joined the crowd. "What's going on?"

"We've got it." Aiden held the wooden box above his head. Being a tall man gave him an advantage over Fallon and Saul, who looked as if they were considering jumping to grab it.

They danced in place nervously next to Aiden, with their attention focused solely on the box as if it were the object of their greatest desire.

I remembered back to the first time Fallon had laid eyes on the box. The enchantment placed upon it was irresistible to humans. That was part of its curse. It could hold within it all the evils of the earth, but no human could help themselves around it. They had to open it and see what was inside.

Both Saul and Fallon were clearly under its spell. Their eyes remained unflinching on the box that Aiden held high in the air. Fallon, in a bold and uncharacteristic maneuver, jumped up and took a swipe at it as if she would be able to remove it from Aiden's hand.

"I said, hands off," Aiden shouted again.

I couldn't believe he actually shouted at Fallon. This was so unlike him; but then again, Fallon was not herself either.

She didn't seem to mind his yelling though, or perhaps she didn't even notice it. Her eyes remained locked on the wooden box.

Two pack members, in human form, placed themselves in between Fallon and Saul, acting as bodyguards.

"You've definitely found it," I said happily. This was it, the last piece we needed. If Saul was right, we might have Lysander free before sunrise.

"Yeah, but we can't let them have it. They'll try to open it." There was no smile in Aiden's voice.

I shrugged. "If what we think is right, it doesn't matter. The box is empty."

One of his eyebrows arched. He cocked his head sideways. "Would the spell still work if the box was empty?"

"My guess is yes." I tried to sound as positive as I could. There was really only one way to find out for sure if the box was empty. Someone would have to open it eventually.

"No offense, but do we want to rely on a guess?"

Saul jumped up this time and tried to swipe at the box. "It has to be open if the witch hopes to put back the spirit." His voice was desperate. "Let me be the one to do it."

Fallon shoved Saul aside. "No. I get to open it."

"Haven't you already had an opportunity to open it?" Saul sounded like a petulant child. "It's my turn."

"I'll open it." I said loudly. "If I'm wrong, then I take all the blame."

"If you're wrong, then we all die. You remember what that thing was capable of?" Aiden said with all the authority his father had once had.

How could I forget? Aniketos had overpowered and killed an ancient vampire, Rozaline. He tore her apart like she was nothing more than a rag doll. Not being bound in physical form, he could be invisible as he struck; he could swarm his victims like horde of bees and rip a body to shreds in moments. Aniketos was not a force I wanted to go up against again. Deep down in my gut, I knew he wasn't in the box.

"Yes, I remember very clearly." I locked eyes with Aiden and put conviction in my voice. "But I know I'm not wrong here. Lysander said he was not alone. The only other spirit around was Aniketos. If he's in the crystal with Lysander, then he cannot be in the box."

Aiden narrowed his eyes at me. "Do we have a backup plan?"

I hesitated before answering. "Not yet. Ariana and Saul were supposed to be working on that today." I glanced around, not seeing Ariana, and wondered where she might be.

Saul gave no indication that his name had been spoken. His eyes remained glued on the box in Aiden's hand.

"Why don't we wait to open this? Let's remove the temptation and see if we can't get some answers first."

I nodded. "Good idea. Take the box to the cabin with my clan, and I'll bring these two to the main building." I grabbed Saul by the scruff of his shirt and grasped Fallon's arm with my free hand. "C'mon, you two."

Aiden trotted down the path with the two pack members still at his side.

Both Saul and Fallon let out whimpers of protest and tried to follow, but I held them tight and pushed them toward the building.

Once inside, it seemed the box's enchantment had waned. The glassy unfocused expressions that had been on Saul and Fallon's faces faded. They blinked and looked at me as if wondering why I was manhandling them.

I blocked the door in case any of them decided to make a break for it. "So, which one of you is going to tell me how we plan to get Lysander back in his body and Aniketos back in his box? Hmmmm?"

"I'll tell you," Ariana said. She stood from the bench where she'd been sitting and walked over with the book in one hand and the crystal in the other. "We need to find a vessel for each spirit to fill. And we'll have to break the crystal to prevent both the spirits from getting back inside."

"Lysander's spirit can return back to his body, right?" I asked. "But what can we use for Aniketos? Where would his spirit go if it had no vessel?"

"His ashes still remain in the box, right?" Ariana asked.

"I think so. We never opened it, though. To be sure."

"If his ashes are there, they might still be of use to us." Though she spoke with certainty, I could see some doubt in her eyes.

"So we call him back to the box?" I asked.

"Sort of." Her face briefly contorted as if she was fighting with what to say. "What we *hope* for is that each spirit will find its place, and when they do, we can seal them both back inside."

"But?" I met her eyes with a questioning gaze, and held my breath expecting the bad news that was certain to follow.

"But… there is no guarantee with this magic. They are both of the same bloodline, and we don't have their original blood to work with. Lysander might just as easily get caught in the box and Aniketos in Lysander's body."

I released the breath I'd been holding. While not the best of news, it wasn't all bad. If Lysander did manage to end up in the box, releasing his spirit was not that hard to do from there. However, allowing Aniketos to take control of Lysander's body, that was something we needed to avoid.

"Is there anything we can do?" I asked.

"Hope and pray," Ariana replied.

"That's comforting."

"Sorry." She shrugged. "But it's the best I can offer."

"I guess it's better than nothing, right?"

"Exactly." She feigned a smile.

"When can we perform the spell?"

"As soon as we have the box."

"I'll tell Aiden to bring it. You three stay here and set up."

27

When I returned, Ariana had transformed the lobby into a Wiccan playground, ready to perform her magic. A large pentagram had been drawn in chalk on the ground, and surrounding it was a circle drawn in a white powdery substance that looked like salt.

In the center of the pentagram stood Lysander's coffin, set up on top of saw horses. An empty table sat next to it with enough space in between for a person to stand.

Saul and Ariana stood over Lysander's coffin, with their heads together, staring down at the book.

"The others are on their way," I said.

"Do you have the box?" Ariana asked expectantly.

At once, all three pairs of eyes were on me.

"No, Aiden is holding onto that until we're ready. He doesn't want any problems, since you three are susceptible to the curse."

Ariana shrugged. "That's fine, as long as it's here for the ceremony." She turned to Fallon. "Red candles on the star points, please. And I need two green and one black candle in between each of the red ones."

Fallon, following orders began setting the red candles as indicated. I joined her and grabbed some green and black candles from a basket sitting on the floor.

"So it's green, black, green, red?" I asked.

"Yep. All the way around," Ariana replied.

I was glad to see that some things were already being done differently and said a silent prayer that this time it would work.

Santino joined us just as I was setting the last of the candles. He made a beeline for Saul. "Need any help, my friend?"

Saul shook his head but didn't look up. "You've done enough. After all my years of research, I can die a happy man having seen the Pandora's Box. Helping to close it again forever is the icing on the cake."

"You are a sentimental old fool," Santino said.

"I should say the same for you." Saul finally lifted his head to acknowledge his friend.

If I didn't know better, I'd say Santino was smiling.

"When this is over, what will you do?" he asked.

Saul shrugged. "I don't quite know yet. Maybe I'll retire and publish my memoirs."

"You'd have to publish them as fiction. No one would believe the things you've seen." Santino laughed.

Ariana looked up from the book. "Did we get the sage smudge sticks?"

Fallon walked over to the basket and pulled out two sticks made from what looked like dried and wrapped leaves. "These them?"

Ariana smiled. "Yes. I'll need those near Lysander's body. If we're lucky, they might help steer Aniketos's spirit away from him."

"What are you going to use to attract him to the box?" I asked.

"Human blood." Ariana picked up her ceremonial knife and sliced open her hand. She held it over a small copper bowl and let her blood drizzle inside.

The scent teased at my nose, and I involuntarily licked my lips.

"See," she said. "Tempting, isn't it?"

I shook myself and turned away. "Very."

Crystal, Drew, and Nicholas walked into the room, followed by Aiden. I could see he held the box in his hands, and it appeared the others were using their bodies as shields.

"We've stationed the remaining wolves around the building to guard. They can be in here at a moment's notice if necessary." Aiden said. "Brady and I will cover the front and back entrances. We'll leave you to perform the magic alone in here." He handed the box to Nicholas. "Good luck."

Nicholas nodded and took the box. "I don't believe in luck. This will work."

"Well, I believe in luck," I said to Aiden. "Thanks."

"Fallon," Aiden called. "Will you be joining us outside or remaining here with them?"

Fallon looked to me and then to Aiden. I saw the hesitation in her eyes. "I... I need to be here for Alyssa this time."

Aiden nodded. I spotted a hint of disappointment in his eyes, but not anger. He walked to Fallon and pulled her in close. "I understand. We'll be just outside. If you need anything, just call out to me. I'll hear you." He kissed the top of her head and then released her and walked away.

Nicholas held the box to his chest, and Crystal and Drew stepped in front of him now to block everything from view. Even with their efforts I could see the pull on the three humans in the room.

Ariana appeared as if she could no longer concentrate. Her eyes kept darting between the book and Nicholas.

"It's now or never," I said. "We might as well get this over with. Otherwise we're going to have these guys mobbing us to open the box, and they'll never get to the spell."

Nicholas took a deep breath. "You're sure about this?"

"As sure as I'm going to get. Just do it."

Nicholas held out the box. He took a deep breath and winced as he pulled it open.

The room collectively held their breath and a deathly silence filled the space.

I shot furtive glances at Saul, Fallon, and Ariana. They too were glancing around the room as if waiting for something.

I remembered back to the first time we'd opened the box. There had been a cold chill that ran through the air, but I felt no such rush now. In fact, the air was eerily still. I took that as a good sign. "I think we're okay," I said.

As if in unison, sighs erupted through the room.

No longer under the compulsion to open the box, Ariana seemed to have regained her composure. She took one last glance down at her book and then looked at Nicholas.

"Please place the box here." Ariana indicated to the table next to Lysander's coffin.

Nicholas's eyes darted all around the room. Though there had been no sign of Aniketos, he still seemed to be on high alert. He joined Ariana at the coffin, gently set the box down, and then backed away.

"Take your places, please. One person on each point. Alyssa and Nicholas, join me here; I'll need your blood again. As the closest links to Lysander, your blood will have to attract his spirit."

Just as before, Ariana opened the lid of the coffin and turned it sideways, uncovering the upper and lower halves of Lysander's body. She set a medium-sized cauldron on the top of the coffin. In separate dishes, Ariana laid out various herbs and incense and then lit them. Instantly, the cavernous room was filled with thick pungent smoke that reminded me of death.

Unlike before, however, she kept her goddess pendant on. A good idea, considering how the magic had affected her the last time.

"I need the crystal," Ariana said to me after she had finished setting up her altar.

Saul walked to the basket where they kept all of the supplies. He picked up the crystal, wrapped in a black velvet cloth, and held it lovingly in his hands. He unwrapped it as he joined us and placed it gently inside of the cauldron.

"And now the blood," Ariana said, and held up her ceremonial knife.

I offered my wrist eagerly. She could take any amount of blood she needed if it meant getting Lysander back.

Ariana sliced quickly and cleanly, and held my wrist over the cauldron allowing the blood to flow into it until my wound healed over itself. Nicholas went second and again

Ariana repeated the process, holding his wrist over the cauldron until it healed.

Ariana sprinkled various herbs into the cauldron, then lit a match and tossed it inside. A small explosion shook the stone, but it remained upright. Smoke began to billow out from the cauldron. It sank down into the coffin and surrounded Lysander's body.

I watched eagerly as she took the bowl that she had previously filled with her own blood, picked it up, and poured its contents inside the open Pandora's Box. Then Ariana began to chant. She spoke in foreign words I couldn't understand.

Smoke from the incense surrounded us like a thick blanket, choking out all the fresh air in the room. My head began to swim from the noxious fumes.

She lit another match and started the two sage sticks on fire. Once their smoke began to rise, she waved the flames out and handed one each to Nicholas and me. "Hold these on either end of the coffin. This should help us ward off the evil."

I did as instructed and moved to Lysander's head while Nicholas took a spot at the foot of the coffin.

Ariana returned to her chanting.

The overhead lights flickered and went out, leaving only the candles to illuminate the room. The gentle twinkling of each flame only added to the dreamy and drug-induced feeling that was taking over.

"Come back to me, Lysander," I mumbled to myself.

Ariana's chanting grew louder and louder, echoing around the room. As she spoke, the air became electrified. My heart sped with anticipation. The crystal began to glow. It took on a hazy white halo. The deep red color inside lightened to an orangey-amber. Within the crystal it looked like liquid was swirling into a mini tornado.

She picked up the crystal, held it overhead and shouted, "Arise and reclaim your body." Then smashed the crystal onto the floor.

I couldn't stop the screech that erupted from my throat. As the crystal broke into tiny pieces, glowing tentacles sprouted up from the floor: one blood red and the other a silvery white. I didn't know which one was which. They both stood up from the ground and swayed like snakes between the coffin and the box.

Ariana jumped back out of their reach. Her hand reached up and held fast to the goddess pendant at her neck.

I did the only thing I could think of and called out, "Here. Lysander. Come back to me." I waved the smoking sage stick in the air like a signal.

Both glowing tentacles responded to my call and slithered toward me.

"Which one is which?" I yelled.

"I don't know." Ariana responded. She looked down to her book and flipped a few pages. She picked up the knife again and pricked her finger. A small bead of blood pooled to the surface. She touched Lysander's forehead with it and then moved to the box and stuck her finger in to the bloody ash mixture there. "Return from whence your spirit came," she commanded.

Both the blood red and the silvery white tentacles responded. They twisted around each other as if fighting over which direction to go. The red stretched out long and headed for the bloody fingerprint on Lysander's forehead. Then the silvery-white one curled around and yanked it back.

Though I could not know for sure, I assumed that the red one was Aniketos. I whipped the smoking stick of sage at the red tentacle, and it jerked backwards.

Still struggling, the two tentacles performed a deadly dance, swerving, curling, and moving around and in between the body and the box.

Ariana franticly ripped through the book, looking for something that might help. "Alyssa, come here," she yelled.

I set the stage stick down and edged around, carefully avoiding the two tentacles, to Ariana.

"You have the closest connection with Lysander. Take this knife, coat it in your blood, and then plunge it into his chest," she said.

My eyes almost popped out of their sockets. "But that might make things worse."

"I'm going to try to call his spirit with your blood, but I think it needs to be inside him to work."

"You think? You *think*? What if you're wrong?" I asked.

"We don't have time for overreacting. Just do it!" She commanded.

I really didn't like that plan, but I had no choice. I took the knife, closed my fist around it, and yanked sharply, slicing my palm. Blood flooded my skin. I coated the blade as I walked back around to Lysander's head.

"I really hope this works." I said, as I held the knife up high and plunged it into his chest.

"Blood to blood, I summon thee, Lysander. Return to your body." Ariana chanted this over and over.

The two tentacles began to break apart. The red one pulled away and headed for Lysander while the silvery-white trailed behind.

I watched in horror as the red one touched the hilt of the knife and slowly slithered inside Lysander's body. The silvery-white one, having nowhere else to go, shot out at Ariana. Her necklace glowed for a moment and reflected the attack, sending the silvery-white one away into the box.

Nicholas jumped into action as soon as he saw the tentacle hit the box. He lunged and closed it.

The room fell silent.

Lysander's body remained motionless. The glow of the tentacle had gone, having sunk deep into his chest. I approached cautiously. There was the faintest trace of a heartbeat. I wrapped my hand around the dagger and pulled it out. Still, Lysander made no move, no sound.

"What do we do?" I asked.

"If he's in there, he needs blood."

"Right." I sliced my wrist open with the knife and held it over Lysander's mouth. Part of me wanted him to move, to do something, but the other part of me worried that Lysander might not be there in his body.

My blood pooled into his mouth for a short while before he finally responded and swallowed. And as soon as he did, his eyes fluttered open.

"Lysander?"

I waited for his response. The rest of the people in the room closed in and watched silently.

His eyes darted around, landing on each person's face surrounding him; then they settled on me.

"Alyssa?" he rasped.

"Yes, baby it's me!" Tears welled in my eyes.

"I thought I'd never see your face again, my love." His voice was a dry purr, but it was music to my ears.

"It's you. It *is* you. Oh, Lysander." I reached into the coffin and pulled him up into a tight hug.

"What about Aniketos?" he asked.

Nicholas held up the box. "We got him this time."

I pulled back and saw the three humans, Fallon, Ariana, and Saul, suddenly stand at attention, their eyes locked on the box.

"Let's get rid of that thing." Santino said. "I'll take it out to the wolves."

"You three, stay here," Drew said. He and Crystal grabbed hold of Saul and Fallon. Nicholas handed the box to Santino and took hold of Ariana.

With the box taken care of, I turned to Lysander again and hugged him close. "Thank you for coming back to me."

"It is you all whom I should be giving thanks to. I wasn't sure how much longer I could hold on."

"Most of the credit goes to Alyssa. That girl never gives up. She's got a never-say-die spirit," Nicholas said. "It's annoying, really."

I shot him a sideways glance. He always had to find a way to poke fun at me. "I can't take all the credit. It took us all working together to make this happen," I said. "And don't let Mr. Tough Guy over here fool you. He was just as adamant about getting you back as I was."

"I'm glad to have my brother back," Nicholas said.

Lysander smiled at both of us. "You all deserve thanks."

I gazed down into his blue-gray eyes, thankful to be able to look into them again. Already I could see the life returning to his face. His waxy skin had begun to soften and the hair was already beginning to regrow on top of his head. Lysander was looking better, but he still had a long way to go before he was back to his old self. And I planned on being right there at his side, nursing him back to health.

"You drink up now. Once we get you all better, we have some Acta Sanctorum butt to kick."

"All in good time," Nicholas said. "Patience. Let the old man rest."

Lysander chuckled. "Haven't you learned by now? Alyssa has no patience."

We all shared a laugh.

"I'll pretend to have some while we're getting you healthy again."

"Then I'll just have to take my time healing." He flashed me the crooked grin that had always warmed my heart.

At that moment, I couldn't have been happier. I had my Lysander back, the Acta Sanctorum was on the run, and my friends were all together and safe. At least for now, life was good. And I planned to enjoy every second of it.

Moonlight
An Immortalis Series Companion Novella
Katie Salidas

Chapter 1

Long pajama pants, a sweat shirt, fuzzy socks, and still I felt frozen. I'd been here a couple of months but still hadn't gotten used to the cold. Boston was an arctic tundra compared to Las Vegas and that blistering desert I'd come from. I'd be warm soon enough, though. Aiden was due back at any moment. That man was hot! Wolves have more than just good looks working for them. They run a few degrees warmer than us humans. And I needed that heat. The thought of him snuggling up next to me, fur coat or not, was enough to keep the icicles at bay for the moment, but I was still cold.

Teeth chattering, I pulled the thick feather comforter up to my chest and snuggled into the fluffy, king-sized down pillows. I doubted I would ever get used to the winter. But, if I wanted to stay with Aiden, I'd have to. As the future Alpha of the Olde Town Pack, he was a Boston boy for life. That also meant I would have to make some life changing decisions.

The thought of that wiped the smile from my face.

Aiden was my love, and I knew he loved me for who and what I was—human. But the pack… they wouldn't accept a human as their Alpha Female.

I buried my head under the blanket as if it would shield me. I'd been avoiding facing the inevitable, but a decision had to be made… soon.

The bedroom door opened with a slight creak.

"Fallon, babe. You still awake?" Aiden called out in a whisper.

Perfect timing! A thrill of excitement ran through me. "Yeah. Come cuddle. I need to steal your warmth, I'm freezing over here."

He gave me a quick sidelong glance then looked at the wall. "It helps if you turn on the heater."

"There's a heater in here? Why didn't you tell me?" I felt a little embarrassed for not thinking of something so simple; but in my defense, I hadn't lived at the sanctuary long.

"Yeah." He tapped a finger on the thermostat mounted to the wall. "Looks like Brady is up to his old games. The thermostat is off." He clicked the switch, walked inside, and shut the door.

Instantly, I heard the fans kick on. Warmth rose to my cheeks, but it wasn't from the heater.

"That bastard!" I said, angrier at myself for falling for another one of his tricks than anything else.

Aiden didn't bother to hide his snicker. "He is who he is. But you probably should have checked the thermostat instead of turning our bed into an igloo."

"That would have been the smart thing to do. But then I couldn't have hot Eskimo sex with you."

Without another word, Aiden tore off his clothes and dove into bed, under the covers. Snaking his arm around my waist, he pulled me in close and nuzzled my neck. My body began to warm, melting against his. Aiden's chin stubble scratched a little but not so much that it hurt. Besides, I loved a little rough touch from my man. His thick scent, fresh from the hunt, filled my nose. There's something about that heady odor of patchouli and cologne mixed with a little sweat that sends my heart racing.

Oh, yeah. This is my happy place. Safe in Aiden's arms, I felt like the world could go to hell and I'd still be okay. *This is love, right?*

Twenty-six years old and I'd never really been in love. Sad to say, I know. But love had never been a high priority on my list. School, family, friends, sure… but men had been merely blips in the radar. They were temporary distractions; fun little bumps along the road of life. With Aiden, it was different. He made me want to stop bumping along the road and find my home, with him.

"How was the hunt?" I scooted closer, reveling in his delicious warmth.

"The new recruits were naturals." Pride filled his voice. "You should have seen them. Everyone transitioned this time, and they're all acclimating well."

"That's wonderful news." *The last group hadn't been so lucky.* "But I couldn't take the cold tonight. I'm still too much of a desert rat."

His warm hand dipped under my sweat shirt. "Your blood will thicken in time." He tip-toed his fingers up to my breasts. "How about your day? What have you been up to while I was playing in the snow?"

"Nerd stuff." I purred. That man had a sinful touch. "I got the new server online and finished configuring the firewall. I still have to set up a few new user accounts, but other than that, not much."

"I have no clue what you just said, but I think it's sexy when you talk computers. Say something else."

"Networking," I said in my sexiest voice. "IP address. Password. TCP/IP Protocols."

"Ooooh. There is nothing sexier than a smart woman."

His cluelessness made me giggle, but the fact he appreciated my skills made me feel special. "Then I must be the sexiest woman this pack has ever seen. Your entire computer network needs an upgrade. Someone has to bring this pack up to date."

"Well, then, we're lucky to have you as our resident nerd. Speaking of that… have you given any thought to what we talked about?" His voice, a bit raspy from being out in the cold, rumbled in my ear like the purr of a big cat. He rolled my nipple between his fingers.

I let out a sigh. I'd been hoping to avoid answering that question. The luscious warmth of his body and the pleasure of his magic fingers were dampened by the reality that we needed to have *the talk* soon. I wanted to give in, say yes, and be with him forever, but it wasn't so easy. That choice was potentially a life-or-death decision. Certainly not something to jump blindly into.

"Forget I asked." He kissed the back of my neck. "I don't want to pressure you. I just want to feel you next to me."

Call it selfishness if you want, but I'd never been the kind of girl who changed for anyone—or any man. *Love me for who I am, or don't have me at all*. That's the way I've always operated. But Aiden was a different case. How could I deny this man? With him, I wanted to be the perfect woman, but that meant I would have to change more than just my hairstyle; I'd have to change my species.

The idea of that was mind-blowingly frightening, to say the least.

I'd been stuck between two worlds in the last few months, and I felt like I was the odd human out. My best friend was a vampire and my boyfriend… he was a werewolf. And not just any werewolf— Aiden's the interim leader of Boston's Olde Town pack. To take the job permanently, he needed a mate. A werewolf mate, and I was a few fangs and a fur coat shy of that.

"You're too quiet," he rumbled into my ear. "I didn't mean to upset you."

"No. It's fine, baby. I'm just tired."

"You're lying, I can smell it."

I looked up at my ruggedly handsome wolf-man. His pitch black eyes locked on mine and all anxiety was forgotten for that moment. "Just shut up and kiss me."

The corner of his lip quirked up as the concern faded from his face. "Getting a little bossy, are we? I believe I am the Alpha here, and someone needs a lesson in pack order." A mischievous glint sparked in Aiden's eyes. He gripped my hips, yanked me on top of him, and met my lips with all the intensity of a starving man at a sumptuous buffet.

He pressed me tightly against him as I ground into his hardness.

An animalistic growl vibrated his whole body. He squeezed me tight and cupped my ass with his strong hands.

"You're wearing too many clothes." Urgency filled his voice. Aiden tossed me back onto the bed and dove at my pants, raking them off with one swipe.

"What happened to foreplay?" I giggled. He was always extra frisky after a good hunt, and I loved it.

"Foreplay later. I need you now." Before I could protest, he rolled me over with lightning speed and pushed my sweatshirt up over my head, leaving my arms partially restrained in the sleeves.

Aiden then gripped my hips and, with a quick tug, pulled me up on my knees.

"God, you have a hot ass." He drew a finger down between my legs. "And you're ready for me too. Good girl." He gave me a playful swat on my right butt cheek and I let out a sharp squeal.

I felt the bulk of his body press against my back. His cock was already hard and ready. He nudged it into my folds, then bent down and nipped at my neck as he drove his silky erection inside of me.

"Oh God." I lost my breath as he buried himself and then stopped. "Don't tease… gimme more." I clenched my muscles around him and tried to move my hips to urge him on.

He growled and bit down harder but not enough to draw blood.

I stilled and arched my back, panting as the pain mixed with pleasure. This was his way of teaching me who was in charge, and I was more than happy to submit.

Slowly and purposefully, Aiden began to rock his hips, pulling out until just the mushroom head of his cock was inside of me. It left me empty and aching for him. Then, when he'd teased me enough, he would slam all the way back in to me, stealing my breath with every purposeful thrust.

Each plunge into my body was punctuated with a growl of pleasure from Aiden. His hands gripped my hips, directing my movement. I tried to rock backwards into him, to urge him to move faster, deeper, harder, but he was too strong. All I could do was let him take me how he wanted. It was sexy and infuriating the way he kept such control.

Every now and again he would bite down harder as he thrust. He was pure animal. I was his helpless prey. And I enjoyed every minute of it.

"I'm so close, baby." I moaned as pleasure began to coil low in my belly. I begged him to go faster. He released his teeth from my neck and replied by picking up speed, slamming into me harder.

Aiden reached around with one hand and found my throbbing clit. "That's it, babe. Come for me." He rubbed my button as he ground into me.

The coiling pleasure became a sudden burst of sensation. I lost control of my breath. My whole body rushed with a warm tingling until the coil released, and like a rocket I took off into the heavens, screaming as my body clenched in spasms of pleasure around his pistoning cock.

He slammed into me harder and faster until he too released with a roar, filling me with his wet heat.

"I needed that," I said breathlessly.

"So did I." He collapsed onto the bed panting. "Now that you've been shown who's the boss, we can take the next round a little slower."

I laughed. "I don't think I've learned my lesson yet."

He put his arms behind his head as he leaned into the pillows with a satisfied grin. "The wild ones are always the most fun to break. But I'm up for the challenge."

"We'll see about that. You've got five minutes to rest up for round two." I found my happy place, snuggling up next to him, and ran my fingers through his small patch of chest hair. I listened to the rushing beat of his heart and let my mind wander.

He was such a good man. What would happen if I said no? Would I lose him forever? Being a were-wolf was not in my life plan. Being the mate of an Alpha. What would that mean for my future? What about my dreams? I'd wanted to go back to school and finish my Masters. Would I be allowed to do that if I turned? Would I be forced to have puppies and be a stay-at-home den mother? How did that work, anyway? So many questions.

"You're doing it again." Concern dulled the timbre of Aiden's voice.

"What?"

"You reek of anxiety. What's on your mind?"

"I'm just thinking about what you asked me. I'm not trying cause problems with us, but I just don't know about going through with the transition."

Aiden went silent, but his heart beat began to race. I listened to the thundering rumble deep in his chest.

"I love you, Aiden, but I'm happy as a human."

"Babe, you don't have to change for me." His words sounded forced, as if he was choking out the emotions behind them. "I'm not going to make you become something you do not want to be."

"But what does that mean for you, or for us? What about the pack?"

Again he fell silent, but his heartbeat betrayed him.

"Now I know you're hiding something," I said.

He let out a sigh. "It's complicated."

"How complicated could it be? If I stay human, you still have a mate."

"You're not able to fully participate in the pack."

"What do you mean? I'm already participating. I've been here every single day since I arrived in Boston, working on your computers, upgrading systems. I'm practically the network administrator."

"It… it's not enough… for them, not for me."

"You mean because I can't sprout a fur coat, hunt, and have puppies, right?"

"Yes. Children." He said the word poignantly. "Werewolf children are a requirement to ensure propagation of the species, but it's not the only requirement to be an Alpha. Don't worry about it, Babe. Just drop it. It's my issue to deal with."

"Hardly. We're together. This is our relation-ship."

"Yes, and your decision puts a strain on my way of life." He couldn't hide the accusation and pain in his voice. "That is something I have to deal with. Please, just drop this for now."

His heart beat raced faster than a stallion at the Kentucky Derby. Things weren't so cut and dried. This was a much more serious issue than he was letting on. I wished I knew more about werewolf politics.

"Sure, baby." I tried to sound light and happy. "Four more minutes and you're back on again."

"Look at you, ordering me around. You'd make quite the Alpha Female." He kissed the top of my head. "I'm going to go take a shower first."

"Sure." *Why didn't he ask me to join him?*

"I'll be back." He scooted out of the bed and made a quick dash to the bathroom door.

I retrieved my sweatshirt and pants and tossed them on. To get to the bottom of this I'd need to talk to another wolf, and I knew just the one to grill for information. If Aiden wouldn't tell me what he was hiding, his brother might.

After pulling on my slippers, I padded into the hallway and headed to Brady's room.

Light blazed under the door, a good sign that he was still awake. *Probably winding down from the hunt.* I knocked lightly on the door.

"I'm busy, Fallon." Brady shouted.

Damn those wolves and their sense of smell.

"It's kind of important. Do you have a minute?"

I heard a woman giggling from behind the door.

Oh. That kind of busy. "Never mind." Guess Aiden wasn't the only one who got frisky after a hunt.

The lock clicked on his door and Brady opened it wearing nothing but a smile. "What do you need?" He sounded amused.

"Seriously, never mind. I didn't know you had company." I averted my eyes, but it was hard to find a spot to look that wasn't hard bodied naked man.

Nakedness was not something that bothered the wolves. Not that I was a prude, but I had not gotten used to how freely they showed their bodies. Around the full moon revelry it was like a furry nudist colony at the preserve. I settled for looking at Brady's dirty blond hair, since looking a wolf in the eyes was seen as a sign of challenge.

Brady chuckled, probably at my appearance: slippers, fuzzy socks and my bright red UNLV sweatshirt. "Is this about the heater?"

"Do you really think I'd bug you about that right now?" I crossed my arms and frowned.

"No," he laughed. "Knowing you, you probably have a plan to get me back."

"Bingo!" I pointed a finger at him and winked.

"So, what's up?" Brady leaned in the doorframe, still not bothering to cover up his nakedness. It was really hard not to inadvertently sneak a peek, and I was sure I was beginning to turn bright red.

I bit my lip to hide a smile trying to spread across my face and turned away. "Nothing. Go back to your fun. I'll talk to you in the morning."

Brady called over his shoulder to the woman in his room. "Diana, take off, love. I'll stop by your cabin later."

An Amazon woman, wearing just enough clothing to fit the part, snarled at me as she walked past.

"Show a little respect." Brady's tone became dangerous. "You know who she is."

"She's not pack," Diana said to Brady as she headed down the hallway.

Brady reached out, grabbed her by the shoulder, and spun her around. "She's Aiden's, and you will give her the respect she is due… now!"

Diana's hazel eyes widened. She gulped and then bowed her head. "Sorry, Fallon."

Reluctance was prominent in her voice, though she wasn't looking at me as she spoke. Her words were directed toward Brady.

"Now go back to your cabin," Brady growled.

With a curt nod, she turned and continued down the hall toward the front lobby.

The whole thing made me feel embarrassed. I didn't need Brady drawing any unwanted attention to me, especially when I'd been trying to win the pack members over in the hopes they'd accept me as I was. "Really, you didn't have to do that."

"She'll be fine." He shrugged. "Just needed a little reminder of the pecking order around here. Some of the ladies have been hot under the collar about you."

"Yeah, I got that feeling while I was making my rounds checking computers. I've been playing it nice with everyone, maybe win them over with kindness."

Brady smirked. "That's not the way to win the hearts and minds of the pack. You need to show them who's boss."

I hadn't thought of it that way, but Brady had a point. "Guess I'd better start pulling rank then."

"Not sure you have it in you, but I'd like to see you try." He patted my head like a pup.

I scrunched up my face in disgust and backed away.

That just made Brady smile more. That man loved to get me riled up.

He crossed his arms and leaned into the door-frame again. "I know why you're here. Aiden told you about the deadline, didn't he?"

"That's news to me. There's a deadline?" Now it was my turn to give him a wide-eyed stare.

His jaw tightened. Guess he didn't want to be the one to let that information slip.

"Aiden didn't tell you that part, did he? Where is he, anyway?"

"In the shower. Don't change the subject. What deadline?"

"Look. I like you, Fallon. I really do. You're great for my brother. But if Aiden's bid for the title of Alpha is going to be accepted, he has to have a mate capable of having wolf children. And he needs to take that mate now."

This whole purebred wolf children thing was really beginning to get on my nerves. It seemed to me that all the pack cared about was kids, and I was only to be used for breeding. My annoyance got the better of me, and I couldn't rein back the tension in my voice. "What does it matter if I can have children with him or not?"

"Pure wolf children are essential for pack stability. They are stronger and live longer than *turned* wolves. They often become the next Alphas, or move on to start other packs, and ensure our species continues."

"But you're a pure wolf." I jabbed a finger at him. "You could take a mate and make pure babies for the pack."

"True." Brady shrugged. "But I don't want the title of Alpha. And I do not want kids!"

"But you're pure and the son of the former Alpha as well."

He shook his head emphatically. "No way! I'm an enforcer, a fighter, and a bodyguard. That's who I am. I make a good *second*, but I don't want the responsibility or the Alpha's title. That's where Aiden has always excelled. He's destined for this job. He'll take the pack far. If…" He narrowed his eyes at me.

The pressure was enough to make me crack. I was getting it from all angles. Turn for Aiden, turn for the pack, or leave. Those were the only options.

"This is ridiculous." I threw my hands up in frustration. "Isn't there any way for them to just accept me as I am? Aiden will be a great leader now, but I need time to consider what's being asked of me. This isn't a simple decision. It's a life-or-death choice. It's, it's…"

"It's unfair, I get that." Brady patted me on the shoulder. Beneath his hard exterior, there was a compassionate man. Every now and again I caught hints of it hiding within the deep chocolate pools of his eyes.

"This is the way the pack works," he said. "We have strong traditions that have served us well for centuries. Just know that if you won't take that title, there are plenty of pack females who will. Any female would jump at the chance to be the Alpha's mate."

I cringed at the thought of another woman touching my Aiden.

Brady softened his tone. "I know this is hard to hear, but Aiden must choose his mate before he can officially take the title. It's already been too long. Connor…" his voice cracked and his mouth drooped. The pain of his father's death was still too close for him to hide the suffering. "Father's death was more than a month ago, and our members are growing restless to regain order. If he doesn't take a mate by the next moon, one will be chosen for him. Or, if worse comes to worst, another wolf might step up to claim the title."

I didn't like the sound of that at all.

Brady regained composure. "We both know Aiden is destined for the job. But, if he abdicates his claim to the title, then it becomes a free-for-all. All eligible males would be pitted against each other to fight for the title. The pack would descend into anarchy. Aiden is not going to see the remainder of this pack destroyed by power plays."

"So the only two ways this works is either I agree to the transition now, or I watch my love take another woman as mate?"

Brady nodded. "That's the bottom line."

"You've said it yourself: The transition is only a fifty-fifty shot. What if I choose to try it and die?" Beyond the fact that once I became wolf, I'd be expected to be a den mother as well, I feared the risk of death in the transition. I may have come from Las Vegas, but I was not a gambling girl. Especially with odds like those.

Brady shrugged. "I don't mean to sound heartless. I really do like you, and I think you'd make a pretty cool wolf. But considering what's at stake, even if you don't make it, isn't love worth the risk?"

Was it? I couldn't quite answer that. Yes, I loved Aiden. Yes, I wanted to spend the rest of my life with him. And yes, I wanted to see him become Alpha. But I didn't want to die.

I opened my mouth to speak but couldn't find the words to say.

"Let me put it to you this way." Brady spoke before I found my voice. "If you don't make the choice and Aiden walks away from the pack to be with you, a dominance war will be started. Those aren't pretty." He narrowed his eyes at me and leaned in close. "Do you know how wolves settle their differences? We fight to the death. Think about the pack, not just yourself. If you're not going to make the transition, then dump Aiden altogether and walk away. Don't give him a reason to follow you. There's more than just your life at stake."

"Brady," Aiden shouted from the end of the hallway. Both of our heads whipped around in his direction. The scowling expression on Aiden's face said it all. He was pissed. He held tight to a blue towel wrapped around his waist and stalked towards us. "I told you not to say anything."

Brady held his hands up and took a half step backwards. "Look, bro, she came to talk to me. She needs to know. You're running out of time, and the pack needs leadership."

"What she needed was to make the decision on her own, with no pressure. You've ruined that now."

"*She* is standing right here. Don't talk about me like I'm not."

Both men lowered their heads and looked at me sheepishly. Even though I was angry, I had to admit, to myself, that it was pretty cool to have such powerful men bowing like that. *Maybe I could consider being an Alpha Female after all.*

I grabbed Aiden by the arm. "Let's go to bed, baby. We can deal with this in the morning." I turned to Brady. "Thanks for the talk."

"You got it." Brady nodded and turned back to his room.

Aiden opened his mouth to speak, but I cut him off. "I don't want to talk now. Please, let's just go to bed."

He let me pull him down the hall toward our room.

Dissension - The great cataclysm wiped almost all life from the face of planet Earth, but tiny pockets of survivors crawled from the ashes, with only one thought: survival, at any cost.

But not all survivors were human.

In the dark, militant society that has risen in the aftermath, vampires, once thought to be mythical, have been assimilated and enslaved. Used for blood sport their lives are allowed to continue only for the entertainment of the masses. Reviled as savages, they are destined to serve out their immortal lives in the arena, as gladiators.

And there is no greater gladiator than Mira: undefeated, uncompromising...and seemingly unbreakable. When an escape attempt leads Mira into the path of Lucian Stavros, the city's Regent, her destiny is changed forever.

Lucian, raised in a culture which both reviles and celebrates the savagery and inhumanity of vampires, finds Mira as intriguing as she is brash. An impulsive decision - to become Mira's patron – changes more than just Lucian's perception about vampire kind. The course of his life is altered in ways he could never have predicted – a life that is suddenly as expendable as hers.

Can Mira prove to Lucian that all is not as it seems? Can Lucian escape centuries of lies, bloodshed, and propaganda to see the truth? Or will the supreme power of the human overlords destroy them both?

Complication - Narrowly escaping death at the hands of the Magistrate, Mira travels west, toward the coast. With three weakened human fugitives accompanying her, she searches for the mythical land of Sanctuary.

After encountering a pack of wolf shifters, headed by the charismatic—and brazen—Stryker, Mira learns that Sanctuary is real after all. Caldera Grove: home of the

Otherkin. Hidden in the mouth of a dormant volcano, it has protected its residents from humans since the early days following the great cataclysm. For Mira— a vampire— Caldera Grove is a land of peace; an escape from the relentless persecution of the humans who once enslaved her, and an end to the daily struggle and bloodshed of being a gladiator.

For the humans accompanying her, Caldera Grove means death. Humans, greedy and untrustworthy creatures, are destroyed before they can penetrate its borders.

To plead her case for entry into Caldera, Mira must abandon her companions, albeit temporarily, and follow Stryker into the heart of the city. What she finds within Caldera Grove presents her with an unenviable decision between her own desires for freedom and peace, or honor and the human companions who risked it all for her.

Revolution - Peace is an illusion. Blood, violence, and death follow Mira like shadows.

Battle lines have been drawn between human and Otherkin, and a bloody war is on the horizon: one that will end in either a shift in the world's balance of power...or ultimate destruction.

In spite of their strength, powers, and a rage known only by the oppressed, the Otherkin are evenly matched by the superior numbers of the human army. To tip the balance in their favor, the Otherkin need more soldiers – and their only options are the Gladiators of New Haven city.

Mira is sent across enemy lines to recruit any able-bodied vampires to her cause. But what she discovers along the way will blur the lines between friends and enemies. Seeds of doubt weaken Mira's allegiance, and she finds herself torn between the old masters who used her as entertainment and the new ones who consider her as nothing more than a weapon.

As the war draws near, Mira will have to decide what she is truly fighting for.

DISSENSION
CHRONICLES OF THE UPRISING
SAMPLE CHAPTERS

Everyone joked about the end of the world, but when it finally happened, no one was laughing.

December 21, 2012.

Mankind's final day had been predicted for years, but no one had believed it would ever come. Why would they? There had been so many dates labeled "the end," and none had yet come to pass.

When the sun rose on that fateful day, everyone made their little jokes. Just one more hoax. Street merchants started selling "I survived the apocalypse… again" T-shirts. Everybody looked around, shrugged their shoulders, and got back to what they'd been doing. The world moved on.

But the day starts at different times across the globe. This particular prophesy — this doomsday prediction — had been made by the Mayan people. It wasn't until the sun rose in South America that the destruction began.

Previously docile fault lines began to quake. As if waking from a slumber, the earth rumbled from deep within like some ravenous beast scenting its prey, to be satisfied only by utter annihilation.

Volcanoes that had lain dormant for hundreds of years suddenly sprang into action, erupting with centuries of pent-up pressure, spewing hot geysers of acrid smoke. Rivers of magma belched out from the mouths of these angry mountains, scorching the land and devouring everything caught in their deadly flow. Thick clouds blanketed the sky, choking out the sunlight. Searing chunks of pumice rained down upon the land, burying entire cities and all their occupants in a rocky grave.

For decades — centuries, even — the Earth had been beaten and bruised, scratched and bitten by her inhabitants. It was only natural that she would fight back. And her retribution was merciless. Whole continents fragmented as fault lines deepened and separated. The surface of the earth ripped apart while its terrified inhabitants futilely attempted to escape the destruction. Nowhere was safe. Giant waves of destruction beat down upon every coast, swallowing islands whole and obliterating coastal cities on mainlands. Never before had the loss of life been so devastating.

No one was laughing now.

It was truly, utterly, the end of days.

In the aftermath, the few that remained alive were forced to band together for survival. Food was scarce; shelter was even harder to come by. People who had never conceived of a life without electricity, running water, and fast food were faced with the ultimate choice: to live, by whatever means possible... or to die.

In the ragged days that followed the destruction, many more lives were lost — or taken — in the name of survival. Those who remained were few and far between.

And not all survivors were human.

Supernatural creatures — vampires — once thought to be the stuff of myth and legend, were forced from the refuge of the shadows. With no place left to hide, their only choice for survival was to reveal themselves to those few humans who remained. Immortality gave vampires the ability to weather the storms, but their weakness to sunlight left them vulnerable and in desperate need of shelter and protection during the harsh days following the great cataclysms. Only through collaboration could both races stand the slightest chance for survival.

It was an uneasy truce at first. The vampires' need for blood, no matter how small a dose, made them objects of hatred rather than companionship; but their ability to protect the former city-dwelling humans against other predators in the night counted greatly in their favor. Eventually, human and vampire learned to co-exist.

Slowly, as they always do, humans adapted to their newly reshaped home. Society rebuilt itself. Life continued on planet Earth and even began to flourish. Over the next hundred years, eight thriving cities rose from the ashes, and humans once again took their place as masters of the Earth.

And with that power came hubris.

Formerly friends and vital allies, the vampires quickly became targets – victims of the humans' drive to be top of the food chain. Rumors and lies spread quickly about what vicious and cold-hearted demons the vampires truly were. Human deaths, even when the cause was not loss of blood, were blamed on vampires. Long forgotten was the help the vampires had given to their human brethren in those early days of reconstruction.

The human race came to see vampires as nothing more than criminals and outlaws. Vermin. Using the vampires' vulnerability to sunlight and starvation, the humans turned their once-helpful protectors into slaves. Hunted down and brought to so-called justice, vampires were faced with the same brutal choice the humans had confronted a century earlier: Succumb to the will of humans, or end their days on Earth.

To live by whatever means possible… or to die.

CHAPTER 1

April 17th, 2210 – New Haven City. *Westernmost* Province of the Iron Gate, Pacific Coast

The roar of the crowd, all twenty-five-thousand people in attendance, rose to a thundering crescendo when Mira delivered a bone-crunching blow to her opponent's ribs. Standing only five feet tall, she might not have appeared a formidable warrior, but the thin, spiky-haired waif of a vampire could hold her weight and more when put to the test. Amplified by the superb acoustics, the sound of bones cracking echoed through the Superdome arena. The defeated, a red-headed male vampire staggered, punch-drunk, and then dropped to his knees. Dirt and sweat coated his face but could not mask the fear in his icy blue eyes. His was a look Mira had seen so many times before. Her opponent's immortal life had finally come to an end, and he was ready to take the final deadly blow.

Above her, Mira knew the fifty-foot mega screen showed her hapless victim in brilliant resolution, ensuring that all who were attending, and those watching from the comfort of their homes, could see these last gruesome moments in crystal clear high-definition.

Mira gazed down at her opponent's blood-soaked face. Though he was her enemy for the moment, she did not relish having to end him. No one should be forced into the arena and told to kill or be killed. It wasn't right. But it was what was demanded of her, and given the choice between her life and someone else's… well, there really was no choice. No matter the cost, Mira was a survivor.

She glanced up to the large private box overlooking the arena. A well-dressed man in deep-purple robes sat, enjoying what appeared to be a dinner of filet mignon and roast potatoes. Even here, in the dusty arena below, Mira's enhanced senses picked up the tantalizing scent of very rare, bloody steak. She could hardly believe that a human could not only watch the murder about to take place, but also sit and eat the dead flesh of a once-living being while doing it. From the smell of it, the poor beast was practically still bleeding on his plate. Who was truly the more savage creature?

Over the crowd's roar, an announcer introduced the well-dressed man, Lucian Stavros, Regent of the Iron Gate. Lucian gently and purposefully slowly set down his knife and fork. He took another moment to wipe his face clean and then smiled, acknowledging the roaring crowd.

Chants of "Death, death, death" rang out from the throng as a single unified demand.

The Regent listened for a moment, making a show of putting his hands to his ears to hear screaming hoard's request, and then held a hand out, with his thumb pointed to the side.

As if the next moment were the most important, the anticipating mass hushed. Eerie silence filled the arena as everyone watched for the Regent to make his decision.

From her vantage point below, Mira saw the steely look of determination cross the Regent's face. If she didn't know better, she might have thought he took this decision seriously; but then, he was human, and they never cared much if her kind lived or died. Lucian Stavros took a cursory glance down at Mira. Their eyes met. It was only a brief moment, but in that short time, Mira saw him waver.

Could it be true, she wondered, or was it just a trick of the light? No human actually cared about the lives of vampires. The moment faded, and the fleeting thought left.

Mira saw the Regent's decision. He turned his thumb down. Death!

The crowd went wild.

The last hope for her defeated opponent had vanished; Mira had to finish him. "Sorry," she whispered to the half-dead vampire on his knees before her. Though her fangs tingled at the prospect of tasting his final dying moments — her reward, if you could call it that, for living through another battle — she did not enjoy what she was about to do. Like her, he was a slave, forced into servitude to the humans as they saw fit. He had not asked for this, and neither had she. But, despite what either of them wanted, it was the will of the crowd, the humans, that had to be served.

Aiming to sever the carotid artery with her fangs, Mira dove at her opponent's neck. His death would be quick. At least she could afford him that luxury.

Hot, sweet, and energizing, his blood flowed freely down her parched throat. She'd been starved for so long. Denied the one thing she needed. And now, free to drink her fill, it was all she could do not to let the beast within her take over. Blood was everything: food, drink, life-giving essence, and pure ecstasy. Even the smallest amount could provide healing nourishment and pleasure all at once. But Mira could not let herself take pleasure from it, knowing the source. This was no willing donor. This was a fallen comrade. A fellow vampire. One of her own kind. His death ordered by the command of the humans. No matter how good his blood tasted, it was not for her to enjoy. She'd take only what she needed to heal from her wounds, and let his death come quickly.

More cheers erupted around Mira. The crowd, despite being entirely human, proved more bloodthirsty than she.

The irony of it was sickening. Distantly, she heard the announcer proclaim her the winner.

With a roar, she threw her head back, ripping out her opponent's throat, spraying what remained of his blood out into the air. They wanted carnage – they could have it. She had to keep her adoring fans happy lest they turn on her. In the arena, the life or death of a gladiator often came down to the will of the crowd. And though she was repulsed by what she had to do, she knew how to play the game.

The satisfying flush of fresh blood in her system and the heady rush that came with it was short lived. The reality of her situation was always close to the surface. Above, the giant dome roof parted, sending a hot blast of UV light down around Mira like a cage.

Not wanting to let them regain their strength, the humans were quick to remind vampires where their place was and who their masters were. Not even afforded a moment's respite for her victory, Mira was already enduring the painful reminder that she was a slave. Worse, a prisoner.

Her skin singed where the light touched. Instinctively, she held up her hands in surrender. The faster she let them haul her away to the prison level, the better.

The crowd around still roared with applause. But were they cheering for Mira, or happy to see her being tortured by blinding light? A bit of both, probably. Humans loved to see any bit of vampire suffering. Though it angered her, Mira would not show it and invite their ire.

Two humans, one male and one female, approached Mira, both wearing standard issue black Kevlar body suits and hoods with a wooden stake and hammer emblazoned across the chest. Handlers. Specially trained to deal with vampires and equipped to kill if necessary. Among their weapons were UV torches, quick blasting light sticks able to direct a powerful beam of ultraviolet light at the push of a button. The female's hand inched towards her UV torch as they approached Mira. She was a new appointee as Mira's handler, who preferred to shoot first and ask questions later. Mira hated the mocha-skinned Amazon wannabe and would have loved nothing more than to rip her to shreds. Few females were allowed to be handlers, and this one had wanted to prove herself from the moment she'd been assigned to Mira.

Once Mira might have acted on her desire to kill the nuisance handler and take whatever punishment she'd be given, but after years in this prison Mira had learned her lesson. Fighting back was best done strategically. Immortality was not invincibility, and she was no fool.

"Arms out, slave." The largest of the two handlers, a male with a deep voice, barked the order at her.

"Come to congratulate me on my victory and adorn me with jewelry?" With a cocky smile, she held out her hands, awaiting the silver cuffs with which they'd restrain her.

"Silence!" The male refused to look at her. He fastened the cuffs around her wrists and pulled back quickly, almost as if he feared what Mira might do.

Silver stung her skin, but Mira wouldn't let on that she was in any pain. "I always did have a thing for the strong silent types." She smirked despite the discomfort the cuffs were already creating. Hives were beginning to pepper Mira's smooth alabaster skin. An annoying allergic reaction, but she'd never admit how much it bothered her. Any sign of weakness could be exploited.

The male handler refused to acknowledge her or engage her further. He continued to work shackling her feet and then connected another silver chain between the two sets of restraints. When finished, he pointed toward the door at the edge of the arena. The female handler pressed a few buttons on a small communicator device around her wrist. Above, the dome began to close, and the shafts of light surrounding Mira vanished.

Thankful to be back in the dark, Mira nodded to her handlers as if to say, "Lead on," and followed as they directed her away from the arena, down to the pens.

Her moment of fame was over.

Chapter 2

Not a word was exchanged between Mira and her handlers as they exited the arena and headed down through the lower levels toward the prison. Only the sound of their bootsteps on the smooth concrete broke the silence. Not that Mira had anything to say to the pair of humans who ushered her back and forth from the arena to her cell, but it would be nice if occasionally she was treated as something more than an unwanted creature whose usefulness had ended the moment she dealt her final blow in the arena.

The silence ended as they passed through a set of thick metal doors. The light beyond dimmed, but the echoes of agony through the corridors became intensely vivid. Deep within the underground, where no sunlight could reach, was where the vampires were kept. Dark and dank, scented with the foul odor of unwashed bodies, blood, and mold, this was the place Mira called home, the only place she'd known for the last thirty years. She was lucky to have lived that long. Countless other vampires had come and gone before her, and many more had been slain at the point of her own teeth. The gladiator's life was all she knew now. Occasionally there were vague remembrances of what life had been like before her capture, but almost her entire vampire existence had been down in these dirty cells.

Fed only with the blood of other unwanted vermin, the humans had practically starved Mira and her kind to the point of savagery. It not only served to keep her kind more eager to fight in the arena, but also reinforced the image of their savagery in the human population's mind.

Rounding one dark corridor and heading down another equally gloomy one, the trio traveled further into the murky underbelly of the arena. Mournful howls and agonizing screams grated on Mira's nerves as they passed by the Hall of Punishment. Vampires who failed in battle but had not been killed were made to suffer unthinkable tortures at the hands of their human owners. Mira had unfortunately seen the inside of that hall on more than one occasion. If vampires could scar, she'd be unrecognizably disfigured from her time within those walls. Her punishments, rather than for failure in battle, had been ordered as attempts to break her spirit. No one, neither her handlers nor her Owner, had any affection for Mira. Free-spirited, uncooperative, and cocky as she was, Mira had not broken. Not once. No matter what vile punishments they'd thrown at her. As long as she was imprisoned in Iron Gate, she had one thought and one thought only... freedom. She'd have it someday, no matter how long it took. But though she loathed the arena and the life she had to lead, she knew that staying alive was the only way to get that freedom she so desired. And to do that, she had to remain a winner in the arena. It was the only reason she was still alive, despite her many attempts at escape and even more episodes of bad behavior. She knew as long as she kept winning, and earning her Owner lots of prize money, she'd be safe from final death.

They passed through a large corridor of prison cells before finally reaching Mira's, a small six-by-eight-foot cage of silver-coated steel bars with an automatically locking doorway. Her door, marked number 8254-A, was locked via an electronic keypad. Mira casually glanced over, trying to be as inconspicuous as possible, as they entered the ten-digit access code on the keypad. 753951...

The butt of a UV torch connected with the back of her head. A lightning fast jolt of pain had Mira hissing through gritted teeth.

"Eyes forward, slave," the female handler ordered.

Instinct more than anger drove Mira to turn on her handler. The fresh throbbing in her head mixed with frantic energy from her recent feed. Mira snarled, fangs bared, ready to strike, and advanced on the female handler.

Gone was the stony expression on the human woman's face. Fear widened her eyes. Realization. Complete understanding of what a vampire is capable of, especially a formidable arena gladiator who'd just fed...

"Stand down, vampire." The human woman tried to put authority into her voice, but her fear was clear, and Mira wasn't in the mood to take orders.

With little effort, Mira snapped apart the silver shackles and grabbed hold of her handler's neck. Ready to squeeze the human woman like a bug, Mira tightened her grip, choking off the handler's air supply as she forced her backwards onto the silver-coated cell bars.

Alarms sounded all around her. The other handler turned on his UV light and shined it in Mira's face. She closed her eyes against the sting but refused to let go. Fangs still bared, she bit blindly at her handler, enjoying the terrified screams, savoring the delicious tremors running through the human's weak body.

An army of heavy-footed steps flooded the corridor. More handlers were arriving. Mira had shaken up the hornets' nest this time. The taste of the handler's fresh blood would not be worth the punishment they'd deliver if she killed the human. Just as she was ready to release her prey, the entire cell block flooded with light. In a fraction of a second, Mira's skin felt as if it had gone up in flames. She, however, was not the only one to suffer. Other vampires peacefully lounging in their cells began to howl in pain as the dreadful light filled every inch of space.

Her whole body on fire, Mira released her prey and balled herself up, trying to hide in the small shadows created by those standing around her.

Something hard connected with Mira's head. She blacked out for the briefest of moments, which was all the humans needed to shove her into her cell and slam the door shut. Once secured, the lights went out and an eerie silence replaced the previous chaos.

"Try that again, you fucking leech, and we'll see you staked out in the morning sun," the male handler spat at her. He held tight to his compatriot, inspecting her Kevlar suit for any signs of damage.

Skin crispy, flaking off of her body, there wasn't an inch of Mira that didn't hurt; yet still she managed to laugh. "Come in here and say that, big man."

The male handler, having finished his once-over of his partner, turned his UV torch on Mira in response.

Already at the limits of what she could feel, Mira continued to laugh through the burning blast of light.

"She's fucking crazy," the female handler yelled over Mira's cackling laughter.

The male handler nodded stiffly and clicked off his torch. "What do you expect, she's a leech."

"Yeah, because humans are so sane," Mira retorted. Though she tried to sound cocky, she couldn't hide the edge of pain in her voice. There was not an inch of her body that was not raw and angry at that moment.

"Don't let her taunt you. File an incident report on that crazy leech, and she'll get what's coming to her." The voices trailed off.

Mira stared up at the ceiling. The coolness of the concrete floor was a small comfort to her searing skin. Her wounds were already beginning to heal, thanks to the blood she'd been able to drink in battle, but Mira knew that was the last she'd taste for a while. No doubt the handlers would report her to her Owner, and she'd be given some archaic punishment for her crimes. Even in their heyday, vampires had never been as cruel as the humans now were to them. Some deserved death, sure, but the rest just wanted to live their eternity in comfort and peace.

"Good job, Mira," George, a male vampire in the adjacent cell groaned. "Did we all need to suffer for your midnight snack?"

Mira huffed in frustration, at war with herself over what she'd just done. Part of her felt guilty for what the other vampires had endured because of her actions, but another part was not going to stand by idly while the humans attacked her for no reason. "You're just jealous because you don't have the balls to try it yourself."

"I'm not that stupid." George's dark bald head appeared at the bars. Though he sounded angry, none of it showed in his concerned expression. "This is a maximum security facility. There are cameras, monitors, sensors. Face it, honey, we're stuck in here until the day we die."

"Well, as I recall, you were the one doing the fucking last night. You were gone more than five hours." Her muscles protested every movement, but Mira slowly rolled over on to her stomach and gingerly pushed herself up to her knees. She was healing, but not quickly enough for her liking. "Is it true? Did you get a new Patron?"

"I know how to play the game." A cocky smile replaced the look of concern. George flashed her his perfectly white, perfectly sharp teeth. Tall, well-built, dark skinned-for a vampire – and that beautiful bald head human women seemed to just adore. That man knew his strengths; he was a handsome devil who flaunted it every chance he got, and it worked wonders. He hadn't been in the arena for well over a month, too busy with his ever-growing list of admirers. "Yep. Got myself a hot vein and a little free time. Which is more than most of us can hope for."

"Well, have fun being a human's play toy," she grumbled. Jealousy burned in Mira's gut. She may not have been a traditional beauty, but she was the best fighter in the place, and she'd never attracted a Patron. Fresh blood. Small comforts. The ability to leave your cell, even if it was only to service your Patron. Those were luxuries she'd never been afforded. George was a pretty face, he wasn't even that great a fighter, and somehow he had managed to get Patrons lining up around the building for a few moments of his service.

"Oh, I will. Beats the punishment you're about to endure."

Mira lifted her head just enough to see a pair of expensive heels walking down the way toward her cell. She knew the familiar clip-clop of her Owner's stilettos. *Damn.* She'd hoped it would be a little while longer before her Owner had gotten wind of Mira's disobedience.

Speaking of traditional beauties… her Owner, a former runway model and a pretty little princess in her own right, seethed with anger as she approached the cell. Mira didn't need to look up to know the deep hazel eyes of Olivia Preston were staring down at her through impossibly long and thick eyelashes. Her perfectly pink lip would be curled upward in a dangerous sneer. Olivia was the worst kind of Owner Mira could have landed: beautiful, spoiled, and self-important. "Stand up, slave. Show your master some respect!"

Respect. The woman didn't know the meaning of the word. Olivia Preston was well known for treating everyone — vampire and human alike — as if they were her things. Try as she might, Mira could hardly hold back her contempt for the pampered little princess. "The fact that I haven't attempted to rip your throat out is a show of respect all its own."

Unaffected by Mira's threat, Olivia continued to stare down the imprisoned vampire. "If you weren't such a damn good fighter, I'd have you put down like the dog you are."

"I should be so lucky."

Olivia wouldn't follow through with that threat; Mira knew that, though she could do many worse things. She wouldn't kill her prize fighter. The money Mira earned her for all the battles she'd won had paid for every piece of expensive clothing she wore, all the way down to her gaudy, gem-encrusted heels.

"I had come here to congratulate you on your win to-day…"

Mira waited in silence, refusing to look up at her Owner, who was impatiently tapping her heels on the concrete ground. She knew there was nothing at the end of that sentence that she really wanted to hear.

Olivia's foot came to rest. "…Instead, I get a report you attacked your handler."

"She threw the first punch." Mira laughed. "Too bad she couldn't back it up." She shouldn't have said it, but couldn't hold her tongue.

"This was meant to be your reward."

Mira had to look up this time to see just what her Owner was holding.

Clutched in her pale pink claws, was a small vial with red liquid inside.

Instinctively, Mira began to salivate. Blood. As much as she enjoyed disrespecting her Owner, this might not have been the best time to do it.

Recognition flashed in Olivia's hazel eyes. "Yes. Now I have your attention, don't I?

She dropped the small vial to the ground, where it shattered.

The sweet scent of that crimson liquid wafted up to Mira's nose. *Such a terrible waste.* It almost brought a tear to her eyes. If she hadn't already fed today, she'd probably have licked it off the floor, shards of glass and all. Other vampires in the area had caught wind of the smell too, and they whined and begged for a small taste.

Olivia sneered at Mira. "You need an attitude adjustment. You want to smart off and be disrespectful to me… you'll pay for it."

Here it comes: the punishment. There was nothing for her to say; she'd already said enough to piss off her Owner.

"Forty-eight hours in the lightbox. No blood after. Perhaps that will teach you a little respect." She turned on her heel and stormed away.

"Respect. Ha! I haven't learned it yet. And you haven't earned it," Mira shouted back to her Owner. She was already in for the worst punishment possible – might as well get in a final jab while she could.

"Damn, girl." George whistled. "Humans do love a tan, but you're going to be one crispy thing after forty-eight hours."

Mira had no reply. He spoke the truth. The lightbox was truly the worst kind of punishment a vampire could be given. Intermittent flashes of light just long enough to burn but not long enough to kill. It was with methods like this that the humans had enslaved her kind. One weakness was all they needed to exploit. Humans grossly outnumbered vampires, and with this one weakness, they had brought the vampire nation to its knees.

This trilogy can be purchased in individual books or on one complete boxed set.

ABOUT THE AUTHOR

Las Vegas native, Katie Salidas is a Jill of all trades. Mother to three, Wife to one, and slave to the craft of writing, she tries to do it all, often causing sleep deprivation and many nights passed out at the computer. Author of the Immortalis series, Chronicles of the Uprising, and various other paranormal works; writing is her passion, and she hopes that her passion will bring you hours of entertainment.

Find Katie Salidas online at:
KatieSalidas@gmail.com

http://www.katiesalidas.com/

Facebook
http://www.facebook.com/pages/Katie-Salidas-Author/214780936916

LinkedIn
http://www.linkedin.com/profile?viewProfile=&kcy=58814031&trk=tab_pro

Twitter
http://twitter.com/QuixoticKatie